LOCK THE DOORS

VINCENT RALPH

Cover design by Stephanie Gafron/Sourcebooks
Cover image © Stephen Mulcahey/Arcangel
Internal design by Michelle Mayhall/Sourcebooks

Published by Sourcebooks Fire, an imprint of Sourcebooks
P.O. Box 4410, Naperville, Illinois 60567-4410
(630) 961-3900
sourcebooks.com

Originally published in 2021 in the United Kingdom by
Penguin, an imprint of Penguin Random House.

Cataloging-in-Publication Data is on file with the Library of Congress.

Printed and bound in the United States of America.
PAH 10 9 8

ALSO BY VINCENT RALPH

14 Ways to Die

For Rachel

PART ONE

1

Home is where the hate is.

I was eight when I figured that out, watching from my bedroom window as my mother and her boyfriend argued in the garden. His name was Gary, and he drank a lot. And not because he was thirsty.

Mum's words were screeches, Gary's were slurs, and, for a little while, they were only fighting with their voices. Then he threw the garbage can lid at her, and she crumpled, her knees cracking on the path. Picturing her now, I see her arms held tight against her belly and tears dripping on the flower bed.

Mum says most memories are Post-its on the fridge door of your life. But a few, she says, are tattoos on your soul. This is one of those memories. What I learned is that anything can be a weapon if you know how to use it.

The lid was metal and dented. Gary held it over her, casting a shadow across her pleading face. He yelled things I didn't understand. Then Mum caught my eye, and Gary turned and smiled and waved.

The worst part? I waved back. I still hate myself for not doing anything—for not knowing what to do.

When bad things happen miles away, it's easy to say you'd be a hero. But, when it happens to you, especially when you're eight, it's not so easy.

Gary's arms stiffened, then he brought the lid down hard and fast, my mother screaming as it stopped inches from her face. He laughed, tossed it aside, and went to the pub.

All night, Mum made crying noises, tiny ones she whispered over, like she was shushing them to sleep. I lay awake, too scared to touch her, because, sometimes, the easiest things in the world, like a hug or a smile or an "Are you okay?" feel impossible.

In the morning, I watched her secretly, in between cereal bites and toothbrush brushes, and, when she caught me, she smiled a smile that didn't reach her eyes.

My mum had a lot of boyfriends, but some were worse than others.

2

Four tiny holes in my new bedroom door. That's the first thing I notice.

And then a bigger one on the frame, flaking at the edges, and a curve where the dark wood turns light, a crescent just deep enough for a bolt to slide back and forth.

My stepsister's door has eight holes, each set of four not quite level, as if whoever drilled them was fixing a mistake. I hunt for holes and find them everywhere, except for Mum and Jay's room. Their door is perfect, the frame untouched, and that's when I realize what happened here. Our dream home, the house Mum fell in love with the moment she saw it, was someone else's nightmare, because these holes aren't where you'd expect them to be. The locks weren't on the inside to keep people out.

They were on the outside, keeping someone in.

3

"They've taken it off the website," Mum says, looking up from her phone.

"I should hope so," says Jay. "We *own* it."

"Still, it's nice that it's official."

Jay stares at the piles of boxes, then jangles the house keys. "It's been official for a while." But Mum's not listening. She's spent so long looking at the place online that she can't stop.

Although we finally got our "dream home," no one seems that happy. Mum prefers the tidy house in the pictures, Jay looks exhausted from shifting all our stuff, and my stepsister, Nia, is already moaning about reception and how long it'll take to get, like, *anywhere*.

New house, same life. Except that's not totally true, because this life is a lot better than our old one, before Mum met Jay.

"We should leave the unpacking until tomorrow," he says, and, even though Mum looks disappointed, she agrees.

Then we all sit in the gaps between the boxes and eat takeout pizza, pretending this isn't a massive anticlimax. Mum looks at her photos, the ones she took when we visited to measure, and Jay doesn't try to stop her because that's how arguments start. Instead, he looks at me and says, "So...what do you think?"

"There are holes in the doors," I say. "It looks like they locked people in."

Jay doesn't respond like I want him to. He just says, "We'll fix that when we decorate."

He does that a lot—asks questions and ignores answers. If he could pick a stepson, he wouldn't be anything like me. Sometimes I catch him giving me the look, and I know what he's thinking. *Why can't he be like every other person? Why does he have to worry so much and say weird things?* It could be worse, because some men get angry if you're different. Jay just changes the subject.

"When are we getting Wi-Fi?" Nia asks. Because this is far more important, Mum puts her phone down, and the three of them discuss it while I go upstairs.

The doors are brown with swirls and dark knots, but I don't see the patterns anymore.

I only see the holes.

4

I listen to music until Mum comes in and says, "We're going to bed, now, if you want to...you know."

I nod, but don't reply. It's better when she doesn't say it out loud.

She doesn't ask if I'm okay. We just stare at each other while I watch her settle on a suitable smile. When it comes out, it's awkward and sags at the edges, but at least she tried.

Jay comes up behind her and says, "Good night, mate. You cool?"

I'm most certainly not. But I sigh and say, "Yep."

"Okay, then. See you tomorrow."

They stand there a second too long...and then a few more...until, finally, Mum breathes out and says, "Sleep well, sweetheart."

Their bedroom door closes, and I hear mumbling behind the wall. I could try to listen closer, but I don't want to know what they're saying about me. It's nothing I haven't heard before. Instead, I go downstairs, feeling my way through the darkness.

It always takes a while to get used to a new house. But, eventually, if we stay long enough, I'll be able to move from room to room with my eyes closed. I prefer doing this in the dark.

I feel for the front door and push the handle down once, twice, three times. Each time it holds firm, but only after three can I clap. That's how I know it's locked.

Moonlight hovers over the kitchen counters, empty except for a kettle and a microwave. I check the back door four times, then clap. Then I touch the windows one by one. On my way back upstairs, I check the front door again, because, sometimes, the clap doesn't work. It's supposed to stop my doubts, to remind me I've already done this. But it doesn't always work.

"Clap," I say out loud.

Then I take a deep breath, go back to my room, and imagine who slept here before me.

5

Mr. Trafford comes into the common room and asks for a tour guide.

"We have a potential new student," he says. "She's here with her mother. Who wants to show them around?"

I keep my head down, hoping someone else volunteers. But they all have the same idea, and, when Mr. Trafford looms over me, I know I won't be able to escape.

"Tom," he says, "would you mind?"

Teachers at our school like asking rhetorical questions.

"Mrs. Pearce," Trafford says, "this is Tom. He'll be showing you around this morning."

The girl has her head down. Her mother smiles and says, "Pleased to meet you."

"You too," I mumble, but I can't shake the feeling that I know her.

She looks too neat and tidy, like she's missing all the messy parts that Mum used to hide until Jay said he loved them.

When the woman frowns, I know I've been staring too long.

"You look familiar," she says, but Trafford talks over her.

"Ready to go?"

I look at the girl, and she glances at me, her eyes filled with a sadness I haven't seen for a long time, then back at the floor.

"Amy's a little unwell today," her mum says.

I suddenly feel an extra layer of nerves on top of the usual ones, but I can't get out of it, now.

"Have you just moved into the area?" I ask.

"Not exactly," says Amy's mum. "She's repeating a year. We're looking for a fresh start, aren't we, love?"

When she doesn't reply, her mum says, "Amy goes to St. Gregory's. They've suggested that a change of scene could bring out the best in her."

Amy shivers, then stiffens as her mother touches her arm. When she catches me staring, she says, "Don't worry. Amy *can* speak for herself." But she doesn't. She stays silent for the whole tour.

Sometimes I look at her, then away. "Stolen glances," they call them, which is a nice way of saying you're a wuss. Afterward, the woman shakes my hand and says, "You've given us a lot to think about."

Then I stand outside reception, waiting for Amy to turn round, to smile, maybe, or just look at me. All that happens is that her mum, one step behind, lifts her arm and goes to put it around her daughter's shoulders. But it just hangs there, waiting, then falls back to her side.

At the gate after lunch, Mr. Trafford stops me. "Did you sell the place?" he asks.

"Yeah. I made it sound like Disneyland."

Some teachers think everything's sarcastic; others think nothing is.

"Excellent," he says. "Good job."

But, wherever Amy Pearce ends up, it won't be here. It looked like she couldn't leave fast enough.

And that's when it hits me. I *have* met her mother before. We all have.

6

Amy lived here before us.

That's why I recognized her mother—because she showed us around. She hit it off with Mum right away, telling her what a wonderful house it was. There was a man, too, but he didn't say much. He hung back while she did the talking. Amy wasn't there.

I wish I'd paid more attention, but we'd looked at so many houses. I thought this was just another one Mum would say no to, because there was always something wrong.

"It's perfect," she told Jay afterward. And, six months later, it was ours.

I touch my door and wonder. Why didn't I see the holes that day? Why didn't I look closer? I could have asked about them, but would Amy's mum have told the truth?

I knock on Nia's door, then again, and, when she finally answers, she stares at me until I say, "Can you remember whose room this was?"

"What?"

"When we first saw the house. Was this a girl's room?" Billie Eilish is singing about bellyaches, and my stepsister reluctantly turns the music down and says, "What are you talking about?"

I point at the holes. "This isn't normal."

"You're not normal," she replies. She doesn't smile, because it's not a joke.

I look past her, at the walls already covered in posters and photos and her guitars resting in the corners. There's no telling which of us got Amy's room. They were both identical when we moved in.

Mum says Nia likes me, really, but I don't think so. She's a year older than me, and she's never even pretended to be nice. She comes with Jay, just like I come with Mum—two people who chose to be together, and two who didn't.

"Is that it?" Nia asks, and, when I don't answer, she closes the door. Luckily for her, she can open it whenever she wants.

But, if I'm right, and there did use to be locks on the outside of Nia's door and mine, it wasn't that easy for Amy Pearce.

7

Miss Kiko asks me to stay behind after registration, then hands me a piece of paper and says, “You have a buddy request.”

“Pardon?”

“We have a new starter. And you’ve been chosen.”

Our school has a buddy system, but I can’t remember the last time they used it. We don’t get many new kids here, and my tutor must see my concern; she tilts her head and says, “Are you okay, Tom?”

I glance at the paper, and there it is: Amy Pearce’s name and the time we should meet.

So she picked our school after all, but why has she picked me? Or is this Mr. Trafford’s idea?

“I’d better go,” I say. “Thank you.”

Miss Kiko could have given me this in front of everyone, but she knows I don’t like attention. If she was picking the buddies, she would have paired Amy with someone else. But I’m not that lucky.

I feel a tap on my shoulder, and, when I turn, Amy smiles and says, "Remember me?"

"Yes."

Except the girl I remember was a lot sadder, and, now...

"I need another tour," Amy says. "I wasn't paying much attention last time."

"I noticed," I say, and she smiles—a massive grin that reaches her eyes.

Her clothes are really smart, but "business dress" means something different at St. Gregory's Academy for Girls. That's where Nia goes, and she isn't allowed into classes unless she's "interview-ready."

I stare at Amy, my confusion pushing out my unease. I want to know if she asked to be paired with me, but I'm scared of the answer.

When you're a kid, they tell you not to talk to strangers. We're used to keeping others out, and that doesn't change in high school. The doors to most friendship groups closed years ago.

She tilts her head and says, "I know what you're thinking."

"You do?"

"Yep. You think I'm weird, because, last time, I was moody, and, this time, I'm..."

"Hyper?"

Amy laughs. "I was having a bad day. But I'm better, now."

I step back and say, "I've got to go. You should probably ask for another partner."

"Meet me at break."

"Why?"

"Why not?"

I can feel my panic bubbling like a kettle starting to heat up. I could risk it coming to boil, but it's easier to switch it off.

"I can't," I say, mostly because I don't usually spend time with girls, and partly because this one used to live in my house.

She shrugs and says, "No worries."

I walk away, thinking of the day I met her, when she left and didn't look back. This time, I can feel her watching. I turn and see her sitting on the top step with a book in her lap, looking at me, then the book, then back to me, scribbling like it's the last five minutes of an exam.

Then I think of the holes in my door: the echoes of a story Amy may be too afraid to tell.

I could ignore her until she gives up and bothers someone else. Or I could talk to her and find out if I'm right.

8

You know those songs you hear in the morning and can't get out of your head all day? It turns out some girls are like that.

In class, Amy gate-crashes my thoughts. I keep having flashbacks of her on the steps and that big smile. Most girls look at me by accident, but she did it on purpose.

I should be thinking about her because of the doors. I should see her as a mystery to solve. But I think it might be more than that. She shakes up my thoughts like the insides of a snow globe, and I need to focus.

At break, I go back to reception, and she looks relieved and says, "I'm here for the tour."

This isn't me. I usually avoid being sociable, but, if I want to find out the truth about the holes, I need Amy to trust me. That's why I show her the school again, except, this time, I'm honest.

"The laptops are ancient, and they take the common room away whenever there are exams," I say.

"If you have classes in the trailers, don't take your coat off unless it's boiling outside. And don't turn left after you leave school. They mug kids in that alley. Even the teachers turn right."

Amy nods and says, "It's still better than my last school." I think of St. Gregory's Academy—the redbrick girls' and boys' schools standing side by side—and wonder if she's joking. From what Nia says, it sounds like a different world—a lot better than this one.

At the running track, I point at the extra white line painted on the grass and say, "That's Simon Marlow's head-start line."

Amy tilts her head, and I sneak a glance.

Some thoughts shout, and others whisper. The shout says, *This girl is amazing*, and the whisper says, *You've only known her a morning*.

The shout says, *Who cares?* Look *at her*, and the whisper says, *Remember what happened to your mum*.

Shouts drown out whispers.

The longer I spend with her, the sillier I feel about the holes. I made up a story and cast her in it before I even knew her. She doesn't look trapped. She looks calm. Whatever issues she has with her mum, and, whatever happened at her old school, here, now, she seems happy.

"We were in eighth grade," I say, looking at the head-start line. "It was sports day. But Simon was lightning-quick. He was always going to win."

And then he fell, only, now, I say crumpled. And the crowd all around him—the one supposed to be cheering—was staring and crying and freaking out. Miss Suman was pushing on his chest. Thinking about it now, it was like she was trying to pump a slashed football.

The next day, in assembly, the principal said that there's no age restriction on tragedy.

"Kids don't have heart attacks," I tell Amy.

She bends down and touches the line. "I'm sorry," she whispers.

"When they painted it, they said Simon had a head start in heaven. That's what the line means."

Amy doesn't look up for a long time. When she does, I must be staring, because she says, "What's wrong?"

"I don't normally do this."

"Do what?"

"Talk to girls."

She laughs. "Do you have any more stories like that?"

"Sad ones?"

"They don't have to be."

I think of all the things Mum and I have been through, but say, "Not really."

Amy stands and hugs me, and I wonder what that means. The blush spreads quickly from my cheeks to my ears and everywhere else. She notices, because it's impossible not to. During class presentations, my face could warm the coldest room, but, today, it could heat a whole house.

The tiniest smile dances across Amy's eyes, and my face turns a shade darker.

"Do I scare you?" she asks, and I lie.

"No."

She sighs, looks one last time at the head-start line and says, "I will."

9

I thought I was being stupid. I thought that, for once, there was no terrible truth, just a harmless coincidence. And then Amy said she would scare me, and I doubted my doubts.

I should have more faith in my paranoia. I've been practicing for years.

Does she know what I know? Is she waiting for me to find the holes in her door and ask what they mean?

This house doesn't feel safe, but that's nothing new. I'm used to feeling like this, because, too many times, Mum mistook prisons for sanctuaries. Every time, she thought we were escaping. And, every time, it was worse.

But this feels different. I'm not scared of Jay; not anymore. I'm scared of the doors. I'm afraid of what they're trying to tell me. Every house has a history, and this one doesn't seem good.

I get out of bed and touch the holes in my door, then go online and order what I need to be sure. If I ask Mum to do it, she'll tell me I'm being paranoid. That's her way of saying things are different, now. But I'm only paranoid because of before. I'm only thinking the worst because I've seen it happen.

I imagine Amy lying in the bed that was here before mine. What did she think? I could ask her, but how do you bring up something like that? How do you say, "I was in bed thinking of you last night, and I wondered if we shared the same ceiling"?

I can't shake the feeling that she's hiding something. She was happy today. But, when I told her about Simon Marlow and the head-start line, about the grief we all felt that day, her face slipped, and something dark crept out. For a split second, she forgot to hide. For the tiniest moment, she looked like Mum used to, before she banished her final monster.

10

There are loads of reasons for never having a girlfriend.

There's shyness...or bad luck...or, maybe, you have better things to do. And, sometimes, it's because your mum had too many goes at a happy ending before she got the hang of it. That's my reason.

My parents got divorced after six years together, just like that. One day, they changed their minds, which confused me at the time, because you change your mind about what you're having for dinner or what to spend your birthday money on.

Some decisions, the biggest ones, take the kind of planning I never saw. Not because it didn't happen, but because my parents did it in secret. They hid their problems behind smiles I was too young to see through. And, when even the fake smiles stopped, it was too late.

A few years after that, Mum's latest bad boyfriend full-stopped their relationship with a garbage can lid, and I learned that, whether love ended fast or slow, calmly or violently, on screen or off, it always ended.

When that happens, when most of your Mum-memories involve her crying, you lose faith in the soppy stuff. Love and all its alter egos work for a while, but never forever. People who don't believe that—they haven't fallen asleep while their mum sobs through the wall every night.

I know I'm a little bit broken, and that's okay. I know what happened when I was a kid has left stains on my new life and the people I randomly meet. But Amy wasn't random. She used to live here, in a house I don't quite trust. And now she goes to my school and seems to have chosen me as her friend.

Maybe it was just because Mr. Trafford picked me for the tour. But she wasn't pleased to see me, then, so why did she ask for a second go? Why were her smiles a bit too wide and her words slightly too rehearsed?

She's covering something up. And I can't shake the feeling that it's my job to figure out what.

11

"Why are you so interested in me?" I ask Amy.

I spent yesterday hiding from her, watching from afar and trying to work out if she's got a secret or if she's just a girl attempting to settle into a new school.

She hasn't spoken to anyone else, not while I've been watching. At break, she sat alone in the courtyard, writing in her notepad, and, at lunch, she picked the table closest to the trash. It's as if she doesn't want to be included.

But, this morning, she crept up on me and said, "Eat lunch with me," leaving before I could answer.

So now we're back in the cafeteria, and she grins and asks, "Who says I'm interested?"

"Because you want to eat with me...and, on your first day, you asked for a tour you'd already had."

I keep having flashbacks to the first time we met. This isn't the same person, and that worries me. But I'm still sitting with her, and that worries me more. When she looks away, I stare, trying to make sense of her.

"What you said before...about me being scared of you... why did you say that?"

Amy's smile slips, then fades, but she doesn't answer.

Instead, she packs up her lunch and says, "We all scare each other, sometimes."

I should tell her I live in her house, now. But something stops me.

It feels like a secret I need to keep; a mystery I can control while I try to figure out the one sitting next to me.

12

"Where are you?" Mum asks, standing in my doorway.

"What?"

"You zoned out. Where did you go?"

"Nowhere."

I can't tell her the truth—that I was daydreaming about a girl. When I think of Amy, something swirls inside me, a strange kind of sickness that wraps around my nerves. I was replaying what she said and how she said it, and now it feels like Mum can read my mind.

Mum smiles and sits on my bed. Glancing at the walls, she says, "We should decorate. Whatever you want."

She touches my hand, and I let her because I know what this means. She's waited half a lifetime to choose wallpaper in a house she won't need to escape from and buy ornaments that won't be smashed within a week. This is her forever home.

"Sure," I say, even though I'm not as ready to make this

place our own; not if that means forgetting what happened here before we arrived.

I need to know what that is first. I need to know if the sad Amy who wouldn't look me in the eye suffered the way Mum used to. If anyone should understand why I'm worried about the holes, it's my mother. But Jay has made her forget quicker than I can.

Whatever Mum thinks about her old life, she does it in secret, when none of us are around.

"Do you like it here?" she asks, and I can see the hope behind her eyes.

I can't say no. I can't say not yet. I can't say anything except, "Yes," because her heart is only held together by a few small things and a few big ones.

One of the big things is Jay. He showed her that not all men are monsters. And the smaller ones are moments like this, when I could be honest or I could be kind.

"It's amazing," I say and, for a second, I think I've gone too far.

But Mum squeezes my hand. "It is, isn't it?"

I glance at the holes in my door, then back to my mother. We've spent a lot of time sitting on my bed, but, usually, we've been hiding, waiting for someone to leave or someone to calm down or sober up. This is a new experience for us, and I can't ruin it, now.

"I'm glad you're happy," I say, and Mum beams.

"Me too," she says.

13

My mum won my dad in a raffle.

It's okay if you don't believe me. Most people don't. But, my parents—when they were together—used to perform how they met like a play. Dad always started.

"On the most important yesterday," he would say, "Fate woke up in a very good mood."

Mum met Dad at the fire station in town. It was an open day, there was a raffle, and she bought a ticket. When her number was called, there were only two firefighters left, and she nearly chose the other one.

"But there was something about your dad," she would say. "I missed him when I looked away…even then."

When they got married, Dad framed the raffle ticket and hung it over their bed. And, every morning, I would touch it and say thank you. Mum said they were my first words. She said, while most babies say Mama or Dada first, I said thank you to Fate.

And then, one Christmas, while I was jumping on their bed, I knocked the ticket off the wall.

How people topple from buildings in films...in slow motion...that's how the ticket fell. And, on the carpet, behind cracked glass, it didn't look magical anymore, just dead. I cried a lot that Christmas.

That was the last day I ever saw the ticket on the wall and the last time I thanked Fate for my parents meeting.

When Dad had gone and Mum was putting his stuff in boxes, I watched her find the ticket and stare at it and cry. I don't know where it is, now. But, sometimes, I wonder if they'd still be together if I hadn't smashed the frame. It's stupid, I know. But that was the start of all the shit. And something was the reason, so why not me?

I was four when Dad left. I know divorce works differently for different people, but, for him, when he said goodbye, he meant it. He sends cards when he remembers and money when he feels guilty. But I haven't seen him in twelve years.

Mum replaced him with arseholes and bruises and tears and, eventually, with Jay.

14

No one was home when my package arrived, so I have to collect it from our neighbor after school.

When Mrs. Hawkins answers her door, she's bent over, a stick in one hand and an alarm hanging round her neck. She looks at least eighty, and I feel guilty for making her move.

The package is propped in her hallway, and I watch her slowly pick it up and pass it to me.

"I'm sorry for bothering you," I say, then again, louder, when she points at her ear.

"No bother," she replies. "I'm always here."

She's breathing hard, one hand resting against the wall, so I thank her and say goodbye, because she needs to sit down and I need to get back to my room.

First, I get the screwdrivers from under the kitchen sink, then I unpack the box and spread the instructions on my bed. I've never done DIY before, but this is different. I need to know if a lock fits the holes in my door, so I bought one.

I think back to Mum patching over the holes caused by men's anger. After Dad, she learned to repair plaster and fix door frames. Her DIY wasn't building new things; it was rescuing what others destroyed. If you looked close enough, you could see the cracks in us as well, glued together like the bits of broken furniture.

And now we're here, safe in a house where Amy may have been in danger.

Some want proof before they believe paranoid people, so here goes. I screw the metal plate in place, then close my door from the outside and slide the lock across. It finds the hole perfectly, but I'm not happy. I was right, and that's not a good thing.

I turn the handle and push, but the door holds firm, and I imagine Amy on the other side.

"What are you doing?" Nia asks. She's staring at me like I've killed the cat, but that's just her face.

"It's the wrong side, idiot...unless you want to be locked in."

"I know," I reply. "I'm just trying something."

She doesn't ask what or why. She just sighs and closes her bedroom door.

After I've removed the lock, only for a second, I think about screwing it to Nia's door and trapping her inside. It might teach her a lesson. I could say I'll only let her out if she's a bit nicer to me. But, honestly, I don't care if she's moody. She's angry because her parents split up and took one kid each. Jay took Nia, and her mum took her brother, Aaron.

I didn't have that choice. If I had, I would have chosen

Mum, anyway. But it must be hard for a child to pick a parent when they're pulling from both sides.

Every Saturday, Aaron stays the night, and it's the only time my stepsister smiles. They goof around while I watch from outside their invisible circle. And, when Aaron goes, that version of Nia leaves as well.

I think she misses being a big sister. I'm not an Aaron substitute, and I never will be. Mum says to give it time. She says we're a "blended family," now, which I guess is better than a broken one. But blended families can still have cracks.

I hold the lock in my hand and think about giving it to Amy as a present.

"You can do what you want with this one," I'd say, and she would smile because she'd understand. Then she'd tell me what happened here.

But that's just wishful thinking, and I'm not brave enough to take the risk. Instead, I put it in my bedside drawer and wait until I have the courage to show Mum and Jay that I was right.

15

"This place is awesome," Zak says, running from room to room like I've bought it especially for him.

When I don't reply, my best friend says, "Which one is Nia's?"

I point, and he knocks. When she answers, Zak says, "I'm here for the tour."

My heart stops as I remember Amy saying the same thing at school, but he doesn't look at me; he just walks past my stepsister and says, "Now this has character."

"Get out," Nia says. But there's no venom in her voice. If anything, there's a smile that sits in the corners of her mouth and a warmth in her warning. She likes Zak more than she'll ever like me. Maybe it's because he doesn't care. Or maybe it's because I'm too sensitive.

That's what he thinks. He says, if I stop giving a shit, Nia will stop acting so bitchy. But I *do* give a shit. That's who I am. I can't just turn it off.

"You need to decorate," Zak says. "Your room looks like a prison cell compared to this."

Nia flashes me a look I can't interpret, waits until Zak has left, then closes the door behind him.

"You shouldn't piss her off," I say.

"She loves it! She'd be pissed off if I *didn't* go in there."

"What do you think of her door?" I ask.

Zak glances at it. "It's all right."

"Do you notice anything?"

He looks again, then shakes his head and says, "Not really."

"What about those?"

I point at the eight tiny holes and Zak looks closer. "I don't get it."

No one does. But who's wrong? Me or them?

"Don't you think it's weird? It looks like this locked from the outside. Mine does too."

Zak is quiet for a while, then he says, "That *is* weird."

"You think so?"

"Yeah. Did your mum try to lock you in again?"

"It's not funny. I think something bad happened here."

"You think something bad happened everywhere."

I don't say it usually does. I just take the lock from my room and hold it against the door. "It fits perfectly. I think Amy was locked in."

Zak makes a face. "Who's Amy?"

He's been out sick for a few days, so I tell him everything. And, when I'm done, he doesn't say I'm foolish. He sits in silence for two long minutes, then finally he nods and says, "If you won't ask her, I will."

16

At school, Zak points at every girl he doesn't recognize and asks, "Is that her?" over and over until I shake my head hard.

"Please don't do this."

"Why not?"

"Because she'll think we're weird."

"We *are* weird."

He's right. But that's no reason to broadcast it.

When Amy walks past, he almost doesn't notice. Then he points and says, "Is that her?" And I must be a second too late because he grins. "It is."

He doesn't run over to her like I feared. He watches her walk across the courtyard with her head down. She's alone, and I wonder if she's made any other friends yet. We usually ignore St. Gregory kids in the street or on the bus, but Amy isn't one of those kids anymore. She's one of us.

When she sees me, she smiles and changes direction, and I feel my heart go from third gear to fifth in a single beat.

"Hey," she says. "Hi."

Zak doesn't say anything. He looks from her to me and back again like we're playing tennis. He has a stupid smile on his face, and I know what he's thinking. He's not completely wrong. I like her. But that's just one feeling in a pile of them.

Before I can think about that, I need to know if I'm right about the locks.

Eventually, he says, "I'm Zak," and she nods and introduces herself.

He holds out his hand, and Amy shakes it, then laughs because who does that? Even I think some of Zak's habits are weird, and I've known him since seventh grade.

I slowly realize he's not going to mention my theory, and I feel both relieved and annoyed because I want to know. But not like this, not with the three of us standing awkwardly in the courtyard while teachers shout at us to get to class.

I practice a few sentences in my head, but I don't say anything out loud. I can't ask Amy what I want to without sounding like a lunatic.

A part of me *wants* Zak to say it, just to put it out there. But then she'd know I've been talking about her and, if I'm wrong, that I jump to the wildest conclusions.

I'm smart enough to know I could be mistaken. And yet I feel like I might be right.

17

I didn't pay much attention to start with.

The house I can see from my new bedroom window looks massive. It has a sold sign outside. And then I spot her, Amy's mum, strolling back and forth in the driveway with a phone to her ear.

"What the fuck?" I say to myself.

There had been workmen there, but they packed up yesterday. Now I know why.

Has Amy's family really moved in around the corner?

It's a much bigger house than this one, so I guess they could have upsized. But don't people move to new places? For new beginnings? That's what we've always done.

I guess you don't need to run if you're not being chased. It used to have a wooden gate at the front, but they pulled that down, dug up the trees, and built a wall all the way around. I watched it go up in a day. Now there are spiked railings across the top, and three bright spotlights that come on after dark.

It used to look like a nice country house. Now it looks like a prison.

I watch Amy's mum wave her free hand while she talks into the phone. She looks angry, but, even with my window open, I can't hear what she's saying.

There's a shout from inside, and she marches through the front door. I wait a couple of seconds, then see her through a downstairs window, talking to someone out of view. She isn't holding the phone anymore. No matter how hard I look, I can't see anyone else. They are hidden by walls and window frames, but, if I wait, eventually, they'll appear.

What will Amy think when she knows I can spy on her?

Is it still creepy when you think someone's in danger?

I should tell her we're nearly neighbors. And I will. But not yet. If Amy's parents *were* the ones who put locks on the doors, they might only show their true colors when they think no one's watching.

18

"She lives in the big house on the corner," I tell Zak.

He frowns and says, "Stalker."

"It's not stalking. She literally moved into my line of sight."

"I bet you didn't look away."

I shake my head, but he's right. I spent last night fighting the urge to watch but doing it anyway. I know it's a weird thing to do, but I wish someone had watched over Mum when she was fighting her battles alone.

I only wanted to catch a glimpse of Amy and know that she's fine. But all I saw were her parents and her brother, their faces lit by the glow of the TV. Upstairs, the curtains were drawn, a single light giving her away.

Had they already locked her in? If I knocked for her, would they make excuses while she sat helplessly by her window? And what about her brother? Are the locks just for Amy, now?

From what I could tell, he seemed fine sitting between his parents. I couldn't see his expression, but he didn't look trapped. And he has no reason to pretend in his own home. When I see Amy across the courtyard, she beams, and I'm either overreacting or she's a great actress.

Mum says I worry too much, but that's only because there's so much to worry about.

"Hey," Amy says, like she's been doing this for years.

"Yo," Zak says, winking when I give him a look.

One thing you can't doubt about my best mate is his loyalty. He mucks about and teases me mercilessly, but I know he won't just turn to Amy and tell her I've been spying. Instead, he makes a face behind her back and blows kisses while I try to make small talk.

"What did you do last night?" I ask.

"The usual," she replies.

She doesn't ask back, and I hope she doesn't already know. If she saw me, she isn't letting on.

"So why did you leave St. Gregory's?" Zak asks, a bit too quickly for it to be a random question.

Amy doesn't reply right away. It's as if she's lost in a memory. But, eventually, she says, "It's shit there."

She's not very talkative today, yet she's still said more than me. Even when Zak nudges me, I just stand there, wanting to blurt out something about the locks or last night, unable to think of something less creepy.

"I'd better get to physics," Amy says, and Zak huffs.

"She's too smart for you," he says, then sort of sucks his face in. "Shit...sorry...I...shit."

We all stand there in silence, and my face is so hot I can feel it melting. I can see Zak trying to make things better with a sentence he can't untangle in his mind. But nothing comes. He just stares at me, apologizing with his eyes, until I take a deep breath and say, "She is."

Amy smiles and Zak raises his eyebrows, and everything is happening in silence, but my head feels so loud.

Zak's fighting the urge to bounce on the spot, and I know, if I don't speak soon, he'll do it, anyway. But what do you say after something like that? I think I've just admitted that I like her, and I don't know quite when I decided that.

"So..." Amy says, "I'll see you around."

"You certainly will," Zak says, talking to her but staring at me.

He isn't teasing anymore. He wants me to think of a line Amy will remember all day. I can see the hope in his face that, for once, I get it right. But, for all the thoughts racing through my brain, none of them can form that sentence. None of them form anything.

All I can do is wave until Amy disappears and Zak grabs my hand and says, "Stop it. You are literally waving like a baby."

19

Maybe the holes don't mean anything. Maybe I'm imagining a horror story, because that's just what I do. Not everyone's life is shit. Ours isn't anymore, and maybe Amy's never was. But I still can't bring myself to ask her.

"She likes you," Zak says.

"How do you know?"

"I've known you a long time, Tom. No one looks at you like that."

I laugh because he's right.

In the cafeteria, he points at Amy and says, "It could be destiny."

"You're ridiculous."

"Maybe. But how likely is it that you move into this girl's house, then she moves within spying distance *and* she changes schools? That's one hell of a meet-cute."

"A what?"

"You should watch more films," Zak says, and then, looking over my shoulder, "Don't mess this up."

He packs away his lunch and gets up, even though it's ages until fifth period.

"Where are you going?" I ask.

"I'm just making room."

"Hi," he says to someone behind me, and, when I hear her voice, I feel sick and excited, but mostly sick.

"Can I sit here?" Amy asks.

"Sure."

"I hope it wasn't something I did," she says, nodding at Zak as he leaves.

"No, it's..." I can't finish the sentence because I don't know what it is. All I know is I like this girl, and I need to be honest with her.

"I live in your house," I mumble.

Amy looks confused and says, "I think I'd notice."

"No...I mean...I live in your *old* house. We moved in. And I can see your new house from my window. I wasn't spying. Only I...I saw your mum and realized you live there, now. I just wanted to tell you."

"Oh," she says. "That's weird."

I look for the slightest suggestion that she's freaking out. But her face gives nothing away.

"Why did you move to the next street? Usually, people move farther away than that."

"My mum always loved that house," Amy replies. "We'd drive past, and she'd look at it with jealous eyes, you know? When she saw it was up for sale, she convinced Dad we should move. She didn't want to leave the village. She just wanted her dream home."

I think of Mum saying the same thing about our house. "There are holes in the doors," I say. "In my bedroom and my stepsister's. It looks like there used to be locks on the outside."

It's not a question because I don't know how to ask what I'm thinking. I just want Amy to know I've seen them. I'm scared that, if I don't say it now, it will be something that gets heavier every time I see her. And it feels like I'm going to see her a lot.

"You saw those?" Amy says. She doesn't look upset or nervous. She's not acting like I've uncovered a secret. She just nods and says, "I thought I was the only one."

"What do you mean?"

Amy tucks her hair behind her ear, takes a bite of her sandwich, then says, "My dad used to say I was being stupid. I said it was super weird that you'd lock someone in their bedroom. That's what it looks like, right? But my parents didn't think it was a big deal."

She stares at me until I look away and asks, "How old is your stepsister?"

"She's seventeen. She goes to St. Gregory's."

Amy's face changes. When I mentioned the locks, she was calm, but talking about her old school does something strange to her features. She looks like she did the day we met, when she wouldn't meet my eye and her mother failed to ease the awkwardness.

I want to ask what happened there. Suddenly that feels like the bigger mystery. Whoever drilled holes into the outside of our doors, it looks like they're long gone. But Amy's time at

St. Gregory's did something that causes tremors whenever you mention it.

"What room are you in?" she asks, and, when I tell her, she sad-smiles and says, "That was mine."

I had hoped it was. Somehow, I knew it was. But I don't ask which room is hers, now. I don't want her to know how closely I've watched her new house.

I was looking to see if she needed saving, but I think she's already escaped—not from a house with locks on the doors, but from a school and its own horrors.

20

The holes don't look scary anymore.

I can see how easy they are to ignore and, maybe, in time, I'll stop noticing them. This house might have a horrible history, but it's further back than I thought, and I don't know who lived here before Amy. I could ask her. But, even if she knew, what would I do?

Instead, I lie on my bed, thinking about Amy and wondering if this is what a happy ending feels like.

I never thought I'd think like this. Dreams are dangerous if you let them creep too close, because reality has a habit of getting in the way. But I can't help imagining what it would be like to let Amy in. I could tell her my secrets. I could tell her about the houses we walked into but ran out of.

Leaving Gary was the easiest, but only after Mum realized he was truly dangerous. The one before was so much harder—the closest we've come to a prison. Before Gary, there was Martin—the man who didn't need locks on the outside of our doors.

Our life with him was one big lock.

21

I don't know how Mum met Martin. All I know is we moved in with him in a heartbeat, and it was millions more before we left.

He seemed nice. Any warning signs were hidden by his newness. Mum was happy, so I was happy too. And, even when she wasn't, she disguised it so well that I was allowed to be a kid for a tiny, blissful bit longer.

I spent a lot of time at my grandparents' house over the next few years. They were always excited to see me, but, after a while, their faces showed something else too—worry.

When I went home, there would often be broken things—door panels, windows, anything made of glass.

Mum moved into my room, and we would lie awake on Saturday mornings, not daring to make a sound until we heard the front door slam and the car pull away. The weekends were our refuge. We didn't enjoy them, but we felt less afraid.

The worst thing was the fear that lingered in the corners, creeping forward as the hours ticked away.

On Saturdays, Martin went clay-pigeon shooting. Sometimes—the best times—he didn't come back until we were asleep. On Sundays, we didn't know where he went. But we didn't care. All that mattered was his absence.

Mum did her best to fill those days with good memories, but it's hard to enjoy something when you know it's just a brief escape from a nightmare.

I remember sitting in the bath while Mum rinsed my hair. I remember Martin bursting in and yelling at me to get out.

I remember standing in the hallway, dripping wet and freezing, while the sound of his heavy, never-ending piss filled my ears.

He forced Mum to stay in the bathroom so he could tell her how pathetic I was. When he was done, he walked past in silence while she wrapped me in a towel.

"I'm sorry," she whispered, over and over again.

Every time he did it, she apologized. Eventually, I stopped sobbing, but I could never stop the shivers.

When I realized he did it on purpose, I stopped wanting baths. I would fight with Mum until she gave in and let me wash in the sink with a flannel.

That's what I remember about Martin—all the times I stood outside the bathroom, naked and freezing and alone. That and the gun.

22

The only time Mum fought back, I thought she was going to die.

I don't remember why they were arguing. There probably wasn't a reason. It was just what happened. But, this time, Mum spoke up or hit back, and Martin went to the safe where he kept his rifle for clay-pigeon shooting.

I heard the click as he loaded it and watched as he held the barrel to Mum's head. He didn't shout. He didn't smile. He just stood there, pointing a gun at my mother. I was seven.

Thinking back now, it feels like a story I've made up or a dream that has fractured in the light, leaving only flickers of the facts.

He didn't pull the trigger. That would have been too easy. Martin's game was emotional torture, and he was good at it. But, that weekend, as Mum and I walked around and around the duck pond in a village near ours, crying and not caring who saw, she made a promise that we would escape. And she kept it.

It took a while, and it wasn't dramatic. It wasn't an escape like you see in films. In the end, he watched as the removal men loaded our stuff into their van.

In our new home, I made a fort out of the boxes while Mum and the removal men drank tea round a temporary table.

A while later, Mum met Gary. But that part of our life feels distant, now.

I didn't trust Jay to begin with, and I don't think Mum did either. She wanted to. She said she did. But, when you've seen what she has, you'd be foolish not to be wary. She met Jay in a bar on a night out when she wasn't looking. She was with friends, and he introduced himself. Whatever he said was enough to get her number. Over the next few years, she began to trust him in all the ways she'd never trusted Martin or Gary. It wasn't quick, and it wasn't always easy. But he's a good bloke. He's a "keeper." That's why I believe Mum when she says how lucky we are. Because, if they were that easy to find, everyone would have one.

23

The four of us strip wallpaper with different degrees of enthusiasm. Jay and Mum are having the most fun, I lose interest once the ripping turns to scraping, and Nia would rather be anywhere else.

"We'll do yours next," Jay says, but Nia doesn't answer. I know why my room is the first project. My stepdad thinks it'll help us bond. He thinks we *need* this. I shouldn't moan about a man in our life actually giving a shit, but, sometimes, I wish he wouldn't try so hard.

It feels awkward and fake, because no one moves into a new house and thinks the first room that needs decorating belongs to the sixteen-year-old boy. That's what posters are for. Except I'm not like Nia. I don't like things the way she does. I don't *live* things.

When she talks about her favorite music, or when she plays her own, my stepsister transforms. That's why her room is already a collage of festival line-ups and flyers and photos of her and her best friends, Femi and Esther, at fifty different gigs.

Every time Mum walked in, she frowned at my blank walls and said something about making it my own. It's her way of saying this is forever. But that makes it worse. I'm happy that she's happy. I don't need new wallpaper to feel that.

"So where are these holes again?" Jay asks.

When I show him, he nods and says, "I doubt it's anything sinister."

It worries me how some people dismiss things because they don't want to have to deal with anything "bad."

"Bad" happens...a lot. And there are always clues if you know where to look. But some people suffer too long, and others get away with so much because people like Jay can't or won't see it. That's not me ragging on him. It's a fact. It's why murderers like the Magpie Man and the Tinder Trap killed again and again.

I'll always look for people's secrets and question why a door has more holes than it should.

"You are super paranoid," Nia says, like it's a bad thing. I want to ask her about St. Gregory's Academy, because that's what Amy was upset about. I want to ask if it's bad there. But we don't have actual conversations. Mum and Jay never forced us to like each other. I think they knew that wouldn't work, because my stepsister has two real friends and treats everyone else like a bad smell. She's not a mean girl. She's just selective with who she's nice to. "What the fuck?" she mumbles.

When Jay says, "Nia!," she points at the wall.

I can't see it until Jay steps back and turns to Mum with a

weird look on his face. But, when I do, I can't take my eyes off it.

Under the wallpaper, in tiny black letters, it says *HELP ME HELP ME HELP ME* over and over again.

"That's creepy," Nia says. But it's more than that.

It means I was right about the locks. Even if it happened before Amy lived here, someone was trapped, pleading for help.

Jay touches the words, then breathes out slowly. "We'll paint over that."

And maybe it's my imagination, but, as he leaves, it looks like he glances at the holes in my door, his eyes showing the fear he's been trying to ignore.

24

"Did you decorate your old bedroom?"

Amy raises her eyebrows and says, "What?"

"Your old room—my new room—did you choose your own wallpaper?"

She doesn't reply right away, and, when she does, she sounds doubtful.

"I think so. Dad probably did it. We lived there a long time."

"How long?"

Amy glances over my shoulder, and, when I turn, no one's there. She looks worried, and I wonder if I've gone too far. But I have to know. Did she see the words too? Or, worse, did she write them?

"I was about ten, I think, when we moved in. Why are you asking?"

I don't answer. Instead, I say, "And you had the same wallpaper for seven years?"

"I guess," she says. "Are you redecorating?"

I nod and try to look behind her eyes, but, if she's worried, she hides it well.

"There are words on the wall," I tell her.

It happens so quickly I would have missed it if I'd blinked. But I see it: a flash of fear that leaves the slightest tremor in its wake. Amy doesn't look calm anymore. Her smile wobbles at the edges. Her fingers fidget. Her eyes won't settle on a single spot.

Eventually, almost in a whisper, she asks, "What did they say?"

"Help me. Was it you?"

Amy shakes her head. "Why would I write that?"

"I don't know. Maybe you were in trouble. I can help…if you still are."

She laughs and says, "It wasn't me, Tom. I had no idea it was there."

When I don't reply, she says, "It was probably the former owner mucking about. Maybe he expected us to find it and freak out. But, instead, the joke's on you."

I stare at Amy until she looks away. Whatever this is, it doesn't feel like a joke. I want to believe her, but I can't shake the feeling that she's lying.

"I can help," I say again, just in case, and she smiles.

"Thank you. But I don't need your help."

I know what fear looks like. I saw it a thousand times in my mother, and I can see it, now. Amy's scared. And she won't look me in the eye, because she knows I can see it. Instead, she shakes her head and says, "I should go."

I think about touching her hand or asking her to stay, but all I do is watch her walk away.

If she won't be honest with me, if she won't admit that something bad happened in her house before it was ours, I'll find out another way.

25

Jay wanted to paint over the words the day we found them, but I said no. I pretended it was because I want to choose the color when, the truth is, I can't let him cover up a clue. Those two words, scribbled over and over again, can't be ignored. They can't be dismissed as nothing. The locks might be gone, but this is different. Not even Jay can laugh this off.

When Mum walks in, she glances at the walls and shivers. She won't admit it, but it's taken the gloss off her dream-home high.

Sitting on the edge of my bed, she sighs and says, "I keep telling myself it was a silly game. You drew on the walls sometimes when you were little, so this...maybe it's the same sort of thing."

I know what she's about to say, and I wish she wouldn't. I hate how she's remembering all the lives she's left behind, all the false starts.

"It's okay," I tell her. "You're probably right. It was probably just a game."

"I hope so," she says, staring at the tiny pleas and not looking away.

I could show Mum the lock I bought, because she'd believe me now. I could hold it up to the door and add to the evidence, but something stops me. She looks sad enough, and I don't want to make it worse.

I was too young to save my mother from the monsters.

She had to save both of us. But I *can* save Amy.

I watch Mum for a while, lost in a daydream, then squeeze her hand and say, "It's still nice here."

She smiles, and I hope she believes me. I don't want to take her happiness away, even for a second.

"We did okay, didn't we?" she says.

"We did great."

She nods and kisses me good night. Later, as I go downstairs, I see her through the crack in her bedroom door, still staring off into space while Jay snores by her side. I check the back door three, four, five times, then again once I've tightened the kitchen taps and pushed against the window locks.

I whisper, "Clap," doubt myself, then say it again after the seventh check.

I'm worse when I'm worried. On good days, I can touch everything once and sleep like a baby. On the worst days, I check everything twenty or thirty times and only make it halfway up the stairs before doing it all again. I know it's silly. I know it's irrational. But it's part of me, and it's not going anywhere.

It hasn't always been. It started when we lived with Martin. Before she knew better, Mum called them "nervous tics." I would touch the same thing over and over again or wash my hands until my knuckles cracked, the tiny cuts yawning wider and stinging sharper whenever I moved my fingers.

It wasn't until we lived alone that I began checking the windows and doors.

I used to be scared for just us, but now I'm scared for someone else too. That's why I can't settle even when I'm back in my room.

I look out at Amy's window and will her to pull back her curtains. When she doesn't, I make a promise I'm scared to keep but terrified to break.

I'm going to find out if Amy's hiding something and, if she is, I'll put it right.

26

Tonight is the first costume party of the year.

It's how the student committee raises money for prom. They rent the town's only decent club and charge $5 for entry. A lot of the money comes from the younger kids—the crowds of sophomores and juniors who pre-drink enough to be wasted before they arrive but are sober enough to walk past the bouncers without wobbling. They don't get wristbands, so they can't be served. But the damage has already been done.

Tonight's theme is Geek Chic. You only get a dollar off entry, but, like always, Zak moaned until I dressed up.

He never needs an excuse. Tonight, he has a comb-over and pants pulled up to his waist. I'm wearing thick-rimmed glasses and a curly black wig—basically the only things appropriate left in the costume shop. Without our parties, I think they'd go out of business.

Two junior girls in school uniforms walk past Zak and laugh.

"Dream on," one of them says, and he flashes his teeth.

"Sorry to disappoint, but..." He holds my hand, and they don't know whether to smile or be offended, so they pick one each.

If you only knew this version of Zak, you'd think he was super confident. But it's not that simple. He wouldn't like me saying, but he has something called a do-over diary. Basically, he goes home every night and rewrites his day.

In real life, he stares at a boy, dances at least three meters away, plucks up the courage to speak to him, then bottles it. But in his do-over diary he talks to them all night long.

For an hour before he goes to bed—every single night—Zak reimagines his entire day. He writes scenes where people laugh at his jokes, where he scores the winning goal at lunch, where he gets every question right in class. And, on party nights, he writes love stories.

Zak told me about it during a sleepover, and I thought he was joking until I woke up to find him scribbling at his desk. He says it's practice for when he meets his dream guy; all those fake perfect nights he's written—one day he'll use the best bits for real.

I reckon he's filled at least twenty diaries, and he still wouldn't say hi to someone he liked. I don't blame him. Sometimes the smallest words are the heaviest. But it's funny how he can be super confident in some ways but not in others.

I'm wondering if Amy will show up when she appears out of nowhere and kisses my cheek.

"What does that mean?" I ask.

It comes out by accident, but she grins at me. "It means I'm happy to see you."

She hasn't dressed up. I guess this is just her usual out-of-school self, and I suddenly feel conscious of my wig and the head I'm desperate to scratch.

Zak winks at me but doesn't leave. He stares at us like we're his entertainment for the evening.

Amy turns to him and says, "Looking good."

"Thanks. You too."

The way she smiles, I wish I'd said it first. But it's too late, now. Instead, I say, "These parties are usually pretty lame."

I hope it sounds cool. I hope it sounds like I'm at a party every night and this one is bottom of the list.

"We'll see," she replies. "You mind if I hang with you?"

"Sure," Zak says, and I wonder if this will make it into his do-over diary.

"You want a drink?" I ask.

"I've got that covered," says Amy.

She reaches into her bag and flashes something metal, tucking it away before I can look too closely. But I know what it is.

"Sneaky," Zak says. "You want some Coke with that?"

Amy nods, and Zak heads to the bar while I desperately think of something to say.

"You still think I wrote on my walls?" she asks.

"Did you?"

"Of course not. You have an overactive imagination."

The bass drops, and the sound goes up another notch, leaving us to stare awkwardly at each other while the dance floor explodes and the people standing round the edges yell to be heard.

Zak and I might not be the coolest, but we still fit in here. That's what I like about our school. Despite all the cliques, no one is bullied for being different. We come to these parties because everyone's welcome. We don't dance or get wasted. It's just a different place to chat the same shit. But tonight is different. When Zak comes back, Amy downs half her Coke, then fills the glass with whatever is in her flask.

She doesn't offer it around, and Zak looks disappointed, but I'm relieved. I don't drink because I've seen what can happen when you do.

Amy has other ideas. "You want to dance?" she asks, and, when I shake my head, she huffs and pulls Zak into the sticky mess that is the dance floor.

Zak beams because he doesn't need an excuse. Sometimes, on nights out, I can see him fighting the beat that makes his body sway back and forth like the wind.

Tonight, it's as though Amy has cut his strings. They laugh as they make up their own moves, and I feel happy and a little bit jealous.

After a few songs, Zak runs over and shouts, "Seriously. Suck it up and dance with us."

I shake my head, because it's not that easy. Zak can go from zero to one hundred in a second. But I'll try, then stop, and that's worse than not trying at all.

"She asked you to dance," he says. "You know what that means."

I know what he *thinks* it means, but maybe she's only being friendly.

"Don't let this go in your do-over diary," Zak says.

"I don't have one."

"You will if you mess this up."

I look over his shoulder at a girl I've only just met who makes me feel so many things. Brave isn't one of them. But she's dancing like no one's watching, and, even though people are always saying that, I don't think I've ever seen it before.

Zak puts his hands on my shoulders. "Tom. It's not embarrassing if everyone's doing it."

I don't say that depends what they're doing. I let him lead me on to the dance floor, and Amy says something I can't hear over the music. I move a bit, then try to stop, but they don't let me. They move my arms and laugh, and I try to do what they're doing.

"Are you having fun?" Zak yells.

I'm not. And then, suddenly, I am. And it's my best mate who eventually pulls me away, holding his side and saying, "Cramp."

Every now and then, Amy tops off her drink, then swigs directly from the flask until she turns it upside down and pokes out her bottom lip.

"All gone," she mumbles.

She's rocking slowly from side to side, and, when she leans over to tell me she needs the toilet, her booze-breath slaps me across the face.

A few people are giving her funny looks, and I don't know if it's because she's the new girl or because she's not exactly shy when she dances.

Or maybe it's because, as I guide her to the toilets, she knocks into people and says things like, "Whoops…drunk person coming through."

The tiniest slur creeps into her voice, and I think about Gary and how we got so used to it that he sounded weird when he *wasn't* drunk.

"Are you okay?" I ask. "Do you want some fresh air?"

Amy shakes her head. "Fresh air doesn't help. You sound like Logan."

I think it, stop myself, then say it anyway. "Is Logan your boyfriend?"

She grins and says, "Why? Are you jealous? Don't worry... He's no one."

Amy tries to walk but loses her balance and giggles as I struggle to hold her up. Someone taps my shoulder and, when I turn, a bouncer says, "She needs to leave."

"She's not that drunk," I reply, but he shakes his head.

"She's drunk enough."

Zak looks like he wants to argue, but I say, "Okay. We're going."

"Boo," Amy says, before pointing at the bouncer and shouting, "You take your job way too seriously."

It takes a lot to be banned from Sensorium. But I don't want Amy to push it, so I guide her to the front doors. Zak calls a taxi while she rests her head on my shoulder and says, "This is fun."

I don't move a muscle until the car arrives.

When we're in the back seat, she nuzzles into me again, mumbling about nothing until she falls asleep. And I sit with my eyes closed, thinking about all the times I didn't dance and wondering why.

27

There's a buzzer to get past the gate.

The intercom crackles, and a voice says, "Yes?"

I clear my throat. "It's Tom. From school. I have Amy with me."

The voice doesn't reply right away and, when it does, it sounds uncertain. "She knows the code."

"She's...forgotten it."

I glance over at Amy, who is grinning up at me and whispering, "I'm in the shit, now."

More silence, then a buzz and a clank as the gate slowly opens. It feels like we're walking into a prison.

The front door is open before I get there, Amy's mum standing with her arms crossed and a weird look on her face.

"She's..."

"She's drunk," her mum says. "What did you say your name was?"

"It's Tom. I...showed you around the school."

Amy's mum's face slowly defrosts, and she says, "Of course. And now we meet again."

Amy is starting to feel heavy on my shoulder, and I edge forward, hoping I can bring her inside.

Her mum looks behind her, then back at me, and says, "I'll take it from here."

I feel Amy's grip tighten, and I think her mum sees it, too, because she says, "Okay. Come in."

I nod and step into a house that looks immaculate. This must have been what else the workmen were doing, after they built the walls and fitted the gate, and I wonder where Amy and her family stayed during the refurbishment.

Everything looks newly decorated, not a speck of dust or dirt.

When Amy sees me staring, she says, "I think it's too white. If you look at the walls too long, you'll see your reflection."

Amy's mum marches into the hall with a glass of water and holds it under her daughter's nose. "Drink this."

They stare at each other until I feel nervous, because Amy looks as angry as her mum does. During the school tour, she shrank into herself, letting her mum run the show. But, now, it's like they are squaring off.

Something silent flashes between them, and Amy downs the water in four gulps, then hands it back and smiles. Except it's not a happy smile. It makes her mother cringe.

"Well, thank you for returning our daughter."

I've waited a long time to get inside this house, to see if Amy's new door is the same as her old one and if her walls are as white as the hallway or completely different, but I need to get out.

The air seems heavy. There's a tension I haven't felt since

we lived with Martin. And that's when I hear a creak above us. I know it's Amy's dad, because I've seen him through the windows. But he looks different tonight.

He doesn't speak until he's sitting next to Amy on the bottom step, and, when he does, his voice is softer than I expected. He strokes her hair. "You okay?"

She doesn't reply. Instead, like the day we met, her mum talks for her. "She's fine."

The man looks up at me and says, "Who's this?"

"Tom was nice enough to bring her home."

Amy's dad stands, shakes my hand, and says, "That *was* nice of him."

He squeezes a bit too tight, nods, and lets go. Then he opens the front door and says, "Good night, then."

I look down at Amy, who glances up at me and says, "See ya."

I wait a few more seconds, overstaying my welcome, but who cares?

I could run up the stairs and find out if there are locks on their doors before they could catch me. But then what? Would they let me leave if I'm right? And what would they do if I'm wrong?

"Night," I say.

Amy's dad walks me to the gate, then smiles as we stand on opposite sides. Her brother is watching from an upstairs window, and her mum waits by the front door, but Amy has already disappeared.

When the gate clunks shut, her dad says, "See you around, Tom."

It's just what people say. It doesn't mean anything.

Except, this time, it sounds like a threat.

28

I can't sleep. Instead, I watch Amy's house from my window, the three lights below the rain gutters painting yellow spots on their driveway.

Everything about the place looks secure. There are twenty-five gold spikes on each railing, the metal separated by thick brick columns.

Thirty minutes ago, I was the other side of that gate. And I couldn't wait to leave. Maybe it was just the tension of being between a parent and their drunk daughter. I would never dare do that in front of Mum, because she'd go ballistic. But it felt different. I've seen Jay go nuclear on Nia. I've seen Zak's parents tear him a new one. It feels awkward, but it's never felt unsettling; not until tonight.

Their house looks even bigger in the dark. In horror films, haunted houses look as old as the ghosts inside. But brand-new homes can be a different kind of terrible.

I wish I had Amy's number so I could message her. I wish

I could throw stones at her window and make sure she's all right.

When Mum touches my shoulder, I jump out of my skin, and she says, "Sorry. Did you have fun tonight?"

The party already feels like ages ago, even though it's still going on. "Yeah, I…it was cool."

"You're home early."

I check my phone and say, "It's a school night."

"That doesn't usually stop you."

Mum wasn't always this laid-back. She used to keep me extra close, when it was just the two of us. Sometimes there were stories on the news about kids going missing, and she would say that if I didn't hold her hand, I'd be next.

"What were you looking at?" she asks.

All she sees is a house. She doesn't know what might be happening inside.

I imagine telling her, because I think she'd understand. But I need evidence before I say she might have bought our house from a psychopath.

If I focus, I can still feel Amy's dad squeeze my hand as he shook it. It hurt just enough to not be an accident.

29

"What did her parents say?" Zak asks. "Were they pissed?"

I nod and say, "I finally got into their house. And I wasted it."

"What do you mean?"

"I wanted to see if she has a lock on the outside of her door."

"You asked her about it, right? And she denied it. Why can't you just believe her?"

When I don't reply, Zak says, "I know you and your mum went through some shit, but Amy doesn't seem trapped. She came to the party, didn't she? So there's nothing to worry about."

Zak thinks the writing on my wall is someone's idea of a joke. But he didn't see how Amy's dad looked at me through the gate. Let's just say it wasn't friendly.

"You worry too much," Zak says.

There it is again. It will probably be on my gravestone: *Here lies Thomas Cavanagh. He worried too much.*

But I don't think I do. I think I worry exactly the right amount.

At lunch, Amy sits with us, and Zak smirks and says, "You suffering today?"

"I'm fine," she says, and then, turning to me, "Thanks for last night."

"Were they angry with you?"

"No more than usual."

I flash Zak a look that he parries with a frown, and Amy catches us and says, "What was that?"

We sit in silence until, eventually, Zak sighs and says, "I'm going."

As he passes, he leans in and whispers, "Ask her again if you have to. But believe her this time."

When it's just the two of us, I practice sentences in my head while Amy eats with her eyes down.

Eventually, it's her that speaks first. "You're still worried about me, aren't you?"

When I nod, she takes my hand and says, "Come on. I have a story for you."

30

Amy sits by the head-start line and touches the chalk.

When she closes her eyes, I think of all the films I used to watch with Mum—the ones where boys meet girls. They all had scenes like this, just the two of them, and, somehow, they always knew what to do.

Mum apologized once because I didn't have a dad to give me "life lessons." She said she would do her best, but there were some things she couldn't tell me.

Those father/son moments you see on TV—if I'd had some, maybe I'd know what to do here with Amy. But, instead, I watch her until she opens her eyes and says, "My old school was horrific. There were dramas on top of dramas, you know? I remember my parents telling me how important the eleven-plus exam was. They basically said it was do-or-die. It was as though your life was over if you didn't make it into St. Gregory's. But I made it, so they were happy, and so was I... for a while."

She shakes her head and breathes out, then stares over my shoulder and says, "It's a lot better here."

"What happened?"

I don't think she's going to reply. But then she says, "My dad was attacked. Last year...he was on his way back from football, and they...they got him."

"I'm sorry..." I say, but Amy holds up her hand for me to stop.

"He got really busted up."

"Is he okay now?"

"He's fine," Amy says. "All better."

Her eyes are closed again, and, behind her, the sky is the color of a strawberry smoothie.

"The police found out who did it," she says. "It was that guy who owns the garage, Mr. Wells, and his brothers. Dad said he was mugged. He said they stole his phone and his wallet and his keys, and he never saw their faces."

Amy looks like the day we met. Like someone you'd want to put your arm around but then chicken out at the last second.

"The police came back and said that's not what Mr. Wells told them. He admitted to battering Dad, but said he never took his money."

Amy opens her eyes and stares at me. "He wasn't mugged. That's not what happened."

"What did happen?"

Amy's eyes go wet the way Mum's do sometimes. "They made it up. Evie Wells and her friends made it up just to mess with me. And her dad believed them."

I don't understand until Amy says, "Don't make enemies,

because they'll ruin you. Evie was my best friend. She slept at my house. And then, one day, she hated me."

"Why?"

"I don't know. She just…changed her mind, I guess. That's when the rumors started. She said she was having sex with my dad." Amy doesn't wipe her tears away. She lets them slide down her cheeks and fall on the grass between us.

Why is she telling me this? Why does she trust me when we've only just met?

"They were posting things online. I don't think Evie's dad was supposed to find out. But he saw the posts…and he did something about it."

"I'm sorry."

"That's what everyone says."

"So that's why you changed schools."

Amy nods and says, "It's one of the reasons." I go to touch her, then stop.

"Everyone does that too," she says. "People don't touch broken things…in case they make them more broken."

"You're not broken," I reply, and she laughs.

"Of course I am."

She stares at me with the biggest, most beautiful eyes, and, after two false starts, I hold her hand. She smiles and rests her head on my shoulder.

I want to ask why her dad lied about being mugged. But I don't say anything. I just enjoy the feeling of Amy's head against mine and wonder why I ever worried about the locks.

31

"*Help me...help me...HELP ME!*"

I wake up shaking, the sound of someone else's cry echoing behind my eyes. I turn on my bedside lamp and stare at the words still covering my wall. Why didn't I let Jay paint over them when he suggested it? If Amy didn't write them, I want them gone. They could have been written fifty years ago. I could look and look and still not find out who did this.

I can't get back to sleep, but the house is silent and dark. So I stay in bed, picturing Amy's face when she told me about her dad.

She trusted me. She said something so big I already feel weighed down by it. And I feel both happy and worried, because I don't know if it's changed everything already, shaking up a friendship that hadn't even settled into its first version.

I feel stupid for jumping to conclusions now that I know Amy's actual story. How must she have felt when I asked about things that had nothing to do with her? And why, after that, did she still pick me to tell?

I grab my phone and search for Amy's social media, but I can't find anything. I try different variations of her name, hoping I stumble across whatever she calls herself online.

When nothing comes up, I type in a different name: Evie Wells. The girl who lied about Amy's dad. It takes me ages to find her, but she's there. It looks like she's in college, now, but, when I scroll back far enough, I see her with Amy.

Except that's not quite true. Amy's in the background. She stares sadly at the camera while the people in front of her smile. She hovers in the corners of a hundred different photos.

The way she looks at the camera, it's not an accident. She wanted to be in those shots. And yet there's a creepiness to every single one, because, I think, unless you were looking for her, you wouldn't notice she was there.

She isn't photobombing them. She isn't making faces or doing it for a joke. She looks like a ghost. I can't find a single photograph focused on Amy. They're all of Evie and a group I don't recognize.

Then something catches my eye—a different person; one I'm not expecting.

Nia—slightly out of focus—stands in the background, talking to a boy. My stepsister looks happier than she ever does at home. But I suddenly can't wait for her to wake up because, maybe, she can explain what's going on.

Amy said she was Evie's best friend before things went wrong. The problem is: Evie's Instagram goes back years, and they look like complete strangers.

32

"Morning."

Nia grunts a reply. My heart is racing because I'm about to have an actual conversation with her, or at least *try* to. And that hasn't gone well in the past.

We have an unwritten rule: we may live in the same house, but that doesn't make us family. And it definitely doesn't make us friends. It's Nia's rule. I just accept it.

"Do you know Evie Wells?"

My stepsister doesn't reply right away. I think she's trying to figure out how to answer, because she keeps looking at me then away.

Finally, she sighs and says, "What about her?"

"Is that a yes?"

Nia fills her mouth with cereal, watches me as she chews, then says, "She used to go to my school. She's not there anymore."

"So she was a senior?"

I say this more to myself than to Nia, but she asks, "Why are you interested in Evie? Have you been perving over her Insta or something?"

Not exactly, I think. But, out loud, I say, "Do you know Amy Pearce?"

When she doesn't answer, I pick up my phone and show her an image of Amy standing behind Evie. But Nia shakes her head. "Never seen her before."

"Are you sure?"

"I'm sure."

Nia takes her breakfast to her room, so that's the end of the conversation. It went better than I expected. At least she was polite.

It doesn't help me, though. How can someone go unnoticed through six years of school? I don't know the name of everyone in my grade, but I know their faces. Amy was there. She even went to their parties. Yet she's always on her own. She's always hovering at the back of someone else's moment.

I should have asked about the rumor. That kind of thing would have spread like wildfire. But I've used up my Nia allowance for the day. Instead, I keep searching Evie's social media for any mention of Amy's dad. There must be comments if it happened recently. But, before I know it, I'm seeing Evie and her friends as kids and realize I've scrolled through five years of her life.

Not one mention of Amy's dad. Not one comment about the lie that got him attacked and forced his daughter to another school. That's not how life works. Those kinds of stories take over. Until something bigger comes along, it's all anyone goes on about.

Nia would have known Amy if her dad and Evie were the talk of the school. She would have seen her face and remembered the rumor, because things like that infiltrate every single clique. But she didn't recognize her. She looked like she was staring at a stranger.

A stranger who went to parties but was never seen and seemed invisible in her own school.

33

I look at the holes in my door for the first time in days and run my hands over the words on my wall. Then I scroll through the images of Amy haunting other people's pictures.

She said it had nothing to do with her. She said the holes were here when she moved in, and the words were hidden behind wallpaper her dad put up. But she also said she was Evie's best friend, and there's no evidence of that.

I want to believe her. Yet every thought is tangled with doubt.

"What's up?" Zak says, jolting me out of my daydream.

"Nothing."

He knows I'm lying, but he doesn't push. He just nods and starts talking about last night's TV.

Outside sociology, I say, "Amy's lying about the locks."

"How do you know?"

"It doesn't add up. She's hiding something."

I'm changing my mind so often that it's hurting my head.

Amy opened up to me, but I can't shake the feeling that she was honest about the wrong thing. I need to know for certain if the story about her dad is true. Nia might tell me if I catch her on a good day, except those are few and far between.

Luckily for me, Aaron is visiting soon. He stays with us once a week, Jay and Nia spending Saturday with him and all of us playing happy families for one night.

He's only six, but he can defrost his sister with a single smile. She loves Aaron so much that I wonder why she chose to live with her dad and his second attempt at a happy ending.

I used to think the love she has for her brother should negate whatever anger she feels for her mum. But I've seen the way Nia looks at her when she drops Aaron off. She hates her for cheating on Jay. She despises her for forcing her to make a decision no kid should have to make. Which parent do you want to live with: the one who has your favorite person in the world or the one who did nothing wrong?

Nia chose her dad when it was just the two of them. Now she has a second brother she can't stand and a stepmother who tiptoes round her.

But Aaron could be my secret weapon, because Nia forgets to hate me when he's around. She can help me figure out what's going on with Amy. She's the insider I need to figure out exactly what happened at St. Gregory's.

34

Nia wraps Aaron in a hug he pretends he doesn't want until his giggles give him away.

She laughs so loudly and so genuinely that it catches me by surprise. And then I smile, too, because I enjoy seeing her like this.

We're all happier when Aaron comes over. The cloud that hovers over Nia all week vanishes the moment he arrives. She forgets to be sarcastic. She doesn't roll her eyes or mumble insults under her breath. She loves being a big sister, just not to me.

I called her that once, and she huffed and said, "I'm literally ten months older than you."

I felt stupid for saying it. And I realized pretty quickly that she didn't want to be my anything.

But there are other moments too. Like the time her friends were over and Femi called me weird when he thought I wasn't listening. Esther laughed, and I waited for Nia to agree, but she didn't. Instead, she said, "He's all right."

"Hi, Tom," Aaron says.

I don't hug him, because it's not my place. Instead, we fist-bump, and Aaron grins and says, "It's my turn to choose the film."

Whenever he stays, we have a family film night. Last week Mum picked *P.S. I Love You* because she only watches movies that make her cry.

Aaron will choose *Moana* because he always chooses *Moana*, and we'll joke how we've seen it a million times, then smile as he sings every word.

After dinner, while Mum and Jay load the dishwasher and Aaron pretends to look through our DVDs, I turn to Nia and say, "I have a question...about Evie Wells."

"Are you stalking her or something?"

"No...I...did you hear a rumor about her and someone's dad?"

She makes a face. "What are you talking about?"

"I heard a story...that Evie was...you know...with a friend's dad. It was going 'round school, so I figured it was true."

I have to lie a little bit. Nia is more likely to tell me the truth if she thinks I already know it.

But she shakes her head and says, "I don't know anything about that. It sounds like bollocks. Some kid at your school probably made it up because it didn't get as far at ours."

Nia doesn't talk about the Academy much, but I know that, when gossip happens, it grows and spreads and becomes more than a few whispered words.

"Evie Wells is not the kind of girl to hook up with someone's dad," Nia says. "I didn't really know her, but I don't see it."

I can actually see the moment Nia realizes she's talking to me in a way she never has before. She catches herself, gives me a funny look, then rearranges her features. But the sharpness flattens as Aaron walks back in, holding the *Moana* DVD, passes it to his sister and sings, "You're welcome!"

We all laugh, and she lets me join in the joke.

After the movie, Aaron turns to his sister and says, "Play it."

"Upstairs," she whispers.

"No. Here."

Nia sighs, but she's not angry. She'll do whatever her brother wants because he can only ask once a week.

She gets one of her guitars from her room, then sits next to him and says, "You ready?"

Aaron nods, and his sister glances at me, then she plays the tune I usually hear through the wall—the song she wrote for her brother that doesn't have any words, but is basically perfect.

If I wasn't here, maybe this would be one of those cheesy family moments you see on TV. But I am, so it's not. Nia's embarrassment creeps out between the notes, yet she keeps going.

When she's done, Mum says, "Amazing," and Nia's face lights up the way Aaron's does when she plays.

"Thanks," my stepsister says, watching as her brother burns off the last of his energy.

It's only when I'm brushing my teeth that Nia stands in the bathroom doorway and asks, "What's going on?"

I can't reply without spraying her with toothpaste, so I just shrug and she says, "Where did you really hear about Evie Wells?"

I slowly rinse my mouth, figuring out what to tell her, but, before I can, Nia says, "Don't believe everything you hear."

35

Amy's new house is twice the size of ours.

If you go online, you can see the photographs taken before the builders started work. That was the house Amy's parents bought, but it isn't the one they live in, now.

I only got a glimpse of the hallway, but it's all white now, the light switch and sockets sparkling chrome, the carpet so perfect I felt guilty for wearing shoes.

I look around our house at how lived-in it looks. How could they go from this to that? I can't imagine ever living in a house that looks like a space station with walls I'd be afraid to touch in case I marked them.

I watch Amy's house from mine, putting words to the silent scenes that switch from window to window.

Again, as always, her parents sit on either side of her brother in the living room, their faces lit by the TV's glow. But she's not with them.

She doesn't talk about her brother, and I wonder if it's

because he's the favorite. He looks about eleven, and I make a note on my phone to look out for him at school. Would he tell me something different if I asked about the holes? Or would he think I'm a weirdo and report me to the principal?

Their house is so far back from the street, with a massive driveway and that sliding gate, that they probably don't worry about being spied on. Mum closes the curtains as soon as the lamp goes on because she hates the idea of people looking in. But Amy's parents act like they're invisible.

I see a curtain twitch, then Amy is looking out, staring directly at me. She doesn't smile. She doesn't wave. But my light is off, and I'm crouched down low, only my forehead and my eyes poking above the windowsill.

I'm not spying. I'm just making sure...that she's safe... that I'm wrong...that their house and the people in it are as harmless as ours.

Amy isn't looking at me, anyway. She's watching a moon that fills the sky, making the night feel almost safe. She brushes a strand of hair behind her ear, puffs her cheeks and blows out. Then the curtain falls back into place, and she's gone.

I look back at her dad, whose face shows no signs of the beating he had, and whose arm rests on the shoulders of a wife who doesn't look betrayed.

Amy's brother laughs at something unseen, and his parents smile at each other. And, in that moment, I think of Mum and Jay and Nia and Aaron. This is how they looked last night as we sat watching the same film for the hundredth time. I was there, on the sofa next to them, not hidden away upstairs like Amy is, now. But I think I felt like her.

I felt separate, as if I was watching them. And, when you watch, you see things other people don't, like a girl leaving behind clues she's too scared to admit to and telling lies for reasons you can't quite understand.

36

Before Jay paints over the words, I take a picture, and he gives me a funny look, but doesn't ask why.

If he scrolled through my phone, he'd see lots of strange things, like Amy's house the way it appears from my window, and her parents and brother looking like ghosts through two sets of double glazing. And, now, hundreds of tiny pleas in writing I need to compare with Amy's before I can be certain.

It's not until the room is magnolia all over that I realize how far the words stretched. Without them, the walls look empty.

I message Zak, asking if he's free, and, ten minutes later, I'm watching his dad chase his brother around the living room while his mum feeds his sister in her high chair.

Zak's house is carnage, but I love it. He was an only child, like me, until he was ten, and then, suddenly, he wasn't. Harrison is six, Ivy's nearly one, and Zak's parents look like they need a rest. But they're always pleased to see me, and, sometimes, I wonder how my life would look if Dad hadn't left.

Would I have siblings...real ones that didn't resent me? I can't imagine Mum with another kid, but that's only because of how life worked out. She jokes with Jay that she's too old for a baby, now.

We go to Zak's room for some peace, and he flops on his bed. "How's the spying mission going?"

I ignore him, because that's not what I want to talk about. But he laughs and says, "You know I love you, man. But you have to let this go."

"I didn't say anything. *You* brought it up."

"It's all over your face, Tom. It's literally all you're thinking about. I've seen you worry about a lot of things. I know what that looks like."

"You think I'm being stupid."

"No, I think you watch too many crime shows. Not everything's a clue, you know. Some things are just...things."

He's right. But it's not just the "things" that are bothering me. It's the feelings that go with them.

When I see the holes in my door, I think of what bad people do to keep good people trapped. I think of Martin and Gary and all the monsters I've never met. I think of what happens behind front doors that look just like ours but hide something terrible. We've lived behind those doors, so I know they exist. And I know there are people out there who lock others in, because it's just what they do. And, when I think of the words on my wall, I imagine the person writing them. I feel their fear and picture their frantic hands working in the dark, pleading to no one but themselves. I picture those things because I've lived them.

I remember them because Mum and I felt trapped for so much longer than we should have.

I could tell Zak because he knows about my old life, except, sometimes, I worry that it's a story he doesn't want to hear over and over again. I know he'd listen, and I know he'd understand. But I feel guilty for reminding him of a version of me he never knew.

Instead, I say, "One of us is right."

He nods like he knows it's him, and I sigh, desperately hoping it's not me.

37

I need to know, one way or the other, if Amy wrote the words on my wall. If I ask her, again, she'll say no. But that's not the only possible answer. The only way to be certain is to compare her handwriting with the scribbles now hidden beneath three coats of paint.

Whenever I get too close to her notebook, she puts it away, and I wonder what she doesn't want me to see. Is it what she's written or how she wrote it?

We're at lunch when it happens. Amy stands up and says, "I'm going to the bathroom." And perhaps it's because she trusts us now, or maybe she forgets or doesn't care, but she leaves her bag under her seat. I watch her leave the cafeteria, then pull it close and unzip it.

"What are you doing?" Zak asks, but I don't answer.

Her notebook is wedged at the bottom and, as I pull it out, something else comes with it—a T-shirt way too small for her.

"Put it back," Zak whispers.

"Just tell me when she's coming."

"She'll freak if she catches you."

I stare at him. "Then make sure she doesn't."

I open the notebook to a random page. It doesn't matter what it says. I'm looking at the patterns in the words, the curls and the joins. Then I point my phone at the pad and take three quick pictures. I do the same with other pages, then pull a few more things out of her bag and place it back where it was.

"Hurry up," Zak says, but, when I follow his line of sight, he's still staring at an empty doorway.

It's not just a T-shirt. There's a tiny pair of trousers and a mustard-colored jacket that looks like it would fit Aaron.

I pause, even though I should be rushing, because it's not what I expected to find.

"What do you think these are for?" I ask, and, when Zak shakes his head and lets out a panicked squeak, I tuck them back in Amy's bag, zip it closed, and shove it under her chair.

"What the fuck?" Zak says.

"I needed to see her writing, okay?"

But all he says in reply is, "Amy," and, a few seconds later, she sits down and smiles.

"What did I miss?"

Zak looks at me, and I shrug and say, "Nothing important."

I want to leave immediately, but it's another fifteen minutes before the bell rings for fifth period.

When I'm alone, I scroll through the photos of Amy's writing and then the words on my wall. I zoom in, looking for the slightest suggestion that they were written by the same person. But they don't match.

Amy's writing is neat and flowing while the tiny army of *HELP ME*s are jagged and untidy.

They look as if they were done in a rush, whereas Amy's journal is like art. She embellishes everything, adding hearts and swirls and doodles. It's not until I look past the patterns and read the words that I start to panic.

> *I see it in the way he looks at me. He can't possibly know the truth, but he knows something isn't right. And I don't think he's going to stop digging.*

38

When the doorbell sounds, I ignore it, because it's never for me. It takes three shouts from Mum before I realize I'm wanted.

"You have a visitor," she says, with a smile that makes me nervous. And, when I'm halfway down the stairs, I stop in shock because Amy's there, her grin even wider than Mum's.

"Surprise," Amy says.

Mum lets out a tiny laugh, "Come in…come in."

"What are you doing here?" I ask.

Mum gives me a look that says I'm being rude. But she doesn't speak because she's trying to figure out what's going on, and she's not the only one.

Girls don't visit me. No one visits me except Zak. And my mother looks flustered in case this is a big deal and she should have prepared for it.

"I'm Amy," she says, and, when Mum shakes her hand, she adds, "I lived here before you did. Tom thinks my parents locked me in my bedroom."

Mum stares at me, then says, "He worries too much. I tell him, but...he has his ways."

This is how she explains my OCD and my anxiety. She turns them into a quirk.

I'm surprised Mum said anything, because she's usually too embarrassed. Sometimes she blames herself. She thinks I'd be different if our family had worked the first time around. Mum worries about my worries more than I do. I just live with them.

"So you're...school friends?" she asks.

"Tom was the first person I met at school. He made a good impression."

She's being weird, and we both know it.

Amy catches my eye, and I wonder if she knows I went through her bag. Is this payback? Or is she just fooling around?

Mum leads her into the kitchen where Jay is working on his laptop and says, "Tom has a visitor."

She practically sings it, and he stands and rubs Mum's shoulders. "I can see that."

Amy introduces herself again, and I'm jealous of her confidence. But, then, this isn't unfamiliar territory. I wonder if, in a way, she feels like we're guests in her house rather than the other way around.

"Would you like a cup of tea?" Mum asks Amy.

"No, thank you."

That's not the answer Mum was expecting. There's a faint ripple of panic in her cheeks before Jay says, "Perhaps we should leave them to it."

"It's fine," I say, a bit too quickly. "Amy was telling Mum she used to live here. How weird is that?"

Jay tilts his head and says, "So how do you know each other?"

"I go to the same school, now," Amy says. "I used to go to the—"

I turn to see what she's looking at, and Nia's in the doorway.

"We have a guest," Mum says. But Amy isn't smiling anymore.

She stares at Nia, growing paler by the second, until my stepsister catches her eye and says, "What's this?"

I think of the photos that Amy haunted, the party that Nia was also at. They were almost as close as they are now.

Amy shrinks into herself, like she did the day we met, while Nia stares at her, then me, then back again.

"This is Amy," I say, and my stepsister looks at her for a little too long.

"I should go," Amy mumbles.

Mum looks worried, like she's offended the first proper visitor I've ever had. But it's not her. It's Nia. And Amy's not offended. She's scared.

She walks into the hallway, opens the door, and leaves without looking back.

"See you," she calls. I don't reply because I'm trying to figure out what just happened.

"She's a nice girl," Mum says, even if it sounds like she's trying to convince herself.

"She's weird," Nia replies, brushing past us and going up to her room.

I follow her, because I have to know. Something doesn't add up, and my stepsister is the only one who can help.

"Are you sure you don't know her?"

Nia gives me the death stare until I step back, moving from her bedroom to the landing. "Why would I know her?"

"Because she was at your school. Her name's Amy. She went to the same parties."

Nia shakes her head. "A lot of people go to those parties."

I don't push it. Either Nia's lying, which doesn't make sense, or she genuinely doesn't know her.

There are kids at my school who slip under the radar. I'm probably one of them. But, surely, people would recognize my face even if they forgot my name.

Amy looked genuinely shocked when Nia turned up. We get that, sometimes, when we tell people we're sort-of related, and you can see the cogs turning as they figure out the hows and the whys. It's the same when Mum says her surname is Nkansa and strangers can't hide their surprise.

But Amy wasn't surprised. She was terrified.

39

"She came to my house," I say. "And she carries around kids' clothes and is writing about me in her journal...saying I can't possibly know the truth."

Zak rubs his mouth and says, "Dude. You know I love you, but I think you're self-sabotaging."

"What are you talking about?"

"I've been doing some research, and it's a thing. I think you like this girl...a lot. But you're trying to rescue her when you should be asking her out."

"Did you not hear what I said?"

"Yes. That's the problem. When you were dancing with Amy, I've never seen you that happy. So *what* if she came over? Maybe she likes you."

"And everything else?"

"It's always a mistake reading someone's diary, Tom. You can easily get the wrong idea."

"And the kids' clothes?"

Zak shakes his head. "I don't know. Maybe they're her brother's or her cousin's. Why are you so desperate to solve a mystery that might not even exist?"

"Because no one helped my mum. The clues were there, but no one saw them."

I think of Martin pointing the gun at her and imagine what might have been. It's a thought I have to scrunch my eyes and squeeze my fists to crush before it swallows me.

"I know what you've been through," Zak says. "So why not try being happy?"

I get ready to argue, but he's right. Mixed in with my fear and uncertainty is that night at Sensorium. I was happy. And then Amy's dad gripped my hand and squeezed all that happiness out of me.

But, sometimes, I still see the strobes flash across her face or remember a yelled conversation chopped into pieces by the beat. For once, my anxiety wasn't pushed to the side—it vanished.

"What if I'm right?" I ask.

Zak raises his eyebrows. "What if you're wrong?"

40

I have Zak's words in my head on repeat. It's the only way to drown out the fears.

There's more than one. There's the fear that I'm right and Amy *is* in trouble. There's the fear that I'm wrong, but I'll never stop worrying. And there's the fear that comes when you're about to ask a girl out for the first time ever, but you've forgotten how to speak.

"Do it," Zak says, nudging me until my legs take over, and I'm five...four...three steps behind her.

"Hey," I say.

Amy turns around and says, "There you are."

She talks like we're more than this, and I want my thoughts to catch up to hers. But I've never had a girlfriend. I've never even been on a date.

Zak is staring from across the courtyard, and I can already sense his disappointment. "Maybe next time," he'll say. Only his words will be tinged with the feeling of failure—mine, not his.

I think of Mum taking a chance on Dad...then another on Jay. Not all her decisions were disasters. Then I swallow my nausea and say, "I was wondering if..."

Amy's eyes lock on to mine and don't let go. She knows what's coming. I'm too obvious and too tragic, but she doesn't laugh. She smiles and waits, and, somehow, I squeeze out the question.

"...you wanted to...do something...with me."

"Sure," she says.

She sees Zak over my shoulder and waves. Then she kisses my cheek and says, "I've got to go."

Amy walks toward the science block until she's lost in the crowd.

It's weird how school works. There are hundreds of us, but we only notice a few. If things were different, I wouldn't know her at all.

"Well?" Zak asks.

I breathe out and say, "What do people do on dates?"

He slaps me on the back and shakes his head. "I have no idea."

41

In films, people go to the carnival and kiss on the Ferris wheel, but there are no fairs around here. The only restaurants are McDonald's and some other fast food. When people go out with each other, that's *all* they do. They go outside, and then, when they get cold, they come in again.

But I don't want to stand around with Amy. I want to do something special. I want to feel like we did when we danced.

It's the toss of a coin who I ask: heads is Mum and tails is Nia. It's hard to choose between awkward and hostile.

After best-of-three, I wait until we're alone, then turn to Mum and say, "If Jay was taking you out tonight, where would you like to go?"

"*Is* he taking me out?"

"No. Theoretically speaking."

She looks disappointed, then smirks like she's caught on. "The cinema's always a safe bet."

Except that's not true. It's safe when you're married and

you can sit silently next to each other for two hours, but I'd spend the entire time panicking.

Mum looks like she wants to say more, but she doesn't.

She watches me with a strange expression until I say, "Thanks for that."

"It doesn't matter *what* you do. It's *how* you do it."

I must make a face, because Mum shakes her head and says, "I'm sorry. It's something I read once."

She used to buy loads of self-help books, after Gary and before Jay. She hasn't opened them for a long time, but I guess she still remembers some of the words inside.

I think back to the head-start line and how special it felt sitting there with Amy. Then I think of the courtyard and the cafeteria and Sensorium. Before her, they were ordinary places, but not now.

I hug Mum, and she says, "Oh," then cuddles me back when I don't let go.

"Thank you," I whisper.

42

I said I'd knock for Amy, but she shook her head. "I'll come to you."

I'm waiting outside when she arrives, because it's easier than another awkward family meeting and whatever that was with Nia.

"Where are we going?" she asks, and I hand her two dollars. "For the bus fare. We'll get a limo next time."

She shrugs. "I like the bus."

I thought this would be weirder than it is. But I'm surprised how calm I feel while we take the trip into town. Amy doesn't say much. She looks out of the window and points when she sees something interesting, and I hope she likes what I've planned.

I keep thinking what Mum said: "It doesn't matter *what* you do. It's *how* you do it."

When we get off, Amy looks at me expectantly, and I change my mind because it's stupid. We could have a hot chocolate instead or look around the shops or get the train somewhere else. But anyone can do that.

I want to show Amy something special, even if it's only special to me. It's not somewhere I go anymore, so I'm surprised when we get there so quickly. But my legs are a lot longer these days.

"This is it," I say.

"A fire station?"

It looks exactly the same, but so different, like everything from that time in my life.

I remember Dad in his uniform, lifting me from the ground up to the fire engine's steering wheel, the steps in between like mountains.

I remember open days when he would climb impossibly long ladders while I sat on Mum's shoulders and cheered with the crowd below.

And I remember that framed raffle ticket, lying in its broken frame on the carpet.

"This is where my mum met my dad."

I tell Amy the story, and, when I'm almost done, she says, "That's so romantic."

"It was. But I don't know where the ticket is now. Mum probably threw it away."

Amy's quiet for a while, then she says, "Or maybe they kept half each."

"I doubt that. Dad couldn't leave quickly enough. One day he loved us, and then..."

"I'm sure he still loves you."

I stare straight ahead because I'm *not* sure, and Amy can't be either. That's only what people say to be kind, so I don't argue. Instead, I say, "I'm sorry if this is weird."

"It's not weird. Thank you for telling me."

A sense of fear races through me, then fades. I can't shake every last doubt that Amy is hiding something, but I want to. And days like this will help.

"So what now?" she asks, but I hadn't thought that far ahead.

She can tell because she smiles and says, "It's my turn to show you something. Come on."

She holds my hand, and I don't pull away as I follow her. It's not a warm day, so there aren't many people around, but she doesn't lead me to the normal places in the park. We go past the bandstand and the cafe and the lake. We walk until I'm sure we're going out the other end. Then she turns right, taking a path I've never seen before. The trees are closer together here, and the birds sing over our silence. Amy crouches, points, and whispers, "There's one," and, when I follow her gaze, a squirrel runs across the grass in front of us, then another, and another. When I look closer, they're everywhere.

"How many are there?" I ask.

Amy shakes her head. "No idea. Mum and Dad used to bring us here all the time. My brother called it Squirrel Park." A couple of them run over to Amy, who whispers, "Sorry, lads. I don't have anything for you, today."

The squirrels wait a few seconds, then bound off in opposite directions.

"It might not be where my parents met," Amy says, "but it's still a special place for me."

She zones out, and I watch the squirrels charge about as if every single one of them has overslept. Then I take a deep breath and say, "Remember your first day at school? Why did you pick me as your buddy?"

Amy blinks away her daydream. "Huh?"

"You chose me, even though you didn't say anything on the tour."

She sighs and says, "You looked heavy, Tom. I know how that feels."

I think of my old life with Mum and wonder if I'll ever lose the baggage that she packed away the moment she married Jay.

"You've never had a girlfriend before, have you?" Amy asks.

I open my mouth, but nothing comes out. Instead, I stare at her until she says, "How come?"

I shrug, and she says, "Don't you like me?"

"Yes."

"Yes you don't or yes you do?"

I pause, find some courage and say, "Yes I do."

"So why are you so scared?"

"I'm not scared," I say, even though I am...a lot.

Did I make up a story about Amy being trapped because the alternative terrified me? If there is no mystery to solve, and she's just a girl who actually likes me, I have to admit I like her back.

Amy goes to kiss me, and I move, just a fidget, and, instead of my cheek, she gets the corner of my mouth. She pulls back and looks at me with eyes I haven't seen before. Then she leans in and kisses me again, and, this time, I don't have to move.

43

"Can you remember the code this time?"

We're outside Amy's house, and she nudges me and says, "I remembered it *last* time," but I don't think she did.

When I was last here, Amy was drunk, her mum looked angry, and her dad looked like he was holding something back. Perhaps he was only being protective. Maybe, to a dad with a daughter, *I'm* the threat. That's what I want to think, because, today, everything changed, and my worries are new but just as hard to tame.

Amy's body hides the PIN pad as she pushes the buttons, and I wonder if that's on purpose. Then she turns and says, "I'll see you soon."

I think about kissing her again, then see movement behind her living room window and stop.

Amy looks behind her, as if she can sense my concern, then squeezes my hand. "Today was fun."

No one opens the door for her. She unlocks it and disappears inside. I stand around for a few seconds, waiting for a wave or a smile that doesn't come. Then I go home and fight the urge to watch from my window. Instead, I sit in the living room, watching Aaron and Jay play Xbox while Nia cheers her brother on.

"How was it?" Mum whispers.

I think of the fire station and the squirrel park and the kiss and say, "It was good."

44

They've been there since the beginning, but I only noticed them today. Carvings inside my built-in wardrobe: words and pictures and lines.

The first I noticed were two stick figures, one large and one small. You can't see them from the outside. I only realized when my shirt fell off a hanger and got wedged in the sliding rail, and, there, when I pulled it free, they were. Lying on my side, my head in the wardrobe and my phone shining in the darkness, I saw more stick figures, always two, always one big and one small, and hundreds of vertical lines scored through like tally marks.

卌

The words are different in here. On the walls it said *HELP ME*, but, in here, it says *NO HELP*.

Whoever wrote this gave up.

I throw all my clothes on the bed and crouch in the closet space, then slide the door closed and sit in the phone's light.

There are eight sets of figures in total, all the same, and staring at them makes me feel uneasy. I take as many pictures as I can before I need to get out and suck in three deep breaths.

This was a bad place. I'm sure of it, now. No one would put this much effort into a game. The holes could be dismissed as a coincidence, and the writing on the wall could be someone's idea of a sick joke—a ghost story to scare the next owners. But who would sit in a wardrobe, carving stick figures and making hundreds of slashes?

If I show this to Mum, she'll freak out. She loves this house so much, and I don't want to ruin it for her. Jay would still play it down, and Nia's making the most of her last few hours with Aaron.

I message Zak, because I need to know if I'm being silly. When he arrives, I point at my wardrobe and say, "In there."

He raises his eyebrows. "What's going on?"

"Just get in. And take this." I hand him my phone, but he doesn't move.

"You want me to get in your closet?"

"Just do it. You'll understand."

Zak shakes his head but clambers in anyway. When I pull the door closed, I hear rustling inside, then, "Fucking hell."

"Can you see it?"

"Of course I can. What is it?"

I slide the door open, but Zak can't take his eyes off the markings.

"I don't know. But I think it's all linked. The locks, the writing on the wall, and this. It has to be."

Zak stands up and flops on my bed. "You think it was Amy?"

I picture her in here. This was her bedroom for years. She would have known every last bit of it. She either did it…or she saw it.

I should be telling Zak about our date, but, instead, I'm already wondering if Amy tricked me after all.

"I don't know what to think anymore," I say. "Why would her parents lock her in here but send her to school? Why would she come home every night if she was trapped?"

Zak stares at me, his mouth open and his eyes drawn back to the wardrobe he's just climbed out of.

"We need to know who lived here before her," I say. "We need a timeline. Then we can figure out who did this."

"How do we get that?"

I look out of my window at Amy's new home and the two cars in the driveway. "We ask someone who knows."

45

When I ring the doorbell, I hear a banging inside, then a muffled, "Who is it?"

"It's Tom!" I shout. "From next door!"

There's more banging, then a latch slides back, and the door inches open.

"Hello," Mrs. Hawkins says. "Who did you say it was?"

"Tom. I live next door."

She opens the door wider and grins. "No packages today, I'm afraid."

"That's not why I'm here. I was wondering how long you've lived here."

She pauses, then says, "Nineteen sixty-two. That's when we moved in."

I swallow my excitement because this is exactly what I was hoping for. Mrs. Hawkins has lived here for ages—almost as long as our house has been standing.

"Do you remember who lived next door…in *our* house?"

"Of course. The Morgans. They lived there for forty-odd years."

"Did the Morgans have children?"

Mrs. Hawkins shakes her head. "It was just the two of them. They were good neighbors. We never had any complaints."

"Who came next?"

Mrs. Hawkins rests her free hand against the wall and says, "If you want a complete history, you should come in. I'm not as strong as I used to be."

She turns and wobbles toward her living room, and I watch her slide slowly into a chair. She pushes a button on the side, and the footrest groans upward.

"If you want a cup of tea, you'll have to make it yourself. My sweeteners are on the side."

She smiles, and I feel guilty for using her. All I want is information. But she seems happy for the company, and I make a silent promise that this won't be the last time I visit.

When I've made the tea, I sit on the sofa opposite her and wait for her to carry on.

Her living room is newer than I expected. It's mostly cream with a few framed pictures on the wall. There's a black-and-white image of five girls in a row, and I try to figure out which one is Mrs. Hawkins.

Time scares me. I know it happens, but it doesn't feel real, not until you see someone's history and you realize they come from a different world. Ten years feel like a lifetime to me, but, to my neighbor, it's barely a blink.

"Who came after the Morgans?" I ask, and she reels off a list of the next five owners.

When she gets to Amy's family, I look for any suggestion that they hid something only a neighbor would see.

But Mrs. Hawkins just smiles. "They kept themselves to themselves."

That's what they say on the news sometimes, when a killer is caught or a horrible truth is revealed. It's another way of saying they were hiding but no one was nosy enough to notice.

"There were two children," she says, "but I barely saw them. A lovely big garden, yet they only played outside for the first year. Such a shame. Maybe you'll use it more. I see a little boy sometimes. Is that your...brother?"

She means Aaron, and I say, "Sort of. My mum married his dad, but he only stays with us sometimes."

She nods like she understands. "Modern families. It's different these days."

"Was there anything...odd about the Pearces?"

I can't leave without asking. I'm clinging to the hope that Mrs. Hawkins saw something that wasn't quite right.

"What do you mean, love?" she asks.

You'd know if you saw it. That's what I think. But out loud I say, "It doesn't matter."

They still live too close for me to dig very deep. She could bump into them in the village, and what then? Would she tell them a boy had been asking questions?

Instead, I stand to leave and say, "Thank you for the tea."

It's only when my hand is on the door handle that she adds, "They were very noisy when they first moved in. Nothing to complain about. I liked hearing it. But, after a while, it was as if no one lived there at all."

46

I scroll through the photos on my phone, stopping on the ones of Amy's journal.

He can't possibly know the truth...

I don't know what that means, but I now know there's a truth to be found. And, if no one else can help me, I'll find it myself. There's a puzzle to be solved, and it feels like I'm missing the central piece, so I stare from my window until my eyes sting. I watch every movement and every tiny flicker of curtain.

From this far away, the Pearces are living their life like a game of charades, and it's my job to put words to their actions.

"Tom!"

I turn to see Mum in the doorway. "I've been calling you."

"Sorry...I was..."

"We're going shopping. I think you should come."

I look back at Amy's house and say, "I'm fine here."

Mum touches my shoulder. "This isn't healthy, sweetheart. I know what you're doing. And you need a break."

I start to blush and she says, "It's okay. If you want to be absolutely certain nothing bad happened here, that's fine. But let's have some time out. I'd like you to come."

I try to think of another excuse, but Mum knows me better than anyone. She could make me feel guilty for spying on Amy or stupid for worrying, and I'm grateful that she doesn't.

"OK," I say. "I'll come."

And, ten minutes later, we're in the car, Nia on her phone next to me and Mum and Jay chatting in the front.

My stepsister is only here for the lift; she'll disappear the moment we reach the shopping center. But Mum's right; I need to get out of the house, if only to clear my head. My thoughts have gotten so knotted that I need space to unravel them. And then I can figure out how to solve this once and for all.

When we arrive, Jay says, "Where do you want to go first?" Nia is already off with Esther, and I saw his disappointment when she left with barely a word.

I could disappear, too, but my stepdad looks at me expectantly and I say, "Wherever you want."

"Okay," Jay says, and, next to him, Mum mouths, *Thank you.*

We used to talk like strangers stuck in a lift, but it's easier, now, even if I can still see the nerves behind Jay's questions. He wants me to like him, and I do.

The men that try too hard at the beginning are often the worst by the end.

For the next hour, I follow Mum and Jay into their favorite places and smile whenever they look over.

When I see Amy, I have to blink and refocus before I

believe my eyes. But she's there, walking along the row of shops opposite. She's alone, and I think about shouting out, but something stops me. If I want to know what she's hiding, I need to see her when she doesn't think she's being watched.

"I'm going to look around on my own for a bit," I tell Mum.

"Of course. Text me when you're done."

I nod and walk in the same direction as Amy, careful not to go too fast or look too frantic. There are a few people in front of me, and I dodge left and right to keep sight of her.

She's looking for something, too, and I wonder if her parents are here. I glance back, convinced for half a second that they're following me as I follow her. But I only see strangers.

Amy goes into a few shops, and I keep my distance because it's not the clothes she's looking at, it's the people. It's hard to track her while her head shoots back and forth, scanning the center.

"What are you looking for?" I whisper to myself.

Suddenly she turns and walks straight for me, and I duck into the nearest shop. When I look out, she's already gone, walking faster than before, and I have to jog to catch up.

She's ten paces in front of me when she walks into a shop and only five when she stops and stares at a woman a few meters away. The woman has an armful of clothes, and, when her phone rings, she rests them on a rail to answer it.

Amy steps forward slowly, like she's hunting her, and that's when I see him. It's not the woman Amy is staring at. It's the boy. He looks about three and is wandering farther and farther away from a mother that doesn't notice. Amy crouches next to him and says something, and the boy nods. When she holds his hand, I assume she's taking him back to the woman. But they walk right past her. I open my mouth to shout, but nothing comes out. I can only stare as Amy and the boy leave the shop.

I don't follow right away. I'm too shocked to move. When I do, it takes me a few seconds to spot Amy hurrying through the crowd.

I should tell the woman. But I can't until I know what's going on. Maybe they know each other. Perhaps this is all a big misunderstanding.

Amy turns right, and I see her and the boy go into the women's bathroom. A security guard walks past, but I hold my tongue. I feel sick and anxious, and I have no idea what's happening.

"It's okay," I say. "It's not what it looks like."

I don't realize how far I've moved until Amy walks out and stares at me. The boy is wearing the mustard-colored jacket I saw in her bag.

"What the fuck?" I say, and she looks at me with fear in her eyes.

That's when we hear the woman screaming for the boy Amy's trying to kidnap.

PART TWO

47

"What are you doing?" I ask.

Amy lets go of the boy's hand and says, "This isn't what it looks like."

"Isn't it? Because it looks like you're abducting a kid."

Amy shivers. "I'm sorry." Then she crouches next to the boy and whispers, "This is a silly game, isn't it? Do you want to go back to your mummy, now?"

He nods, and she takes off the jacket and pushes him toward me. "Take him back."

"Me? What if they think…"

"Just say you found him."

The boy's mother screams again, and people around us look toward the sound. It won't be long before we seem suspicious, so I hold his arm and say, "Come on, mate. Let's find your mum."

When she sees him, she sprints toward us and sweeps him into a hug.

"He was..."

"Thank you," the woman says. "Thank you so much." She turns to her son. "Don't you *ever* wander off again, do you hear me? You scared Mummy."

A few people smile at me because they think I'm the hero. But I'm something else. I saw it happening, and I didn't stop it. I gave him back, but I know the truth.

The boy is sobbing, and I feel guilty because he doesn't deserve this, even if his mum is pulling him close and whispering, "It's okay, darling. You're safe now."

Loads of people are staring, but Amy isn't one of them.

When I go back to the bathrooms, she's gone.

I followed her, hoping for answers. But now I have more questions than ever. She tried to steal a child. She was prepared for it, carrying spare clothes around for weeks.

All that time I thought Amy was being trapped by a monster in her home. Now I think Amy might *be* the monster.

48

Everything I thought I knew is bullshit.

I spent so long trying to figure out how to rescue Amy, but she wasn't the victim. And then I believed we could actually *be* something. We kissed, and it was amazing, but now it feels like a horrible trick.

What happens when I see her at school…if she even comes back? Is that why she left St. Gregory's? Did someone catch her doing something bad, and she ran just far enough to avoid seeing them every day?

When I close my eyes, I picture her leading that little boy out of the shop, and her face when I caught them later. What would have happened if I hadn't been there? Would she have walked right out of the shopping center? And then what?

She had the clothes, and she was stalking the shops, waiting for her chance. And, when it came, she didn't pause for a moment. Only the worst kind of people act like that. It was premeditated, and I need to understand why.

I can't tell anyone what I saw without getting her into trouble. I should do it, anyway. She deserves it. Yet something stops me.

The holes and the words and the drawings are suddenly pointing to a different story; one I don't want to hear.

I stare out of my window at a house that already looks so different. I used to think the gate was there to keep Amy in, but she can walk out whenever she wants. And, when she leaves, she does terrible things.

Do her parents even know? And what does it mean about the holes and the carvings?

I think of Amy's journal, how she wrote that I can't possibly know the truth. I have to talk to her. I need to know what's going on.

"I don't understand," I say out loud.

Behind me, Mum asks, "What's that, Tom?"

I jump back and stare at her, convinced she can read my mind.

"Nothing. I was just thinking about schoolwork."

Mum shakes her head. "You know you can talk to me. We used to talk all the time."

We did. But it was different, then. Most of our conversations were whispered and full of fear. We stopped telling each other everything when Jay came along.

I can't tell Mum what Amy did. I'm still trying to make sense of it. Yet, for a moment, I almost say it, anyway. If anyone will understand, it's Mum. She's used to people not being what they seem. But I hold my tongue, and she touches my shoulder and says, "I love you."

"I love you too."

She gazes out of my window. "When Jay first asked me out, I said no. He accepted it, but we stayed friends. And, one day, when I started to trust him, he asked again, and I said yes. Even then, I was waiting for the first sign that something was wrong. I'd promised myself that we wouldn't suffer anymore, so I was on my guard. And I stayed that way for a long time. I always expected the worst, even when all the evidence suggested otherwise."

She points at Amy's house. "If you keep telling yourself stories, you'll never allow for the truth. I know you're concerned about the holes and the walls, but, honestly, Tom, she seems like a nice girl. Don't scare her away with your worries."

Mum leaves before I can answer.

If she'd seen what I had, she'd think differently.

49

"What's up?" Zak asks, but that's a complicated question these days.

Some people tell their best friends everything. And maybe I would, too, if what I had to say wasn't so confusing.

Amy tried to kidnap a child. If there was another explanation, she would have come out with it. But, instead, she looked like she'd been caught red-handed.

"Trouble in paradise?" Zak says, because he likes saying things no one actually does in real life.

"No, it's…I'm fine."

"And Amy?"

"What about her?"

"I haven't seen her for a while. Did you two break up?"

"We were never together," I say, but that hurts because we *were*. For a tiny, brilliant moment, I thought she was my girlfriend. I liked her. She was beautiful and strange and terrifying, and that was okay until it wasn't.

Is this what she meant when she said she would scare me? Did she know I'd find out eventually?

"Hey," Zak says, and, when I turn, Amy's there and I think I'm going to be sick.

I push my fingers together so the tips of each hand are touching, and that calms me down. Then I count the syllables of my thoughts, sorting them into threes and fives.

Sometimes my anxiety is a trickle, and, sometimes, it's a tsunami. No prizes for guessing today's forecast. I can't focus on her face. My head suddenly aches behind my eyes, and I want to shout at her, but not here.

"I'll leave you to it," Zak says.

He thinks this is a lovers' tiff when I'm really face-to-face with a potential psycho. What other reason could there be for Amy carrying children's clothes in her schoolbag and stealing kids when their parents aren't watching?

"Can we talk?" she whispers.

"What were you doing with that boy?"

"Not here," she says, reaching for my hand.

When I pull it away, she sad-smiles, and I follow her to the head-start line.

"Have you told anyone?" she asks, and I shake my head. "Thank you."

"What would have happened if I hadn't been there? Would you have taken him?"

"No," Amy says. "It's just...a thing I do. I don't think some parents look after their kids. These days, everyone is on their phone or their iPad. So I teach them a lesson."

"You kidnap their children."

"No, I show them what it would be like to lose your child forever. But their forever only lasts a few minutes. I wasn't going to leave the center."

I don't believe her, because she looked genuinely terrified when she saw me. I caught her doing something she shouldn't be, and she knows it. So why is she still lying?

As if she can read my mind, she says, "I'm telling the truth. I swear it."

She touches the chalk on the head-start line, and I think of the first time I brought her here. She was a different girl, then, to me, at least. I want to believe her, but I can't. You can only see so many warning signs before you have to accept that there's danger.

"What about the coat?"

She shakes her head. "It gives me more time. If parents find their child too soon, they aren't relieved, they're just angry. For it to work, panic needs to set in. That's why I change what they look like."

"That's fucked up."

Amy closes her eyes and says, "Maybe. But they won't turn their back again. I haven't been completely honest with you, and I'm sorry for that. But you have to believe me. Please, Tom. I was just…trying to make a difference." She reaches for my hand, and I don't pull away. I know I should, but I like how it feels, even when my head is all over the place.

"Will you stop?"

Amy doesn't reply for a long time, and, when she does, she says, "I'll try."

50

The message is short and scary.

Dinner at mine. Tomorrow at six. Please come. Amy x

Do her parents know what she does? Will they call it other names or nothing at all, like Mum does with me? Or is it another secret Amy's keeping from everyone?

I think back to the night I took her home after the Sensorium party and how weird her parents were. Do I really want another evening like that, this time trapped at a dinner table?

But, the truth is, this is what I've always wanted—an invite into the one place that can prove me wrong or confirm my fears.

Maybe Amy is all the things I thought her parents were. Perhaps she's the one to be scared of and they're just ordinary. But, either way, I can't say no to her, so I respond with an okay.

And then I go to my window and watch the people I'll be spending tomorrow evening with. I see Amy in the living room doorway, saying something to her mother. Her brother looks around, but Amy ignores him. She's doing all the talking while her mum looks concerned. I try to lip-read, but I can't make out anything. All I can see is the worry on everyone's faces.

Her dad appears from the back of the room and touches Amy's shoulder, and she flinches. Then he sits on the chair opposite and points at something unseen.

This is the first time I've seen Amy in the same room as them. She's usually hidden away, which is either her choice or someone else's. Tomorrow I'll find out, if they agree to something that I think Amy has decided on her own.

I keep watching until her mum nods, then pulls her brother into a hug and stares back at the TV.

Amy stands for a few seconds, as if she wants to say something else, before disappearing. Then the light goes on upstairs and the curtains close, but not before she stares directly at me and smiles.

51

Sometimes you have to be brave or stupid.

I'm not sure which it is, but I push the buzzer, then hear Amy's voice say, "Hi."

The gate slides back, and I think about going home. But I don't want regrets as well as questions, so I walk up to her front door and knock.

Amy is wearing a dress and the biggest smile, and she looks beautiful.

I was going to ask why she invited me when I'd just caught her doing such a bad thing. But something else breaks through the confusion, something that swoops and soars in my head and my heart, and all I can do is stare at her.

"Hi," she says again.

"I nearly didn't come."

"I know. But I want to show you there's nothing wrong. You thought all the weird things in your house had something to do with me, but they don't. You'll see."

“What about that little boy?”

Amy’s smile shrinks but clings to the corners of her lips. “I’m not a bad person.”

“Do your parents know?”

She shivers. “Of course not. They wouldn’t understand.”

“And I’m supposed to?”

“I hope so. Because, if I can make *one* parent pay more attention and cherish what they have, it’ll be worth it.”

Amy’s mum walks up behind her and says, “Here’s our guest.”

She’s smiling, too, but it looks awkward on her, like she’s read about smiles in a book but never actually seen one.

“Hello, Mrs. Pearce,” I say.

“Call me Jane. And this is Chris.”

Amy’s dad nods but doesn’t hold out his hand. I have a flashback to when he gripped a bit too hard and a little too long and feel relieved, then uneasy.

“You’re our first dinner guest since we moved in,” Jane says.

That’s weird, because they’ve lived here for months, but she’s right. All the times I’ve watched this place, and I’ve never seen a visitor. The only person who gets close is the mailman.

“Come in,” she says, and I follow Amy into the living room.

I’ve seen this room so many times, but not like this. I can suddenly see everything, and it’s a lot bigger than it looks from my window. There are whole sections I couldn’t see from there, and now I can figure out where they disappear to.

“Do you like it?” Jane says, and, when I follow her gaze, I realize I’m staring at a photograph of Amy and her brother.

"Yes," I say. "It's nice."

"I hate it," Amy says, and her dad sighs.

"Amy dislikes all her photos."

"Not *all* of them," she replies.

No one says anything for a few seconds, and I'm already feeling awkward. I swallow my nerves and say, "Did Amy tell you I live in your old house, now?"

Her parents both give her a look I can't interpret, then stare at each other.

"No," her mum says. "She didn't."

"Surprise," Amy says, just as her brother walks in.

"When's dinner?" he asks.

He doesn't sound like he looks. His voice is deeper than I imagined, and he takes up more space than he does from across the street.

"This is Will," Jane says. "And this is Amy's friend Tom."

"Hey," the boy says.

He looks about ten or eleven, but he doesn't make eye contact. He just walks past, sits at the table, and starts playing on his iPad.

"You can't get more than two words out of him when he's on that thing," Jane says.

Mum says technology has made us smart in some ways and stupid in others. Her thinking doesn't go down too well with Nia, but I know what she means.

"We're having chicken casserole," Jane says. "Is that okay?"

I nod and wonder how this is actually happening. I waited so long to get in here, and then Amy took a kid, and I think that's what got me past the hallway. After our kiss, she seemed to get smaller the closer we got to her house, and she couldn't say goodbye quickly enough. But, now, she's trying to prove something.

Everything feels super weird, but, then, Mum and Jay would be exactly the same if we were hosting. Parents are awkward when they're trying to impress. Only the coolest ones pull it off. Chris doesn't seem bothered, so Jane's trying for both of them. And I'm already starting to like her more, because she has the same nervous tics as my mum.

She twirls her hair around her finger and keeps trying different smiles as if she knows it's not quite right. I was nervous about coming here, but it seems Jane is nervous too. That makes me feel better.

"It won't be long," she says. "Maybe Amy could show you around while I serve dinner."

Her dad looks up from his newspaper just long enough for something silent to pass between him and Amy. Then she stands. "Come on. I'll give you the tour this time."

52

"See," Amy says. "No holes."

We're standing by her bedroom door, the white paint unmarked and identical to every other one on the landing. "And no weird words on the walls," she says, walking inside and waving her arm dramatically.

"I see that."

Amy sits on the edge of her bed and pats the duvet for me to do the same, but I don't.

"I keep thinking about that boy," I say, and she stands and pushes her door closed.

"Is that allowed?"

"What do you mean?" Amy asks.

Jay has a rule with Nia. No boys behind a closed door.

"Won't your parents...worry?"

"Should they?"

"No."

"That was a bit too quick, Tom. I thought we had something."

She's playing with me again, acting weird like the day she came over. But she's also trying to change the subject.

"The boy," I say. "What were you really doing?"

I think back to that afternoon. She was searching for something, and I can't shake the look in her eyes when she found it. They were completely focused, but, now, they're wide and innocent.

I try to see something in her reaction, a secret hiding between her words, but her face gives nothing away.

"I told you. I hate it when parents don't pay attention. I'm reminding them what they can't afford to lose. They should thank me."

I laugh, and Amy looks offended and says, "It may not be 'normal,' but that doesn't make it wrong."

I want to believe her—that all she's doing is some kind of twisted community service—but it's a ridiculous thing to do.

Her mum shouts that dinner's ready, and, in the hallway, Amy says, "Please don't talk about it in front of them."

I watch her for a few seconds, then whisper, "I won't."

I think about kissing her, but I'm scared. So far, Amy has kissed me first. I can imagine Zak telling me to go for it, and I almost do before remembering where we are. This is the house where something isn't quite right.

I know what horrible homes feel like. Mum and I breathed them in for years. You can sense the cracks and the bad memories. You just need to know where to look.

Back downstairs, Chris points at the dining table and says, "Sit."

Amy slides in next to me and squeezes my hand.

Will is already eating, and no one tells him to stop. Mum would let her dinner get cold if there was someone missing from the table, but there are different rules here.

I still wait until everyone is sitting, then focus on my food and hope someone else starts talking.

"So," Jane says, "how is Amy settling in at school?"

"I've told you, I'm fine," she mumbles.

Her mum looks annoyed. "I'm just making conversation."

Jane turns to me, like she still expects me to answer, so I say, "It feels like she's always been there."

It catches me by surprise, and I'm not the only one. Amy makes a weird face, then smiles to herself, while her mum looks at me differently and says, "That's nice."

Even now, with everything that's happened, I like Amy. I think about her in so many ways and not all of them are about the holes and the walls and the little boy. Some of them are nice thoughts, like me wishing we could be more than whatever this is.

When I look up from my food, her dad is staring at me, and he doesn't look away. His eyes force mine back to the tablecloth and the plate I have no choice but to scrape clean. It's the only thing I can do to feel less anxious. Eventually, Amy takes it from me and carries the rest of the dirty dishes into the kitchen.

"I'll help," I say.

"No," says Jane. "You're our guest."

But no one else moves, not even her brother, and we watch in silence as Amy slowly clears the table.

"What grade are you in?" I ask Will, because I have to say something.

"Sixth," he says.

"So you'll be coming to our school next year?"

"Will got into St. Gregory's for Boys," Jane says, just as Amy walks back into the room, and I see her body stiffen.

"He's still going, even though Amy moved?"

Jane nods. "Boys aren't so… We think he'll be fine."

I remember how much Amy hated her time at the girls' Academy and hope her brother has better luck at the boys' school.

"Well done," I say, even though I don't mean it, and Will half-smiles but doesn't make eye contact.

"Shall we take a break before dessert?" Jane asks, and her husband and son stand in silence, then sit down on separate sofas.

The scene looks so different from the one I see every night through my window, when Will is always between his mother and father.

"Come on," Amy says, and I follow her back to her room. Every other door upstairs is closed, but she was right—there are no holes and nothing suspicious. The only thing that's odd is how clean it all is. "Can I use the bathroom?" I ask.

"It's that one."

I don't need to go. I need to breathe. And I can't do that down there with her parents. It's as if they don't know how to talk to people, and I don't feel welcome here. Her dad acts like he hates me, her brother has the same vibe as Nia when we first met, and Jane is trying too hard.

It was Amy's idea to invite me, but she knew what I'd see. Unless that's the point.

When I open the bathroom door, the hallway is empty, and I can hear Amy humming to music in her room. I might not get another chance, so I walk to the nearest door and hope the handle is as new as it looks.

Please don't creak, I think as I gently push down and pray.

It opens in silence, and I hold my phone up, spraying its flashlight through the darkness. It's her parents' room, and everything is perfect. The bed is made and the closets are closed and there's nothing out of place.

I close the door and move to the next one, quickly glancing up the corridor to make sure Amy's not there.

Her singing grows louder, and I smile to myself because it's cute, then open the next door. The light is on, and it catches me by surprise, but no one's there.

This must be Will's room, because there's loads of Marvel stuff. He has a thing for cars, and there are gadgets everywhere. He has his own set of decks, a guitar that Nia would be jealous of, and a massive unit full of Funko Pops and Blu-rays.

Amy's room is practically empty compared to this, and I walk over to his desk where there's an open sketch pad.

He's good. There are loads of drawings of superheroes and animals and his family. There's one of the photo downstairs, and he's managed to capture it perfectly. Except something's different. Downstairs they're all smiling. But, in this sketch, they are flat-lipped and serious.

He's got Amy spot-on: the sadness in her eyes that creeps in when she thinks no one's watching.

I turn more pages, all the way to the back, and I stop dead because there they are—two stick figures, one big and one small. They fill the final few pages of his book, over and over again, just like the carvings in my wardrobe. “Fuck,” I whisper, quickly flicking back to the first drawing I saw, then stepping into the hallway just as Amy leaves her room and stares straight at me.

53

"I got lost," I say. "There are too many doors in this house."

Amy doesn't reply, but the smile falls off her face. And there it is—the same sadness Will drew.

"We should go downstairs," she mumbles.

She leads the way as I try to figure out what to say. She's not stupid. She knows I didn't muddle up the rooms. I was snooping, and she could tell her parents. Instead, she walks over to Will and ruffles his hair until he wriggles away and says, "Stop it!"

I have a flashback to Nia and Aaron on our sofa, goofing around, but Will doesn't laugh like my stepbrother does. He scowls.

Back at the table, Jane says, "What are your plans, Tom? For when you finish school. Do you have any ambitions?"

I don't, but people hate hearing that. They always look disappointed, like I'm insulting them just because I haven't figured out my life yet. Mum says it's fine, that it's wrong to think you can map your future out at sixteen.

I don't know if she had plans when she was at school. But, if she did, I doubt they included a Gary or a Martin. I'm not even sure they included a me.

But that's what she got—a kid and a divorce and a photo album full of arseholes and then, eventually, Jay. But that's not all she got, because my mother is making up for lost time. She loves cooking and does evening classes, now. It's Mum's dream to open a restaurant, and she's all the proof I need that I'll figure stuff out in the end.

"I'm not sure yet," I say. "I'm keeping my options open." Chris lets a laugh slip out.

Everyone else pretends they don't hear it, and Jane says, "Amy wants to be a teacher, don't you, darling? She loves children."

There's another tiny shiver, then a smile as Amy says, "That's the dream."

I picture her holding the boy's hand, leading him farther and farther away, teaching his parents a lesson they didn't ask for. Then I imagine her standing in front of a whole class.

The person she is, sometimes, would be a great teacher because, she's kind and funny and patient. But that's not all she is.

"What about you, Will?" I ask. "What would you like to be?"

He looks surprised, opens his mouth, but doesn't reply.

"Will's going to be an artist," Jane says. "You should see his drawings."

I catch Amy's eye. But, if she knows my secret, I know hers. She won't tell them I was in his room, because I can tell them about the boy. Instead, she looks away, and I wonder how much longer I have to stay here.

If this was the other way around, Jay would be busting out the board games, and Mum would still be fretting. But I feel like a burden. No wonder the Pearces don't have many guests. They're terrible hosts.

When Chris turns the news on, we watch it in silence for ten minutes until I stand and say, "I should go. Thank you for having me."

"You're very welcome," Jane says. "We'll have to do it again sometime."

I don't believe her, but nod like I do.

"I'll show you out," Amy says.

Will and his dad don't say anything.

"Thank you for coming," Amy says. "I know it was a bit awkward, but I wanted to show you we're normal…ish. What I did has nothing to do with them. And all those things you worried about…you shouldn't have."

She goes to touch my hand, but I pull it away. "I thought…"

Amy doesn't need to finish the sentence because *I* thought it too. I thought we were more than friends because we kissed and it was great. And then, just as quick, I watched her do something unexplainable.

"What you did with that boy…please stop."

Amy sighs. "I told you I'll try."

I feel disappointed and relieved at the same time because I like her, but I can't do this. Maybe one day, but not yet. Love scares me more than I can explain, because, if you let it, you lose control. And there's no telling where it will lead you.

While the gate slides back, I almost tell Amy I saw her brother's drawings and that he was the one who carved them in my wardrobe. But she's spent all night trying to convince me not to worry. I can't tell her I've got the proof I was waiting for.

Instead, I smile and walk away, wondering with every step what to do with that proof and what it means for a family that is anything but normal.

54

They look like they always do—Jane on one side, Chris on the other, and Will in the middle. I've been home for less than five minutes, and, already, they're back in their places.

It felt right before, but now it looks odd. Because I've been there, and I've seen how little they say to each other and how distant Will is. I've seen the looks Chris gives Jane when she's not watching. They aren't a happy family. They didn't even pretend to be. So why are they sitting on a single sofa when they could have one each?

Will drew the stick figures. I thought Amy was the answer to the puzzle, but it's her brother. This must have been his room, so why did she say it was hers? And it still doesn't explain the holes in both doors. Two locks for two bedrooms.

"How was it?" Mum asks.

She's at it again—catching me by surprise. But, then, she spent years tiptoeing around monsters.

"It was weird."

"In what way?"

"Amy's parents are odd. It just felt a bit awkward."

Mum sits on the end of my bed and smiles. "We should still return the favor," she says, and I imagine her running around, trying to make everything perfect and freaking out about the smallest imperfection.

Mum wants everyone to be happy in her happily-ever-after. Mostly we are, but she overreacts when we're not.

"Maybe one day," I say.

"You like this girl." It's not a question, so I don't answer. I just watch her until she says, "It's okay if you do."

"I don't."

"Okay. But, if you do, embrace it, Tom. I know what you've seen, and I know what you think. But, if you don't try, you'll never know. Your dad and I weren't meant to be. It wasn't a mistake. It just wasn't forever."

She's right. But that doesn't mean I'll listen.

Mum found the love of her life when she was forty, which I used to think was old until I saw her face when they got married. She looked younger than she had in years. And, yes, that repaired some of the damage, but I've still seen what love does when it's mislabeled or when it sours.

I don't think I love Amy yet. But I like her more than I should. That's where it starts, if you let it. And that's why I'm shutting it down.

"If you ever want to talk, I'm here."

"I know," I say, wondering what she would do if I *did* talk, if I told her about the carvings and Will's sketchbook and my fears.

Mum is most properly Mum when it's just the two of us. I like it, but I feel sad at the same time, because it hasn't always been like this.

She looks at Amy's house through the window, then closes the curtains and kisses me good night. I could pull them back and spend all night watching. But *this* is the haunted house. This is the one with the ghosts.

I don't go downstairs to check and clap and repeat.

Instead, I lie in bed, trying to piece everything together.

That's when I figure out my next move. I'll go straight to Will.

55

I should have photographed Will's drawings, but there was no time.

Now I sit in my wardrobe, shining a light on the carvings and comparing them with what I saw last night. They seem the same, but anyone can draw a stick figure. The one thing that makes me certain is the pairing. Always two, always one big and one small, like a parent and a child.

"What are you doing?" Nia is standing in my doorway, looking confused. "Why are you in the closet?"

"Come here and I'll show you."

"You're so weird."

"Not as weird as this. Just look. Please."

Nia's face softens, and I get out so she can get in.

I can't show Mum, because she'd only worry, but my stepsister will be honest. She'll tell me if this is something or nothing.

She doesn't need to know who drew them. But I suddenly

have the urge to show her and to prove, or at least try to, that I'm not the odd one.

But Nia doesn't move. She just sighs and says, "I'll leave you to...whatever this is."

She's not like Zak. She doesn't trust me without question.

But, the more people I show, the more real it will be.

Last night already feels like a dream, and I need to cling to the facts, to the unease I felt in their company and looking at those drawings.

"Please," I say again, and something happens behind her eyes. For a split second, Nia looks at me like she looks at Aaron.

She nudges past and pokes her head around the corner, then edges in farther and waves her hand at me. "Pass me your phone."

"What do you think?"

Nia doesn't reply for a long time. I can't read her face, and, when she does finally speak, her voice is different.

"Did you do this?" she asks, even though she already knows the answer. She wants me to say yes. She wants to dismiss this as just another Tom thing.

I shake my head and she stares back at the carvings, then looks at the wall where she discovered the words. She opens her mouth, but nothing comes out. I don't think I've ever seen Nia shocked before, and certainly never speechless.

She gets it, now. She knows we moved into a house with secrets, and the latest warning can't be painted over.

I think back to the day Amy came over, saw Nia, and freaked.

"Are you sure you don't know Amy Pearce?" I ask.

My stepsister shakes her head, but her eyes tell a different story.

"What's Amy got to do with this?" she asks.

"She lived here before us. This was her brother's room."

Nia walks over to my bed and sits. This is already the longest she's stayed in my room, and it doesn't look like she's leaving any time soon.

"We used to be friends," she says. "But I haven't spoken to Amy since we were eleven."

"Why did you say you didn't know her?"

Nia shrugs. "Because I don't. I *knew* her...years ago. I don't know her now. That's how school works. People change. People disappear. Not everyone is best friends with the first kid they met in seventh grade."

She means like me and Zak, although she smiles when she says it, and I know she's not being mean. She likes him, and, for now, at least, it feels as though she likes me too.

"What was Amy like?" I ask.

"She changed, but so did everyone. We used to laugh all the time. It pissed the teachers off. But then she went serious and just sort of...faded away."

"She went to the same parties," I say, remembering the photos on Evie's Instagram.

"She never looked like she was having fun, though. I made new friends after Amy, but...I'm not sure if she did."

"And now we're living in her old house."

Nia looks around my room, then back at the wardrobe. "Do you think she carved those?"

"No," I reply. "It was her brother."

I don't explain how I know, and Nia doesn't ask. She just nods as if that makes sense and says, "Will. She talked about him all the time."

"Did you ever meet him?"

"A few times. When her mum picked her up from school. But he was just a baby. I don't know if he grew into the kind of kid that would write 'help me' all over his walls."

I do...because this wasn't Amy's room. It was her brother's. He's the answer to the riddle. I just need to figure out the question.

56

Evie Wells goes to the University of Chester, now. I know because her Instagram is full of pictures from freshmen week and all the weeks that followed.

She has a lot of friends but the same smile for everyone. It's different from the one at the old parties with Nia and Amy in the background.

I draft my message for hours and delete a few false starts before finally clicking send.

> Hi. My name is Tom Cavanagh. I know a friend of yours, Amy Pearce. Could I ask you a few questions?

She replies almost instantly.

> What do you want to know?

It is not the reply I expected, but it's better than being ignored.

I want to know why Evie lied about Amy's dad and if there was anything suspicious about her parents or her brother. She was a closer friend than Nia was. At least, that's what Amy suggested.

"We were best friends," she'd said. "And then, one day, she hated me."

I heard a story about her dad. What can you tell me about that?

I sound like I'm interrogating her, but it's too late, now.

When the reply comes, my nerves spike.

It says *call me*, followed by a phone number.

If there was nothing to say, Evie would ignore me. And that scares me more than dialing the number, because, whatever information she has, she wants to say it out loud.

I stare at my phone for so long it goes blurry. Then I blink until the world snaps back, take a deep breath, and call.

"Hello."

"Evie?"

"Yes, is this Tom?"

"It is."

"Cool. I have to say your message caught me by surprise."

"So did your reply," I say, and she laughs.

She doesn't sound like I imagined she would. I thought Evie's words would have sharp edges, but she seems genuinely happy to talk.

"How do you know Amy?" she asks.

"She goes to my school," I reply, and then, because I want

to say everything, "and I moved into her old house and can see her new one from my bedroom."

Evie laughs, then stops when she realizes I'm serious. "Oh. That's a bit creepy."

"I know how it sounds, but it's not like that. I met her parents. Her dad seems..."

Protective...scary...strange? What I really want is Evie to finish the sentence for me, but it turns out she can't.

"I never met him," she says.

"So the rumor..."

"The rumor is bullshit. And how did you even hear about it?"

"Amy told me."

Evie doesn't reply for a long time, and, when she finally does, she sounds like she's carefully selecting every word.

"Well, I guess I know who started it, then."

"Why would Amy set up her own dad?" I ask.

Evie breathes down the phone, then says, "Amy did a lot of strange things."

"But you were friends."

"Not really. She was the year below me. I only knew her because of my sister, Pippa."

"How did they know each other?"

"Amy mentored her. They do this thing at St. Gregory's where they pair an older kid with a first year. My sister got Amy. They were supposed to meet once a week to discuss any problems Pippa might have had. But Amy wouldn't leave her alone. My sister didn't mind. She thought it was great hanging out with an upperclassman. But we thought it was weird."

Just when I think I'm starting to get it, I realize Amy has told more lies. She said this was her room when it was Will's. She said Evie was her best friend when they hardly spoke. She said Evie started the rumor about her dad.

"I don't understand anything," I say as much to myself as to Evie.

"What do you mean?"

"The rumor was that you got with Amy's dad."

"I know."

"But there's no reference to it online. Wouldn't a story like that be everywhere?"

"You've been stalking me," Evie says. It's not a question, and she doesn't sound angry. "Look, all I know is my dad came to me raging because someone told him I was doing Amy's dad. It took me ages to convince him it was bullshit. He said he'd already taken care of it, and I didn't ask what he meant because I was scared of the answer.

"No one outside my house ever talked about it. It wasn't a rumor. I shot it down before it could fly. And then you started asking, and I thought it was happening again. But, if Amy is the one talking about it...either she started it or she knows who did."

"Or she still believes it."

57

Evie told me to call back if I had any more questions. She sounds like someone I could be friends with. The exact opposite of the girl Amy made her out to be.

I *do* have more questions, but Evie can't answer them. I think only Amy can.

When Amy told me about her dad, she looked genuinely heartbroken. She believed what she was saying. I cling to that, because the alternative is too scary to accept.

What would she gain from lying? I didn't know her father. I still don't. He's just an angry face and an awkward presence.

She opened up to me, and I promised to be there. Unless that was the trick. Did Amy make up a horror story so I'd feel sorry for her? Did she listen to me talk about the head-start line and invent her own tragedy?

Evie said Amy did a lot of strange things. And, knowing her, I can believe that. Some people get labels they can't shake, and everything they do is the wrong side of right. There are kids like that at school.

At St. Gregory's, Amy was the girl who hung out with the seventh graders. She haunted other people's pictures. She changed enough for Nia to forget all about her. And yet she's not hiding now. She's taken center stage in my life, and I can't shift the spotlight. When I close my eyes, I think of her, and, when I open them again, she's there.

What happened to turn her from the almost-invisible girl Evie knew to the one who danced at the costume party and kissed me in the park?

Amy's echoes are in the walls. I couldn't escape her if I wanted to. But I need to figure out why her brother carved stick figures into the wardrobe and wrote HELP ME.

I've seen Amy's family close up. I've felt the weird energy when they're all in the same place. And I saw her face when she caught me leaving her brother's room. She knew what I saw, and she was too scared to say it.

Her dad may not have done anything with Evie, but there was a reason for that rumor.

"Hey," Nia says from behind me. "You coming?"

She's been nicer to me since we talked about Amy. She doesn't look at me like a bad smell, and Mum and Jay are starting to notice.

It's family film night with Aaron, and hiding in my room isn't an option. He hunts absentees down and whines until we join him.

"Here he is," Jay says, and I sit on the sofa and ask whose turn it is.

"It's mine," Nia replies, "and I choose..."

Aaron starts chanting, "*Moana...Moana...Moana*," and his sister grins and says, "No way, dude. I want to watch something romantic."

"Gross," Aaron says, and we all laugh because Nia is only messing with him. She always chooses something he'll enjoy, and today's no exception.

"How about...*Toy Story* ?"

"Which one?" Jay asks.

"All of them!" yells Aaron.

Mum watches this with a massive smile on her face. She always wanted a family, and I'm glad she finally has one. She doesn't join in with Nia's and Aaron's silliness, but she loves it. What's ordinary for one person is magical for another.

It's hard to feel happy when my head is such a mess, so I get a drink from the kitchen, then try to sneak back upstairs as the movie starts.

Aaron won't move until it's over now, but Jay says, "Tom. You're missing it." He points at my spot on the sofa, then snuggles into Mum.

We only end up watching the first film, but no one complains. Aaron has a ninety-minute attention span, and Jay says he doesn't want to waste all their time together sitting in silence.

He's a good dad. He's a good stepdad, too, for what it's worth. And he's a good husband.

I'm not sure where my real dad is now. I don't know if Mum and I were a rehearsal for a life he now prefers. Maybe he got it right the second time around, or, perhaps, like us, it was further down the list. Wherever he is and whatever he's doing, I hope he's not lonely.

We have takeout and talk way past Aaron's bedtime, and tonight feels different.

Nia is including me, and Mum notices because, a few times, she tilts her head and grins. She doesn't know we connected over a girl made of secrets.

It's not until we say good night that I realize I haven't watched Amy's house for hours. Mum must have drawn my curtains, and I could pull them back, just for a minute. But, instead, I get into bed, close my eyes, and whisper, "Clap."

58

“Amy’s keeping her distance,” Zak says.

I follow his stare across the courtyard, see her disappear into the English block, and say, “We kissed.”

“*Seriously?* When?”

It already feels like weeks ago, that day when my anxiety evaporated and I barely thought of anything except us.

“The Saturday we went out. She took me to see the squirrels.”

“Is that a euphemism?” Zak asks. Then, when I don’t answer, “Why didn’t you tell me before?”

“Because I found the carvings, and I didn’t know what to think. Then she invited me to hers for dinner…”

“On the second date?”

“It wasn’t a date. It was like a weird dream.”

“What do you mean?”

“It was her brother who carved those stick figures.”

It feels like, the more people I tell, the more things will make sense. This isn't my secret to keep. If Amy's not being honest with me, I'll talk to people who are.

"I have a theory," Zak says. "What if you're so afraid of actually falling for this girl that you're..."

"Making it up?"

"No, but...how do you know her brother did that?"

"I saw the same drawings in his room. Trust me, mate. Something's not right. If you'd been there, you would understand. It felt like everyone was holding their tongue. I know I'm paranoid, but, sometimes, paranoia is being first to the truth."

Zak looks at me like he's not so sure. "So what did the brother say?"

"Nothing. I didn't really speak to him."

I know I should. But the problem is the house. I can't just walk up to the front door and hope Will answers.

The buzzer and the gate mean no one can sneak up on the Pearces. I had my chance to look closer, and I took it. But what's the use of knowing who made those carvings if I don't know why?

Jane drives Will to and from school. The car doors only open once the gate has clunked shut. He's never on my side of the spikes, so I can't talk to him. Would he even answer if I did?

He hardly said a word that night, but, maybe, I was asking the wrong questions. If he knows I've seen his drawings and his pleas, that could change everything. If he really wants help, or if the carvings are some kind of warning, perhaps it would be enough to tell him what I've found out.

Amy has barely spoken to me since I left. She knows what I found. Or, if she doesn't, she knows I went looking. And that shows I don't completely trust her.

Is she figuring out that she can't lie to me anymore? Is she disappearing like she did at St. Gregory's? Or will she turn up in a few days, acting like everything's normal?

"Amy's brother goes to the same school as Harrison," I say.

Zak nods, gives me a funny look, then says, "Are you thinking what I'm thinking?"

"I want to use your brother as a spy?"

Zak laughs. "He's six. What could he possibly do?"

"Pass on a message."

I could post it through the metal mailbox next to their gate, but Amy or her parents might read it first, and then they'd know.

If Harrison can put it in Will's hand, at least he'd have a day to think. At least whatever decision he makes will be his own.

"What do you want to ask him?" Zak says.

"I just want him to know what I know. I've seen the carvings, I've read the words, and I know about the locks. He can talk to me."

"What if it's all a massive misunderstanding? If you put something in writing, you can't hide that from Amy."

"I'll take the risk."

"So now you're saving her brother instead?"

I stare at the sky, remember a life that feels like a half-forgotten nightmare, and say, "I'll save whoever needs saving."

59

"Do you recognize this boy?"

Zak's brother nods. "He's in sixth grade. I'm in second." Harrison is the same age as Aaron, but what choice have I got? Besides, it's only passing a note. It's nothing that can get him into trouble.

I hand Harrison an envelope and say, "I want you to give him this. Not his teacher or his mum or dad. It has to go to him. Do you understand?"

Zak's brother nods. "Okay."

Inside, it says:

> **Hi, Will. I've seen the stick people. What do they mean? If you want to talk, you know where I live. —Tom**

If Amy reads it, she won't be happy. But that's a risk I'm willing to take. I'm sick of not knowing what I'm worried about. That didn't use to be a problem. I could see what

I was scared of because it hid in plain sight. But this is different.

"Don't lose it," Zak says. "And don't let Mum see it." This is why he's my best mate. He knows this is important to me, even if, sometimes, I catch him questioning everything with a look or a pause. He's not all-in like I am. But he still wants to see it play out.

"One last look," I say, showing him the photo of Will that I took from my window. He had stopped for a moment, glancing back at the gate that had closed behind him. Just enough time for me to zoom in and snap.

"I know what he looks like," Harrison says. "I won't forget."

60

I can't see Will's bedroom from my window. You can only see it from the street, so I wait until Mum and Jay have gone to bed, then go downstairs. Only, this time, I'm not checking that the front door is locked; I'm opening it and walking into the night.

Amy's house stands out like a circus in a village of churches. Our homes are small and quiet, a couple of lights shining behind drawn curtains. Hers is massive, the spotlights above the guttering painting the bricks a shimmering white.

Our street is almost silent, just the murmur of a TV through an open window and the distant yowl of a cat.

Most people think darkness is dangerous. They think the night is something to hide from. But outside can be a lot safer than inside if you live with the wrong people.

The closer I get to Amy's house, the bigger the walls seem. From my window, they look like something you can almost jump over, but, up close, the spikes are out of reach. I step back, figuring out which room is Will's and waiting for a sign. Their living room was dark when I left the house, so he must be in his bedroom.

Did Harrison give him the note, and is he planning a response? I pick a stone from the ground and think about throwing it at the window. I don't know what he wants yet, though. He may hate what I said. I may have pushed him too far in the other direction. But I had to try something.

The curtain moves, and I swear I see Will looking out, but it falls back into place so quickly I doubt myself.

The spotlights are making my eyes blotchy, and I look away and blink, then stare back at his window and see him staring down at me.

I hold my hand up, drop it when he doesn't copy, and watch for any sign that he's happy to see me. He stares, unblinking, until I finally look away. If he's trying to creep me out, it's working. I'm the one spying on him from a dark street, but he doesn't look scared. He looks like he was expecting me. Then the window opens, and I hold my breath, waiting for him to speak.

He leans out, and I strain to hear. But there's no sound. Instead, something falls from his hand—small white patterns that appear and disappear in the darkness. When one falls at my feet, I pick it up and see that it's part of my message, torn into so many pieces that they dance through the air like a tiny snowstorm.

More fall on either side of the wall, and I wonder if Amy's parents will find them and understand, or if they'll be blown away by morning.

Harrison did what I asked, but Will didn't do what I hoped. I thought he would explain everything. Instead, he watches the final pieces fall, closes his window, and turns off the light.

When I get home, it takes ages to complete my checks. I doubt myself over and over again, pushing the front door handle ten, twenty, thirty times, and cursing myself when I go back for more.

I can be outside past midnight and not be scared. But, in here, with locks to check and things to unplug, the fear grows fast.

I push my fingers together, my right hand meeting my left at five separate points. It's another way to balance myself, and it's easier than when I had to touch something with all ten digits. Sometimes it would be a single button on the TV remote or a random spot on the wall. When it was really bad, my toes would need to touch the baseboard while I split the sentences in my head into threes and fives.

Those days are gone. But, sometimes, if I'm still downstairs this late, I worry they've come back. I'm scared that I'm losing myself in my search for something that might not be there. If Amy doesn't need my help, and Will doesn't want it, there's nothing left to do but stop.

No one saved Mum when she was trapped. She saved herself. Is that what they're doing? Or did we get our wires crossed...twice?

61

STOP LOOKING

The words are carved into our icy car window, their edges trickling in the early-morning sun. I quickly scrape them away before Jay sees, then curse myself for not taking a photo. It's my job to deice the car before school, and someone clearly knows. Either that or they don't care who sees.

Was this Will? Did he sneak out early after what happened last night? Or did he tell Amy and this is her way of warning me to stay away? Or is it worse than that? Did Jane or Chris see me standing below their son's window or find scraps of my message and take matters into their own hands?

I walk to the end of the street and stare at their house. The gate is closed, but both cars are already gone. It could have been any of them. Chris leaves for work early while Jane takes Amy and Will to school.

Whoever it was, it means I'm right. Mum would say I'm

making something out of nothing, but this is proof that they're rattled. This is the type of warning only bad people send. Or scared people.

"Morning," someone says behind me, and, when I turn, our neighbor, Mrs. Hawkins, is putting her trash out.

"Hi," I say, and then, because it's worth a shot, "Did you see anyone in our driveway this morning?"

She thinks for a moment. "There was someone, yes. But I couldn't see their face. It's cold, see. I thought it was one of you with your hood up."

She points at our house and says, "I should have known better. They were looking through your window."

I stifle a shiver. "Could you tell how big they were?"

"I'm sorry, love. I didn't get a good look. Is it something to worry about?"

"No," I lie. "Everything's fine."

Mrs. Hawkins nods and creeps back to her front door. Whoever she saw didn't just leave the message. They were watching us.

Is it payback? Do they know how much I can see from my bedroom window? Or have I pushed too hard and they're looking for different reasons?

The problem is I can't stop now. I'm on to something, and someone is trying to stop me. If I was hoping for a sign that I'm right, it was drawn into the frost, now melting at my feet.

62

Amy teaches bad parents a lesson. That's what she told me. But do you need to change a child's clothes to do that? People wear disguises to escape. They hide the truth in something else, like a kid who's not yours in a mustard-colored coat.

If I hadn't stopped her, would she have taken that boy from the shopping center? I should have let it play out. I should have watched Amy from afar, not walked headfirst into her game. And then I'd know. Because I'm not sure if she was giving that mum a brief moment of terror or something worse. Maybe she was planning on making that boy disappear long enough for the lesson never to be forgotten.

The thought makes me dizzy, and I wait for Amy to walk across the courtyard, then run after her.

"Hi," I say, and she turns without smiling.

"Hello."

It sounds strange, and I wonder if she stopped trusting me the moment I walked out of her brother's bedroom. Or was it when I passed him a note asking for a truth Amy couldn't give?

"Someone wrote a warning on our car window today."

I drop it in the space between us and see what damage it does. But Amy just creases her eyebrows and says, "What kind of warning?"

Okay, I'll play. "It said 'Stop looking.'"

"That's weird. What do you think it means?"

"I think I've pissed someone off."

Amy looks over my shoulder and says, "It wouldn't be the first time."

"What?"

"I saw you come out of Will's room. You were snooping. You still think my family's hiding something, and it upset me."

"Enough to send a warning?"

Amy's face changes instantly. Her eyes narrow, her lips curl downward, and she practically growls at me. "You think that was me?"

"You said it yourself: I was snooping."

"But there's nothing to find, Tom. You can look all you want. I don't care."

A tear falls down her cheek, and, once again, I wonder if I'm wrong about all of this. When we're apart, I know for certain that I'm on to something. But, when we're together, I doubt everything.

Amy looks betrayed. I pissed her off when I snuck into Will's room. But blaming her for the message on our car window—it looks like I've gone too far. I don't think she knows about the note I wrote to him. She's angry because I still doubt her. And the only thing I know for certain is that one of us is right. Either Amy's a great actress or I'm digging a hole I'll never get out of.

If Will isn't prepared to help, the only way to find out the truth is to get back into that house. I need to keep Amy on my side or risk carrying these questions forever.

"I'm sorry," I say. "I believe you."

A moment of surprise flickers across her face, quickly replaced by an uncertain smile. "You do?"

"Yes."

Amy reaches for my hand and squeezes it, and I flash back to when her dad did the same. When he shook my hand, he was warning me. He held it too hard and too long. But Amy's grip is only just there, sitting in my palm so gently that I can't tell where her skin ends and mine begins. She's happy again, and I wish that was the end of it. I wish I didn't have this nagging doubt. Because, if there were no holes and no words and no carvings, if there was no creepy brother and no icy warnings to spur me on, I could fall in love with her.

My head spins at the thought, but it's true. Amy is amazing. There are moments with her when I understand why Mum and Dad framed that raffle ticket and why they clung to the magic until it leaked through the cracks.

When I'm with her, I *feel*. But I can't let that win until I know if I'm making a mistake. I would hate myself forever if the first girl I fell for was in trouble, and I chose to ignore it. If I can convince Amy to trust me, she might invite me back to her house. And, if she does, I won't waste my second chance to help.

63

I'm so tired after school that I dump my bag in the hall and am on the third stair before Mum calls, "Tom. Come in here, please."

That's the voice she uses when she wants to impress someone, and I hear another voice I can't quite place, then my mother's nervous laugh. It's only when my hand is on the kitchen door that I realize who's behind it. I could leave, but the door is already creaking open.

Mum turns and says, "Hi, darling. Good day at school?"

I don't answer, because Amy's mother is sitting opposite her, a cup of tea in her hand and a fixed smile on her face.

"Look who's here," Mum says.

Jane says, "Well, how often do you get the chance to revisit your old house for a cuppa?"

Mum laughs, but she doesn't mean it. I can tell she's thrown by this visit and is hoping Jane doesn't judge her for the unwashed plates and the pile of clothes that it's Nia's job to sort.

First Amy comes over unannounced, now her mother. But this feels different. After the warning on our car, I can't help wondering...

"I like what you've done with the place," Jane says, and, while Mum thanks her, I can see the sarcasm in her eyes.

"We haven't changed much," Mum says. "You did such a good job decorating."

"But you've made a few changes upstairs," Jane says. It's not a question, and I wonder what else Amy has told her.

I haven't said anything yet, and Mum is looking anxious, so I say, "We stripped the wallpaper in my room. And we might change the doors."

Mum gives me a funny look. "I don't think so, Tom. The doors are fine." But I'm watching Jane.

The tiniest grin tickles the corner of her mouth before she says, "We never did get 'round to the upstairs. Well, I tell a lie. We decorated *our* room."

She winks at Mum, and they share a laugh that sounds so fake that it sits in the air for a few awkward seconds too long. Amy said her dad decorated her room. Now Jane is saying he didn't.

"You'll have to come over when it's all done," Mum says.

"I'd like that."

"They should come for dinner," I say.

Mum looks terrified because that's a lot bigger than boiling a kettle, but I've suddenly had an idea. If Amy's family do have secrets, they're more likely to be found where they are buried.

I might not be able to get Chris or Will to talk, but Jay won't take silence for an answer. Chris won't be able to just wander off and stare at the TV. And Will...

"We should do it on a Saturday," I say, "when Aaron's here. I think he and Amy's brother would get along."

My brain is working so fast that my mouth can't keep up. But this is perfect.

I was so desperate to get back into Amy's house that I ignored the obvious. We take the Pearces out of their comfort zone. We force them to make a mistake. And, even if they don't, I could learn something.

This isn't what Jane expected. I could tell by her face that she enjoyed catching me by surprise. If she was the one who left the message, this was her attempt to finalize it. But I'm not as weak as she thinks. Neither of us are, even if Mum is struggling to say anything, now that I've invited a bunch of semi-strangers over for dinner.

"That would be lovely," Jane says, finishing her tea in one gulp and standing up.

One–nothing to me.

"We'll let you know," I say.

Mum adds, "Yes, we'll...it will be lovely."

When Jane's gone, Mum turns to me and says, "What was that?"

"I'm just being nice. It's called returning the favor."

"So are *you* going to cook?"

"If you want me to."

Mum smiles because we both know that's a terrible idea, and she'll want to show off her skills.

"It's just...I didn't think you liked that kind of thing. I was surprised you accepted *their* invitation. You told me you didn't like Amy."

Mum knows me better than anyone. That's why she's looking at me with suspicious eyes. But she'll only agree if she thinks I'm genuine, so I say, "I *do* like Amy," which is not a lie, and then, "and I like her family," which *is* a lie. "I just thought it would be nice."

Mum tilts her head. "She seems nice."

I'm glad she focused on the truth. Even if the chances of Amy being my girlfriend for more than one amazing afternoon could fall to zero if I force her parents to slip up.

64

“Whose stupid idea was that?” Nia asks. She can’t stand still, and she keeps tossing out evil looks like they’re grenades and we’re the enemy.

Don’t say mine. Don’t say mine. Don’t say…

“It was Tom’s idea,” Jay says, “and I think it’s a good one.”

Nia turns all her anger on me. “Saturdays are *our* night. It’s Aaron’s night.”

“And this one will be too,” Jay says. “But it’s nice to meet new people.”

“I don’t *want* to meet new people. I’m happy with the people I know.”

When Nia gets like this, Jay calls it regressing. He says she’s acting like a kid, but she’s not. She’s being a big sister, upset that the one night with her brother has been changed without her permission.

“I’m sorry,” I say. “I just…”

"You know I'm not friends with Amy anymore. So this is going to be super awkward."

That's what I'm hoping for. I hope it's so awkward that Jane or Chris slip up. If you're forced to talk for long enough, eventually something important comes out.

"Is this about those fucking carvings?" my stepsister asks.

"Nia!" says Jay. "Enough!"

If she hadn't sworn, Mum would have asked what she meant. But Jay raises his voice so rarely that, when he does, he sucks everyone else's from the room. Nia goes upstairs and slams her bedroom door.

"She'll get over it," Jay says, but I can't take that chance. If this is going to work, I need her on my side, so I knock until she answers and say, "I know you hate me right now. But please, hear me out. And, if you still hate me afterward, I'll convince Mum to cancel."

Nia doesn't reply, but she doesn't slam her door either. I tell her about the warning on the car and how uneasy I felt at Amy's and how, if she lets me, we could finally trip them up.

"Are you done?" Nia asks, and, when I nod, she says, "I love Aaron more than anything."

"I know."

"So, if I'm going to give up an evening for a bunch of randoms, it better be worth it. If you're wrong..."

She doesn't finish the sentence, but I know what she means. If I'm wrong, I've wasted her time and dragged people into a horror story of my own making. I'll have spent hours talking and stressing about something that's not true.

But if I'm right...

That's what I cling to as I thank Nia and go to my room and ring Zak.

"I have a job for you," I say. "How good are you at climbing walls?"

65

"Are you trying to get my whole family arrested?"

"That's a bit of an exaggeration," I say. "Your brother only handed over a note."

"What about me?" Zak asks.

"Well, you *could* be arrested."

"Fucking right I could. You want me to break into Amy's house while her entire family are eating dinner at yours. How long have you been planning this?"

"A couple of hours."

Zak laughs down the phone. "I worry about you."

"Thanks. Is that a yes?"

"I've seen that place. It's a fortress."

Except that's not entirely true. There may be a wall all the way around, but the spikes stop beside the garage. If you climb up there, directly under Will's window, you could be up and over in seconds.

"I don't want you to break in. Only an idiot would do that.

But they keep their curtains open. I just want you to look closer. If they had anything to hide, it wouldn't have been out when I was there. That doesn't mean it's always hidden."

At first, I only wanted Jane and Chris out of their comfort zone. But this is an opportunity. They'll all be out of the house, and I can't waste that.

They don't look like the kind of people who leave a key under the mat. When they go out, the blue light of the burglar alarm dances from left to right and back again. But, if you live behind an electric gate, you might not be so quick to tidy away your truth.

If I could do it, I would. But I can't disappear from a meal I invited them to. Zak's my only chance.

"What if I get caught?"

"Don't."

I can literally hear him thinking down the phone, and, eventually, he says, "If you're right and this is something serious, I want proper credit. None of this 'I solved it on my own' crap. Equal partners."

"Deal."

What we both know is that Zak has always dreamed of being a hero. That's why he has a do-over diary—to transform a boring life into a brilliant one. For one night, he won't have to write it…unless something goes wrong.

"Do they have any pets?"

"Nope."

"Security lights?"

"Just the spotlights. They come on after dark, so stay close to the house."

"Trip wire?"

"What do you think this is? No, they don't have trip wire."

Zak snorts and says, "If I was hiding something, I'd have them."

"Then it would be pretty obvious, wouldn't it?"

Their house looks normal. Absolutely massive, but normal. "There are no trip wires or trapdoors or laser rooms. That's why I think getting over the wall is key. They have patio doors at the back and windows at both sides and the front. Look closely and take pictures, and, if anything seems weird, it probably is."

Zak sighs, and, for a moment, I think he's changed his mind. I wouldn't blame him. I'm getting carried away. But, eventually, he says, "Okay."

"That's it?"

"If it shuts you up, yes. You enjoy your dinner party with your sort-of-but-not-really-girlfriend and her potentially psycho family, and I'll try not to spike my privates."

"Thank you."

Zak doesn't say anything for a while, then sighs. "I know the stick figures are proper creepy, and Amy's a bit odd, but how far are you prepared to take this?"

"There is something," I reply. "I'm certain there is."

"You know I love you, Tom. But this is starting to feel a bit much."

I get what he means. I'm not daft enough to think this is normal behavior. But too many things have happened for it to be just one big coincidence.

"I'll do it," Zak says. "But only if you agree that, if we're no closer to answers after Saturday, you'll quit."

"Deal."

66

"Have you finished the bathroom?" Mum asks, and Jay turns to me.

"Do you see what you've done?" He has a smile on his face, but Mum doesn't see the funny side.

"It's clean," he says. "Everything is clean. You can take a breath, now."

She starts walking away, but Jay pulls her into a hug and whispers, "The place looks amazing."

A dinner party is one of those things Mum has always wanted to do, but, at the same time, it terrifies her. She wouldn't like me saying it, but she's still fragile, and there's nothing wrong with that. Even now, her nerves creep out sometimes, causing the final word of a sentence to tremble or her eyes to fidget like a fly with nowhere to land.

I love her for it, and I'm not ashamed to say that. When you've seen what we have, you don't hide your feelings. For a long time, they were the only things that kept us strong.

"When are they coming?" Aaron says as he runs past, and then, when he's done a circuit of the house, "Are they nice?"

He never stops for an answer, but you can tell he's excited. There's not much that *doesn't* excite him, to be honest. He's like the Energizer Bunny on steroids.

Mum gives Jay a look, and he says, "Be careful, Aaron," because she's still not comfortable telling her stepson off.

Now that she's won him over, she doesn't want to upset him. Unfortunately, not upsetting Nia is an impossible challenge. Aaron's presence certainly helps, but, whenever he leaves the room, her face falls a tiny bit more.

I check my phone, half-expecting a message from Amy saying they've canceled. She was wary when I invited her. She looked nervous, as if it was a trap. After I snuck into Will's room and then accused her of writing that warning on the car, I don't blame her.

"This is going to be fucking horrible," Nia mumbles.

"Just ask lots of questions. The more they say, the likelier they are to slip up."

"This is ridiculous."

"Maybe. But imagine if I'm right. I'll be saying I told you so for years."

Nia looks at me and smiles. "You're an oddball, you know that?"

"I do."

Aaron bursts in from nowhere and jumps on his sister. I can see that, for the briefest moment, she wants to moan at him. The words "Get off" rest on her lips before she pushes them together and they crumble.

"Are you ready to be charming?" she asks, tickling him until his giggles fill the room.

When he's got his breath back, he says, "I'm always charming."

We don't notice Mum and Jay in the doorway until the doorbell rings, and Jay says, "Right, troops. Let's do this."

67

We always eat at the table, but never like this.

When we first moved in with Jay, Mum made a point of doing things differently. We'd gotten used to eating on trays, first in bedrooms, and then, when it was just the two of us, in front of the TV.

But Mum wanted to do things "properly" now. She wanted dinner to be an event, not something to do in secret or in silence. She liked asking people to pass her things, even when she could reach them.

This is that turned up to eleven, because the table looks like it's been set for Christmas, with the special-occasion plates and three sets of cutlery. There are tall glasses for wine and small glasses for water and not enough space for all the food.

"Does it look okay?" Mum whispers, and I nod.

Even with Jay to calm her nerves, she still turns to me, sometimes, and I love that. We're a team. We always have been.

"This looks wonderful," Jane says, and, when she coughs, Chris hurries to agree.

Friendliness doesn't suit him. He looks like he's trying on smiles when he's shopping for scowls.

"Thank you," Mum says.

She's made Parmesan risotto with roasted shrimp for the second time this week, and she's nailed it. She didn't need to practice, because she's a great cook, but rehearsals calm her nerves.

I wanted her to do one of her own creations, because Mum has a whole notebook of them since starting her course. But, for now, those are reserved for us and her teachers.

Amy sits next to me with her head down. She smiled when she came in, but the tension between her and Nia is obvious. Will is beside Aaron, but, without his iPad, it looks like he's broken down. Only the adults are talking.

"So," Jay says to Chris, "what do you do?"

"I'm in recruitment."

Jay smiles like he knows what that is. Whatever it means, it must pay a lot for them to afford that house.

"I used to be an accountant," Amy's mum says, "but I haven't done that for a while."

"Jane keeps us ticking along," says Chris.

He's already said more than he did the entire night I was at theirs, and that only makes me more suspicious. He's pretending, and he's good at it.

"I wish I could be at home more," Mum says, "but we do what we must."

"I understand," Jane replies. But I've seen the inside of her house, so I don't think she does.

My phone vibrates in my pocket, and Amy looks at me and raises her eyebrows. I don't check it until she's looking the other way, because I know who it's from.

Are they there? it says, and I quickly type, Yes, and click send.

Okay, Zak replies. I'm going in.

My heart cranks up a couple of gears, and, when I tuck my phone back in my pocket, everyone's looking at me.

"Tom?" Mum says.

"Yes."

"Jane asked you a question."

"Sorry, I..."

"And what did I say about phones at the table?"

Nia smirks because it's her least-favorite rule, and Amy gives me another confused look.

"I was asking about your room," Jane says. "You said you'd decorated. I'd love to see it."

Is she mocking me? Does she know I was playing with her when I mentioned it, and now she's returning the favor? Before I can reply, Jane's already out of her seat and heading toward the stairs, saying, "Come on, then."

"Now?"

I look at Mum because the plates haven't even been cleared, but she looks relieved, as if Jane's presence at the table is wringing her out.

"That would be nice," Mum says. "We should take a break before dessert, anyway."

Jane's in the hallway, so I jump up and follow her. No one else comes, not even Amy. Why is she so interested in what my room looks like now?

"This is lovely," Jane says, walking toward my window and looking out.

Her new home stares back at us, lit up by the spotlights that could give Zak away any second.

I try to find him in the shadows, but he's not there. If he does what I told him, he'll move from window to window, searching for clues, eventually walking straight into Jane's line of sight. I reach for the curtains, but Jane doesn't budge.

"I didn't realize quite how much you could see from here," she says. "You could spy on us if you wanted to."

She says it with a smile, but neither of us laugh. Has she noticed me watching? Is everything I've seen been an act?

My phone buzzes again, and she says, "You're popular tonight."

"It's just notifications. Nothing important."

Jane puts both hands on my windowsill and stares out. She can't possibly know what we're doing, but I don't think she trusts me. Every look and every word come with a hidden meaning. She's one of those people whose eyes tell a different story from their mouth. And, the more time I spend with her, the more I think she's the one to be scared of.

Chris is hardly there. He's like a ghost, haunting the edges of rooms like Amy in those photographs. But Jane's different.

When she turns her back, I quickly check my phone.

You need to see this.

Zak's found something, and I have to fight to keep everything in check. My heart is beating so fast I'm sure Jane will hear it. My palms are hot and clammy, and I can't keep still.

I think I see Zak move in the half-light outside my window, but blink and he's gone.

Jane has turned to look at me. "Are you okay?" she asks but doesn't wait for an answer. Instead, she goes over and runs her hand over the paint now covering those words: *HELP ME.*

There's a creak in the floorboards, and, when I turn, I see Amy in the doorway.

"Tom's really making it his own," Jane says, but her daughter doesn't reply. She looks over my shoulder and, for a moment, I'm terrified she's seen Zak.

Amy's eyes change, but she doesn't say anything. Maybe it's just the feeling of being in this house. Maybe it's bringing back the memories I'm so desperate to unlock. Or, perhaps, she feels as uneasy in her mum's presence as I do.

Jane follows Amy's eyes to the window, and that's when I see a shape in the Pearces' driveway, appearing and vanishing in the dark. Jane steps slowly across my bedroom floor until she can almost touch the glass, and, if Zak moves again, she'll see him.

I hold my breath and hope I look calm even though my insides are doing somersaults. Then I watch Amy, trying to figure out if she knows what she saw or thinks it's her eyes playing tricks. She's barely said a word since they arrived, and I don't know if that's because of me or her parents.

"Dessert is served!" Jay shouts up the stairs, and I breathe out too loudly.

"Come on. Mum's desserts are awesome."

On the way down, I reply to Zak.

What is it?

And he messages back instantly.

I'm not sure. Just come.

That wasn't part of the plan. I can't leave the meal without attracting attention...unless they don't know I'm gone.

"I'm just going to the toilet," I say, but, while everyone is distracted, I gently open the front door and leave. I run to the end of the street, then dial Zak's number.

"I'm outside," I whisper. "Where are you?"

I hear stones crunching from the other side of the wall, then a grunt just before Zak's head appears a few meters away.

"Come over," he says. "You'll want to see this."

When I don't move, he says, "This was your idea. Come on." But *this* wasn't my idea. I should be having awkward conversations with the Pearces; we shouldn't both be trespassing. How am I going to explain this if we're caught?

"Tom," Zak hisses. "Quickly."

He's pushed the brown garden waste bin against the wall so it's easy to climb over.

"How's it going?" he asks. "Did you save me some leftovers?"

"This isn't funny."

"I'm not laughing. I'm just hungry."

Zak smiles, but I don't have time to muck about. He's making light of this because it's his way of coping. If he didn't joke, he'd convince himself the police were on their way.

"What did you find?"

He starts walking away from the house, deeper into a garden that feels infinite in the dark. Amy's house is lit up through the patio doors, and I'm tempted to try them. Another look in Will's room could give me the evidence I'm searching for. But, whatever Zak has found, it's in the opposite direction.

"Where are you going?" I whisper.

"You'll see," he says, his voice far enough away to make me nervous.

I know I said I wasn't scared of the dark, but that changes when you don't know what you're walking into.

He stops quicker than I expected, his phone's flashlight piercing the gloom. He's pointing it at a tree.

"I looked through their windows, but there was nothing weird," he says. "It's just a house. A lot tidier than ours, but... nothing out of the ordinary. I was coming back when I heard the wind chimes."

Zak moves the flashlight slightly until I can see the slivers of silver hanging overhead. Every now and then, the faint breeze catches them just enough to make them tinkle. But that's not what I'm looking at. There's something else: a box hanging from the same branch with a flower drawn on the side.

I've seen the same drawing in Amy's journal—hundreds of variations of that intricate design.

"Can you see it?" Zak asks, and I reach up, my fingers brushing the bottom of the wood.

"Yes."

With a stretch, I can just manage to unhook it, placing it between us on the grass and stepping back.

Opening boxes isn't always a good idea, but what choice do

we have? I run my fingers over the wood, and it's surprisingly smooth. Whoever made this spent a lot of time on it.

Zak holds the phone closer as I lift the latch, then peer inside. Nothing jumps out; nothing changes. All we can see is paper.

I should be at home by now. Someone will be asking where I am. But, instead, I reach inside and unfold the top sheet, then another, then a third. In Amy's handwriting, they all say the same thing:

I'm sorry.

68

"We need to put it back," I say, stuffing the notes in the box and reaching for the hook.

"Why?" Zak replies. "Isn't this important?"

"I think so. But if she knows we found it…"

This isn't an answer. It's another question. What's Amy sorry for? And why is she hanging it from a tree? I can't be certain who wrote the words on my wall, but I'd recognize her handwriting in a heartbeat.

This is how she writes now. It's identical to the words I photographed when she left her journal unguarded. She wrote some of these recently, at least the ones on top.

I check my phone and see that I've been gone for nearly ten minutes. If they haven't already sent Aaron to check on me, they will soon.

"Come on," I say.

I don't wait for Zak to answer. There's no trash can on this side of the wall, but, a few feet down, there's a stack of garden chairs.

If we move them, they'll know. But we can't get over the spikes, so what choice do we have? After dragging them to the safe spot, I point for Zak to go first. There's just enough height for him to reach the top row of bricks and pull himself over. When I hear a thud on the other side, I copy him.

I'm banking on no one noticing the chairs, or everyone thinking someone else moved them. It's a risk, but they won't know it's us, and nothing is missing.

Back on my street, I turn to Zak and say, "Thank you. I owe you one."

"You're not inviting me in?"

He smirks, and I pat him on the back. "Maybe next time."

A curtain moves next door, and I see Mrs. Hawkins disappear. But I don't have time to worry about that.

I turn my key as quietly as I can, close the door with the slightest click and avoid all the creaks in the hallway.

"Where've you been?" Aaron is standing at the top of the stairs with his hands on his hips. The noise in the dining room doesn't stop. There's even some laughter.

"Come here," I whisper.

My stepbrother plods down the stairs, not caring who hears, and, when Mum shouts, "Did you find him?" I hold a finger to my lips.

"He did," I reply.

"Hurry up," she says. "You're missing all the fun."

I crouch down next to Aaron and say, "I was in the bathroom, okay? I know you saw me coming in from outside, but that's a secret. Are we cool?"

I hold my fist out, and he bumps it. "Yep."

Aaron's a good kid. His sister's animosity toward me hasn't rubbed off on him yet, and I hope it never will.

"Where were you, though?" he asks, and I squeeze his shoulder.

"I'll tell you. I promise. But not yet, okay?"

He nods, then walks into the dining room and shouts, "Tom was in the bathroom a long time!"

When you're six, there's no such thing as subtle.

Everyone laughs, even Chris, and I wonder what's changed since I left.

I sit down next to Amy and try to look as calm as possible. She's smiling, but her eyes look strange.

"What's so funny?" I ask.

Jay says, "I was telling everyone about your theory. Remember when we first moved in, you thought Chris and Jane were locking the kids in their bedrooms."

A freezing chill shoots through me, and I take a bite of my cheesecake to buy a few seconds. I glance up and that's when I see the difference. They are all laughing, but only Jay means it.

Mum is shrinking into herself, desperate for him to stop. Chris looks angry, his lips switching from a smile to a scowl and back again. Jane has the same look in her eyes as the day she came over for tea, like she's daring me to do something. Nia seems embarrassed, and Amy...

The note we found said she's sorry, but for what? "Whatever gave you that idea?" Jane says, and there it is—the dare.

She wants me to tell her everything I know. But I know more than she thinks. I open my mouth to speak, then catch Mum's eye. I've seen that look so many times—the moment before she cries. I always wanted to stop it but couldn't because I was too young or too scared or too helpless.

I could tell Amy's family everything and force it out of them. Maybe not the truth, but something real, a glimpse of whatever they're hiding. But, instead, I say, "I know, right? I saw a few holes and let my imagination get the better of me."

Jane's laugh is like the last trickle of an empty tap. Mum smiles at me, relief washing over her face. And then Amy's hand touches mine. She doesn't look at me. Her eyes are fixed firmly ahead. But she's thanking me in her own way. Everyone knows I could make a scene because there's enough evidence to shake it all out on the table and see how it lands. But I won't do that to Mum. She's worked so hard to make tonight perfect. I can't take that away from her.

When I do finally challenge Amy's family, they won't be able to laugh their way out of it.

69

Once the table is clear, Amy whispers, "Thank you."

"For what?"

"For believing me."

How can I ask about the wind chimes and the box full of apologies now? She thinks I've finally admitted defeat when I'm preparing for a knockout blow.

"Why don't you two play?" Jay says to Aaron and Will, but, while my stepbrother jumps out of his seat, Amy's brother doesn't move a muscle.

When Jane nudges him, he mumbles, "I'm ten," and Aaron looks offended.

"I'm seventeen," Nia says, "but we still play together, don't we, mate?"

Aaron beams and looks at Will with the same eyes that get him a new toy whenever he wants.

"Fine," Will mumbles, following him into the living room and sitting with a face on while my stepbrother explains everything in his toy box in fine detail.

Amy watches them, then turns to me and says, "This was a good idea."

She's still holding my hand under the table, drawing circles in my palm with her thumb. It tickles just enough to feel nice, and, when I've finally solved whatever's going on, I hope she still does it. Because, when Amy touches me, I feel nervous and excited and a hundred other things, and I wish this wasn't so confusing.

I wish I'd found nothing in her garden. I wish this was a normal dinner party with normal guests.

I want to lose myself in this moment. And I want to enjoy Mum's smile that has come back strong since I turned my fears into a joke. I think she'd smile even wider if she could see Amy holding my hand.

I don't blame Mum for wanting something else, now. She lived in the darkness for too long. But, if I didn't know it would upset her, I'd ask her to take a closer look at our guests.

I thought Amy was the key, then I was sure it was Will—two kids leaving notes and signs and warnings they were too scared to explain. But now I need to solve this the old-fashioned way.

70

Aaron is exhausted by the time he finally goes to bed. Nia tucks him in while Jay and Mum load the dishwasher, and I tidy the house.

When they think no one's watching, they kiss until Mum giggles. She looks like the photographs she hid for most of my life—twenty years younger and one hundred times happier. She nuzzles into Jay's shoulder and closes her eyes, and I back away.

"Night," I say from the hallway, and Mum comes out and hugs me.

"Thank you for tonight," she says. "It was a lovely idea. Everyone seemed to enjoy themselves."

"I think so."

Mum looks me in the eye. "Did you?"

I nod because it's easier than saying I only enjoyed certain parts—like Mum's smile and Amy's hand on mine.

"I was worried when you disappeared for so long. Were you feeling all right?"

Mum knows me better than anyone. But, if she suspects I did something stupid, she hides it.

"Yeah, I'm fine."

"Will you be coming back down?" Mum asks.

What she means is: did tonight make me feel better? After a posh meal and a few hours with a girl I like, will I still need to make sure that we've locked up?

"Maybe," I say.

"I understand."

I'm sorry that the last smile I see is her sympathetic one. I'd rather have gone to bed with the memory of how Mum looks when she's alone with Jay. But she can't hide her disappointment that OCD rarely takes a night off.

Nia is stroking Aaron's hair when I walk past. His breathing is already loud and steady, the late night taking its toll. She turns and smiles, and I smile back.

Whatever she thought of the meal, this is the moment she'll remember. Nia loves putting Aaron to bed. Tonight she doesn't go straight to her room. She knocks on my door and whispers, "Well?"

"What?"

Nia grins and shakes her head. "What did you find at Amy's house?"

"How did you..."

"If Aaron makes you a promise, he won't tell anyone," she says, "except me."

"He didn't know where I went."

"But you went somewhere...and I'm the smart one in this family."

Nia realizes what she said; I can see it in her eyes, but she doesn't correct herself.

"So, was it worth it?"

I walk past her and close my door, then pull out a notepad and start writing.

"If you're the smart one," I say, "help me figure out the clues."

Clues

- Holes in the doors where locks have been.
- Words written under the wallpaper: Help Me.
- Stick people carved into the wardrobe—one big and one small.
- Will's sketch pad—he's drawn the same pictures over and over again.
- Amy's journal—"I see it in the way he looks at me. He can't possibly know the truth, but he knows something isn't right. And I don't think he's going to stop digging."
- The box hanging from a tree, full of notes that say "I'm sorry."

Possible clues:

- Amy took boy from his mother at the shopping center to teach her a lesson—suggests she hates bad parents.
- Rumor about Amy's dad and Evie Wells. Amy says Evie started it. Evie thinks it was Amy.

- **Will tearing up my note in front of me.**
- **Chris's handshake.**
- **Jane's surprise visit.**

71

"What do you mean, she took a boy?"

Nia is holding the paper, staring at me as though what she's reading is ridiculous.

"I followed Amy around the shops and watched her take a kid when his mother wasn't looking. When I caught her, she said it's to make sure parents pay more attention."

"That's fucking wild."

"She thinks she's doing something good."

Nia shakes her head. "Well, she's not. And that should definitely be bumped up to a clue. If she's targeting 'bad' parents, what does that say about her own? You might be on to something."

"You think so?"

"Yes, but I don't think we can have handshakes and surprise visits on the list."

"It was a hard grip," I say. "I think it was a warning."

Nia laughs. "Probably to stay away from his daughter. Dad does the same whenever a boy comes 'round."

I think back to the only time Nia brought a boy home. Jay wasn't anything like Chris. He was his usual happy self, and they talked about football for hours. I think Jay liked him more than Nia did.

"It was more than that," I say, but I cross it off the list anyway.

"You've tried talking to Will, and he's having none of it," Nia says, "and Amy was pissed off for you even suspecting something's wrong. Her dad is super protective, and her mum's playing happy families. But here's the thing...you don't need any of them."

"I don't?"

"No, because everything you have so far has come either from our house or from you being a stalker guy."

"I'm not a stalker."

"I know, but you followed her when she was 'shopping,' and you got her whole family here so you could break into her garden. They're not going to suddenly open up now."

Nia waves the clues in front of me and says, "I'm sorry I made fun of you before. Whatever this is...I think it's worth investigating."

"The handshake," I whisper. "Is *not* a clue."

"Unless..."

Nia said *whenever* she has boys over, and I've only seen one, but that's because we haven't lived together for long.

Chris met me, so maybe he met others as well. Maybe there were other handshakes, other warnings...

"What are you thinking?" Nia asks, talking over thoughts that are racing through my mind so quickly I can't catch them.

"Logan," I say. "She said Logan."

"Who did?"

"Amy. She said Logan by accident. What if that was her boyfriend and he did something, and now Chris is extra protective? Or maybe he always has been, and, if I find this Logan guy, he'll be able to fill in the blanks."

"That's a big leap," Nia says.

"I know. But, like you said, I've found everything out on my own so far. If Amy let something slip by accident, I have to check it out."

There's a knock on my door, and I tuck the clues in my pocket as it opens.

"Oh," Mum says. "This is…"

"We're bonding," Nia says, standing up and kissing Jay good night.

"About time," he replies. "Sleep well, mate."

He leaves Mum and me alone, but she doesn't sit. She smiles, and I know what she's thinking. She thinks tonight has changed everything. She thinks Nia and I are finally getting along.

I hope she's right.

72

If you google "Logan," you get tons of stuff about Wolverine and, eventually, the origins of the name. I refine my search, but there's nothing useful.

Amy doesn't have any social media, so I can't find anyone called Logan that way. Evie has changed her security settings since our conversation, so I can't see her friends either.

I type in our school's name, then search for St. Gregory's Academy for Boys, then the girls' school. But there are no links to any of them.

I google "Logan I'm sorry," "Logan stick drawings," and "Logan and Amy," and get nothing useful every time. The internet knows everything, but only if you ask the right questions.

I pull the list of clues out of my pocket and renumber them, and that's when I think of it. Nia said one of the possible clues was a definite: the boy at the shopping center. So I type something else into my phone—"Logan child abduction"—and scroll down and hold my breath. I don't breathe out until I've read the whole story.

Logan Connolly was four when he disappeared. It was lunchtime on a quiet street near a park, and he was never seen again. It happened when Amy was eleven. They didn't find the boy. They only found his clothes.

PART THREE

1

The new house is awesome, and we have our own rooms. Plus, Dad has an office, so it's basically perfect. Will is running around like a maniac, but no one shouts at him, because this is a good day.

Mum's talking about counter space, which is apparently a big deal. She talked about it a lot before we moved in, and she's still going on about it now.

My room's ugly, but Dad says we can change that. So I grin and bear it.

The old lady next door has already been over with a card and a bottle of wine.

Mum said, "This is a good neighborhood," because, where we used to live, no one even looked at each other.

When we're all settled, Dad hugs me and says, "What do you think, Amy?" and I tell him it's perfect. And he smiles like that's the right answer.

11

Will loves the garden. He runs around, screaming, because he's three and that's what he does. When he stands still, I tell him this place is our Magic Kingdom, and he nods, all serious, and whispers, "Yes."

Then we make up stories about the creatures that live in the bushes and up the trees and behind the shed. They're all different, but they get along because the garden is so big that they have enough space not to fight over it.

"Who lives there?" Will says, pointing to a hole in the fence.

"That's where the queen lives. She's in charge, so we don't bother her."

I can tell my brother anything, and he'll believe me. That's why I stick to good things. Mum says he has an overactive imagination and I make it worse. But I think I make it better.

There isn't really a queen behind the fence. It's a water-pumping station, whatever that is, and it's out of bounds. Our parents watch us from the other end of the yard.

We have outside furniture now and a massive umbrella, and they're so happy.

"Don't run around so much or you'll be sick," Mum tells Will.

He bounds over to her and holds his tummy, pretending, and Dad scoops him up and says, "It's coming. He's gonna blow."

Will's laugh isn't like any other sound in the world. It bursts out of him and carries the rest of us with it.

I didn't want Will until he arrived. When Mum said she was pregnant again, I was already seven, and I thought it was too late for a brother. Then he was born, and I changed my mind as soon as I held him.

He still likes being cuddled sometimes, but he has to choose. And it's usually when he's tired. The rest of the time, he's playing, which is fine by me.

I think ten is a good age to be a big sister.

III

When I get into St. Gregory's Academy for Girls, Mum screams, and Dad hugs me and says, "Well done, sweetheart."

Will gives me a card that is supposed to say congratulations on the front, and, even though he doesn't know what that means, it's the thought that counts.

"What's St. Gregory's," Will asks.

Mum says, "It's where all the smart kids go."

I should be happy, but my friend Kasia said, if you want to get in, you need to be rich, not clever.

When I asked Dad if we were rich, he laughed and said, "No, darling. But we're happy."

I didn't tell them what Kasia said, because I didn't want to upset them. They always wanted me to go to the girls' Academy, so now they've got their wish.

They're nearly always happy since Will arrived, but now they're even happier. And I'm the reason.

"Let's eat out," Dad says. "Wherever you want."

"Anywhere?" I ask, and, when he nods, I tell him and wait for him to say no.

But Mum thinks it's a wonderful idea, so Dad says, "Okay. But we'll have to wait until tomorrow."

Where I want to go is the castle with the restaurant where my parents got engaged. But it's not close, and it's not Pizza Hut, which Dad probably expected me to say. We went to the castle once, when it was just the three of us, and they told me the story and I never forgot it.

It's not a secret, but it's not for sharing. Mum says some history is everyone's, and some is just for us. So I won't tell.

It sounds better when Dad tells it, anyway.

////

"This is where I did it," Dad says. We're at the lake by the castle, and it's beautiful.

"It was perfect," Mum says, and I believe her.

Sometimes, when people say something was perfect, it's not true, but it's magical here.

The castle isn't just ruins, like some places we've been to. It's still all there, and you have to be quiet when you walk around, which is easier for me than Will.

It's okay seeing all the rooms, but it's better outside. The sun makes the water look like tinsel, and there are gardens with flowers so red and orange and yellow it's as if they've been painted. You can sit in a boat while someone pushes you along with a stick, but we don't do that because Will is saying, "Maze...maze...maze."

"Come on, then," Dad says, scooping him up and doing Superman until my brother is too tired to laugh.

Sometimes I think Will needs a leash like a dog, because he

always likes to see what's next. He's always running around corners and charging ahead, but at least he's safe in the maze.

"It's not that way," he says, and, "Come on," and then, when the fun wears off, "We're lost."

That's when Dad puts Will on his shoulders, and he can see the people at the top. They point, and my brother guides us. And, when we climb the steps, the maze looks like a beautiful pattern, not just bushes.

This was a good way to celebrate getting into St. Gregory's, even if I'm scared of what comes next. They reckon you have to be supersmart to keep up, and I'm not. Mum says I'll be fine, but that's just what parents say. Some lies make you feel better, but that one doesn't.

When we're in the restaurant, Mum tells Will that he needs to be on his best behavior, and he nods. He isn't naughty, though. He's just energetic.

Dad holds his glass up. "To Amy. We're so proud of you."

"To Amy," Mum says, and we clink glasses. Will giggles, and a few people look at us and smile.

Our parents have their lovey eyes tonight, which means they look at each other like there's no one else in the world. I think they always looked like this before I was born, but now they save it for special occasions.

When we're done, we walk back to the car in our line. Mum is on one end, Dad's on the other, and I'm in the middle with Will. We can only do that when it's quiet or we'd take up the whole sidewalk. But it's one of my favorite things, because it makes me feel strong.

"Look," Dad says. "A star."

"It's a plane," Mum says.

"Make a wish anyway."

"You don't wish on a plane," I say.

And Dad says, "Well, maybe you should."

So we all say a wish, one after another, out loud because our secrets are safe with each other.

卌

I'm frightened because today's my first day at St. Gregory's, and it doesn't feel exciting anymore.

Dad sits next to me on the stairs and says, "It's okay to be scared. But everything will be okay. I promise."

"How do you know?" I ask, and he smiles.

"Because we've all had that first day…even me."

I try to imagine Dad when he was eleven, but it doesn't work.

Mum rushes into the hall with pink cheeks and a puff and says, "Are we ready?" Then she crouches next to us. "I'm so proud of you, Amy."

"Wish your sister luck," Dad says, and Will shouts it without looking away from the TV.

In the car, I cry a little bit, and I can't get out right away. We watch the other kids go through the gate, and Mum holds my hand and says, "One day, it will be your brother's first day at secondary school. And you can tell him how amazing it is."

She wants me to be brave, so I am, even if I'm full of butterflies. I'm strong all the way to the hall where a teacher tells us the rules. And I'm strong in the classroom where Mrs. Solomon says she's our homeroom teacher.

The girl sitting next to me whispers, "I'm Nia."

"I'm Amy."

She smiles, and I don't feel scared anymore.

We sit next to each other in every lesson, and she's good at making me laugh even when we're not supposed to. At the end of the day, she hugs me and says, "See you tomorrow."

Mum and Dad and Will are all in the car, and they ask so many questions. I answer them all, but my favorite one is, "Did you make any friends?"

"Yes," I say.

Dad smiles. "I told you it would be okay."

𝍸 𝍷

"I need you to look after Will," Mum says.

"For how long?" I ask.

"As long as it takes."

I don't ask what "it" is because Mum doesn't like talking about work. Well, she does, but only on the phone and only to other people.

Bending down to my brother, she says, "Be good for Amy, okay?"

He nods hard and pushes his lips together like he does whenever he makes a promise.

"I won't be long," Mum tells me. "Thank you."

We wave goodbye, then watch TV until Will says, "I'm *boooored.*"

You can tell how bored he is by how many o's he uses, so I turn the TV off and say, "Let's play outside."

He jumps up and runs to the back door, and I have to wrestle his coat on and force a hat over his head because it's not summer anymore.

"What shall we play?" I ask.

"Creatures," he says, so I tell him about everything that lives in the places we can't see.

He searches the bushes and climbs the apple tree, and I just watch because it's harder to enjoy yourself when it's cold.

Eventually, I say, "Come on. It's time to go inside," and Will pretends he can't hear me.

When he does it to Mum or Dad, it's funny, but my cheeks are tingling. And I'm a bit annoyed because Mum's still not back and it's been ages.

"Come on!" I shout, but he doesn't come.

When he was a baby, we'd say, "We're going now," and he'd chase after us and shout, "No, no, no." But now he knows the difference between real threats and pretend ones, and that's a problem when you want him to behave.

I could go and get him, but then he'd cry so I say, "I'm going inside," and I don't look back.

I can see him from the patio doors. He knows I'm watching because, sometimes, he checks, just to be sure, then carries on playing Creatures.

My phone pings, and it's a message from Kasia saying,

I'm bored. What you doing?

And I smile because it feels like everyone is bored and it's my job to entertain them. I take my phone back to the windows so I can reply, but Will's gone.

I run outside and shout his name, but he doesn't answer, so I look in all the places we hide. He's not in the shed or the garage or the bushes. He's not anywhere. I go back inside and check his bedroom and the bathroom and every other room, and my heart is beating too fast. It hurts in my chest, and I start to cry because I'm in charge and he's not here.

"Will!" I yell, inside and out. "Where are you?"

That's when I see it, and I'm happy because I know where he is. I look through the hole in the fence and call his name again.

"I know you're in there, William. Are you looking for the queen?"

I climb through the hole and look left and right, but all I can hear is the pumping station humming and water sloshing.

And then I see him.

~~IIII~~ II

He's doing that thing again where he pretends he can't hear me. He has his head down, and he's moving funny. And that's when I realize he's in the water.

"Will," I whisper because, sometimes, he listens better when you're quiet. But he doesn't look up, he just moves from side to side. It sounds like he's in the bath, except there are no toys and it's cold, and my brother still has his face in the water.

"Get out," I say, and, when he doesn't, I grab his arms and pull hard, then harder, until I fall back and he lands on me.

"What were you doing in there?" I ask. "I said, what were you doing?"

He's heavy, and he doesn't get off and, when I push him, he falls to the side and lies still.

"Will?"

His eyes are open, but he can't see me. He's looking at the sky, and his lips are blue. I know what I need to do, but I've forgotten.

I push on his chest and blow into his mouth. I push on his chest and blow into his mouth. I push on his chest and—

It's not working. On TV it works, but I can't do it. I shout for help, but no one comes.

Will has a cut on his head, so I wipe the blood away with my finger. I can still help him if I stop the bleeding. I need to call an ambulance, but I don't want to leave him. He's too cold and too wet, and I've already left him too long. I try to pick him up, but he's so heavy.

"I'll be right back," I whisper. "I'm just going to get my phone."

I crawl through the fence and run toward the house, and that's when I see Mum in the living room by the patio doors. She's saying something I can't hear. She looks angry because she saw me come out of the hole, and we're not allowed in there.

"I'm sorry," I say, and I think Mum can hear me through the glass because her face changes.

"Where is he?" she says, but I can't reply because I don't like the answer. So I cry, and she runs outside and past me to the hole. And then the world goes black.

~~||||~~ |||

"What happened?" Mum asks, but I can't tell her because I only know some of the answer.

She holds my arms too tight and shakes me and says, "Tell me what happened!"

Will isn't behind the fence anymore. He's in his room, but not like he used to be.

I know what that means, and Mum does, too, because she cried a lot before she spoke to me.

"Have you called an ambulance?" I ask, and she shakes her head.

"It's too late for that," she whispers.

That makes me cry, and she grips me tighter and says, "Don't you dare. This is your..."

I think I know what she was going to say, and I don't like it because it's not true. I didn't tell Will to go through the hole. I said we should never disturb the queen. But he tried to find her, and something happened and he fell in the water. That's what I know, so I tell Mum and she takes lots of deep breaths and says, "Okay. I need to think."

She's still thinking when Dad gets home, and she tells me to stay in my room while they talk.

I hear noises I don't like, and Dad's voice comes through the floorboards. Mum's crying again, and I hate myself because it *is* my fault. I was supposed to look after him, but I walked away. I wasn't watching him, and now he's gone.

I sit on the stairs so I can hear my parents better, and Mum is saying, "But she's eleven, and I left her alone with a four-year-old. How does that look? They'll take her away from us. I'm sure of it. And they'll charge me with..."

My foot makes the step creak, and my parents come to the bottom of the stairs and look up at me.

Dad's face is scary. He always looks tired when he comes home from work, but, tonight, he seems different. Mum's face is red and blotchy, and I want to hug her but don't know if I'm allowed.

"I'm sorry," I whisper, and Dad comes toward me. I'm scared, but he lifts me up and hugs me, and his tears make my shoulder wet, but I don't complain. Over his shoulder I see Mum and think of what she said about them taking me away.

"I don't want to go," I say.

Dad says, "You're not going anywhere, Amy. We love you, and we'll keep you safe."

They said that about Will, too, and he's not safe anymore. But I believe Dad because I have to.

"What are you going to do?" I ask.

Dad puts me down and looks at my brother's bedroom door.

"I don't know yet," he says. "But it'll be okay."

~~IIII~~ IIII

They take Will away when I'm at school.

I didn't want to go, but Mum said, "You have to, darling. We must pretend that everything's fine."

"Why are we pretending?" I asked.

"I've lost one of you. I can't lose both. You understand that, don't you? We'll be in trouble if anyone ever finds out."

Dad drove me to school, and, at the gate, he said, "Are you all right?"

The answer was no, but I nodded because it was easier than lying out loud.

Will's bedroom is weird now that he's gone. It's as if he's haunting it, because I can still feel him there. Sometimes I hear his voice, but it must be in my head.

I have nightmares, so I sleep in my parents' bed, and, sometimes, one of them wakes up screaming. I thought you grew out of bad dreams, but I was wrong because Mum's screams are the worst.

When I wake up, I think he's still here, and then I remember the truth and don't like life anymore.

Mum and Dad's smiles aren't really smiles. I know they're trying for me, but I wish they wouldn't. I wish they'd just be sad all the time so I know what they're saying is real. That's why I like it when Mum sits on the end of my bed and cries and says, "I want you to do something. You might think it's bad...but it's actually good."

It doesn't matter what she wants me to do. I'm happy that she's being honest, and I say, "Okay."

"We'll need to practice," Mum says. "You can't get this wrong."

"What happens if I get it wrong?" I ask, and she cries a bit more.

"Then I'll lose you as well."

𝍸 𝍸

“Watch closely,” Mum says. “This is really important.”

We’re in town, but we’re not shopping. We’re looking at people in secret.

“Not all mums are good mums,” she says. “That’s what we’re waiting for.”

“A bad mum?” I ask.

“Exactly.”

“But we also need to find a boy that looks like…” Her voice wobbles, and she looks down at me and says, “I’m sorry.” I don’t know what she’s apologizing for, but I say it’s okay. She smiles and says, “We need to find a boy that looks like Will.”

“Why?”

“Because we’re going to save him.”

Mum’s eyes are wet, so I give her a tissue. She hugs me and says, “It’s all going to be okay.”

They both keep saying that, and I want to believe them, but I don’t. How can it be okay when my brother is dead and it's my fault and my parents are so, so sad? And now Mum is talking about things I don't understand.

"What are we saving him from?" I ask.

Mum pushes her lips against my ear, and it tickles, but I don't laugh because nothing is funny anymore.

"We're saving him from a bad life," she whispers. "We're going to give someone what Will had."

She seems strange, and I have to look away.

"Like that boy," she says. "See how his mum isn't paying him any attention? Anyone could take him if they wanted to."

"But that's wrong," I say.

"It *is* wrong. But not if you're rescuing him."

All afternoon, Mum points out the good parents and the bad ones. She tells me what to look for, like people on their phones and kids being allowed to wander off. She says not everyone is cut out to be a parent, and I block out the tiny feeling pushing through, because she left me on my own with Will and I didn't want that.

At dinner, Mum says, "Tell your dad what we learned today," and it feels like a trick.

I stare at her, and she says, "It's okay. Your father and I have discussed it, and we think it's for the best." But the look on his face says something else. He just stares at the table until I ask to get down.

When he kisses me good night, I ask if he's angry, and he says, "No, sweetheart. I'm not angry with you."

"Mum wants me to..."

"It's okay. I know what your mum wants. But you don't have to do anything you don't want to."

There's a noise behind him, and she's standing outside my room and doesn't look happy.

He kisses me again and closes my door, but I open it and listen to them arguing.

"We need help," Dad says. "This won't solve anything."

"You're wrong," Mum says. "This is the *only* solution. What do you want to do...tell the police our son is dead because I left him with our daughter, and we hid it for weeks because... why? They won't believe me. It will be the end of us."

I can't sleep, because my eyes sting. I stay in my own bed, even though I need a cuddle, and think of Will.

Dad said I don't have to, but I do.

There are only three of us left, and it feels like we're falling apart.

𝍸 𝍸 𝍷

"Are you ready?" Mum asks, and I nod because we've been practicing a long time.

"This is different," she says. "This is real."

She doesn't need to point at them, because I knew right away. There are three children and two adults.

The dad is pushing an empty cart, and the mum is shouting at a girl who's probably about eight. The other girl is older and seems angry, but it's the boy I'm focused on. He doesn't look like he's with them because he's so far behind, and no one checks that he's following them, not even his sisters.

When Will was alive, Mum or Dad would hold his hand, and he would get annoyed and say, "Amy, Amy," until his fingers gripped mine. This little boy has no hand to hold, and he's losing sight of his family, but he doesn't cry, because he must be used to it.

"Come on!" the woman yells. She still doesn't look around, and it's like she's calling a dog.

I remember everything Mum told me. This is a test I need to pass, and then she'll be happy, so I walk toward the boy and check that no one is looking, then touch his shoulder and say, "Hi."

The boy stops and looks up, but there's no smile because he doesn't trust me. I'm a stranger, and he's smart, even if his parents are arseholes.

"Are you bored looking 'round the shops?" I ask, and the boy nods.

"Do you like toys?"

He nods again and almost smiles, and I hold out my hand and he takes it. Then I walk slowly in the other direction, and he follows.

I keep walking and count one, two, three, all the way to twenty, then turn round and look for his parents. They're farther away than I thought, so, when I go back, I have to walk fast to catch them.

The boy's legs are too short, and he moans, but I ignore him because I know Mum is watching. When his parents are just a few steps ahead, I let go of his hand and say, "Go on. Or you'll get lost."

He runs up to his mum, and she grabs him and says, "Speed up."

Then I go back to Mum and say, "Why couldn't it be that one? I think he needs rescuing."

She shakes her head. "It's not time. You need to be perfect, and so does he."

We used to go to swimming club on Saturdays, but now we do this.

"Let's go home," she says. "It won't be long now."

Dad never comes with us, because he hates what we're doing, but he doesn't argue with Mum anymore. He pretends this isn't happening and hopes we fail.

But we won't.

~~IIII~~ ~~IIII~~ II

We have a family meeting, because there are important things to discuss.

"It will happen soon," Mum says, "so we have to be ready."

She has a list, but Dad refuses to look until she bangs on the table and says, "This is important."

Dad isn't Dad anymore, but then Mum isn't really Mum either. Dad used to talk all the time, and his laughter filled the house, and he always got home early so he could play before bed. Now he works late and only speaks when he's spoken to, and he never laughs. Mum pretends to be happy, and we let her because it's better than hearing her cry.

We used to sit around the dinner table every night, but this is the first time we've done it since Will died. I still can't say the word out loud. I can think it, but even that hurts. I miss him so much, and I know it was my fault even though Dad says it wasn't. He said accidents happen, but they don't when you're careful.

Mum hasn't said it's my fault since she almost did the first time, but I know what she's thinking. I can see it in how she looks at me. Sometimes I don't think she likes me very much, but I'm all she has left.

I know Will was her favorite because he was younger. You become boring when you're older, and, if she could choose, she would have kept him and lost me. But you don't get to choose the big things; they just happen.

If I could choose, I would have stayed outside until he got tired or taken him back in even if he cried. I wouldn't have left him, and I wouldn't have checked my phone.

I have dreams about what I saw, and I wake up, scared, and sometimes Dad is asleep in the chair next to me and sometimes he isn't. When he's there, he whispers me back to sleep, and, when he's not, I try to do it myself, but it's not the same. Mum is never there because she has her own dreams to worry about.

I'm sorry for what I did. I'm sorry I messed up and that some mistakes are too big to repair. *I'm sorry I'm sorry I'm sorry*, but it doesn't help.

I used to say it every day until Mum shouted: "Stop apologizing!" so now I only say it in my head.

Dad says she doesn't mean to get angry, and I know he's right, but I also know I'm the reason.

I want to ask if it gets better, except I'm scared it doesn't. And I still want to say sorry because keeping it in makes me feel heavy and ready to burst. So I whisper it, and it feels better even if they don't hear.

I'm sorry.

~~////~~ ~~////~~ ///

“You don’t have to do this,” Dad says, but Mum says we do. She says we have no choice if we want to stay together.

“Amy…I…” His mouth stays open, but there are tears where the words should be.

I touch his hand, and he pulls it away, holding it to his face while he cries. Except it’s not a cry. It’s a moan and a shout and a sob all mixed into one, and it’s horrible.

“It’s okay,” I whisper.

But he shakes his head. “It’s not.”

Mum sniffs behind us, and I move closer to Dad, because we’re not supposed to do this. She only gets upset in private, and I try my best.

The floor creaks, and I close my eyes, waiting for her to yell. But I feel the bed drop slightly, and, when I look, she’s sitting next to us.

Mum takes Dad’s hand away from his face and kisses him. Her fingers tell me to come closer, so I do, and she pulls me into a hug with Dad in the middle. He's shaking, so I grip tighter, and then I see Mum is shaking too. Her eyes are closed, but the tears are there, sticking her eyelashes together.

I think the words, then say them out loud. "I'm sorry." This is my fault. Mum gave me a job, and I messed it up.

"I know," she says, and I feel lighter, because she isn't telling me off or blaming me. And then I think of Will and feel heavier than before. He used to sit on Dad's shoulders and laugh at the sky. I was too small to carry my brother that high, but now he's there, pushing me down.

I guess he weighs more now that he's gone.

~~////~~ ~~////~~ ////

Dad breaks more often than Mum, and it takes longer for him to mend as well. The day after Mum cries, it's like I dreamed it.

She says we need to focus on the plan. But I'm scared, because, even though we've practiced and Mum says it's the right thing, I'm worried it's wrong. There are different types of wrong, and the worst kind is what happened to Will. But that doesn't make this right.

"I don't want to," I whisper.

And Mum says, "What did you say?"

It's too hard to repeat it, so I don't. But she heard because she stares at me. "You're the reason for all of this. If you had been a better sister..."

I think she's going to cry again, but she doesn't. Her eyes go thin, and she breathes out and whispers, "You want to make it better, don't you?"

I nod because I do. If the police find out, they'll take me away, and Mum will go to jail and Dad will live here on his own.

He's fixed the hole in the fence, and Mum said something about horses and gates, but he shouted, "I had to do something! I couldn't stare at that fucking reminder anymore."

Dad swears as well, now, and he doesn't care if I hear. Their arguments used to be whispers, but not anymore. Now I'm the only one who whispers, and I hope my brother can hear me even if I'm not sure about heaven. Dad said that's where he's gone, and Mum made a face like she didn't believe it. I keep changing my mind.

If he's not there, he's nowhere, and I hate thinking that. I wish we'd never played Creatures. I don't like the garden, but I still go outside because it feels like he's there. If I close my eyes, I can see him running toward me, and, if I concentrate, I can hear his laugh. And it feels nice until it doesn't.

Remembering him makes him real again, but it also hurts.

I hate pretending nothing's wrong. I didn't go to school for a while, and Mum said I was ill, but now I have to be strong for the family.

No one talks about Will at school, because people don't care about little brothers. Before I went back, Mum said, "It's not going to be easy. But you can't tell anyone what happened. Do you understand?"

She says that a lot, now, and I always nod because it makes her happy.

Before we take the boy, she says it again, and I say, "Yes."

"And what do you do if it goes wrong?"

"I say I was just playing a game, and then I say I've lost my mummy."

She smiles and kisses my forehead. "This will all be over soon."

~~||||~~ ~~||||~~ ~~||||~~

"That's the one," Mum says. "Don't let me down."

The boy is crying, and I wonder if Mum's made a mistake, but she pushes me forward and says, "Do it."

He's not like the children I usually follow. He seems dirty and upset and not someone I'd want in our house, but he does look a bit like Will. And Mum knows best.

I turn to her, and she shakes her head and points forward. We're not supposed to be together, because, if one of us gets caught, we both do. But I don't want to do this anymore, so I stand still.

We're not at the shopping center this time. We're on a street I hadn't seen until last week, when Mum drove us here and spent ages looking for cameras.

"Security cameras are everywhere these days," she said, but that's not totally true. It's not here, where I'm standing, and it's not where we're going if this works.

I turn around one last time, and Mum looks angry. So I

do what I did at the beginning. I dare myself to take one step, then another, then another, and, after enough dares, the boy is in front of me.

"Hello," I say, and he squints like he's looking into the sun, but doesn't reply.

"Would you like to play?"

He turns, but his mother is nowhere, and not even I can see her.

"Play what?" the boy asks.

"Whatever you want."

There are lots of words to remember, because children can say so many different things, and Mum has prepared me for all of them.

He looks one last time for his mum, then nods. "Okay."

I hold out my hand, and he takes it.

The park is five minutes away, and the disabled bathroom is big enough for two people to change clothes at the same time, but the boy won't do it.

When I show them to him, he says, "I've *got* clothes."

"But these are better."

"No," he says, shaking his head too hard, but I know what to do. So I take out the sweets, and his eyes go wide.

When he reaches for them, I say, "Not until you've changed," so he does and then he eats the whole packet of candy like it's a bag of chips.

After I've changed, I stuff my other clothes in my bag but leave his on the floor because they smell, then say, "Are you ready to play now?"

He nods and reaches for my hand, because I'm winning him over.

Mum is in the car with the engine running, and she has a hat pulled over her face. When the boy sees her, he says, "Who's that?"

"That's my mum," I say. "She's nice. Is your mum nice?"

The boy nods and gives her a funny look, but she smiles her old smile, and it reminds me of Will.

I help him into the car seat and strap him in and he asks, "More sweets?"

Mum turns and says, "Of course, gorgeous. You can have all the sweets you want."

𝍸 𝍸 𝍸 𝍷

There are no sweets at home, because Mum says they're bad for you, so the boy is going to be disappointed. But her lie worked, because he walks into our house and up the stairs and into Will's old room, and she says, "What do you think?"

He doesn't reply. He just walks over to Will's toys and starts touching them, which I'm not happy about.

Mum turns to me. "Well done, sweetheart," and my heart jumps because she hasn't called me that in a long time.

Dad isn't smiling. The look on his face is new and strange, but Mum hugs him and says, "It will be okay."

It's what we all keep saying, and I hope it's true.

I watch them as they watch the boy pick up my brother's things. Mum's smile slips a bit, Dad blinks his eyes dry, and I try to feel better.

This is what she wanted, but she doesn't look pleased. She looks like she's trying to be, the same way I do when someone gives me a present that I didn't ask for.

When Dad leaves, I go with him, but Mum doesn't move. Eventually, she comes down, holding the boy's hand, and she's wearing her old face, but you can still see her new face underneath.

"What would you like for dinner?" she asks, which is weird because she never asks us. She says you get what you're given, but the boy says, "Nuggets."

"Nuggets it is."

When it's ready, the boy sits in my brother's seat and gobbles it down so fast, and Mum just laughs.

"What's your name?" I ask, and she shoots me the worst stare.

"You know what his name is. His name's Will."

"No it's not," the boy says. "It's Logan."

"No," Mum says. "It's Will."

He looks confused and stops eating. "Where's my mummy?"

"She's gone away for a while," mine says. "She's asked us to look after you."

The boy's lip wobbles, but he doesn't cry. He doesn't say anything else until Mum asks if he wants ice cream. I know what she's doing, and it's working.

Once, she said the way to a man's heart is through his stomach, and I didn't know what she meant, but now I do. She's bribing the boy with treats, but that only works until you start feeling sick.

~~||||~~ ~~||||~~ ~~||||~~ ||

"I want to go home!"

The boy is shouting, and Mum's trying to soothe him, but it's not helping.

"Come here," she says to me. "I need you to play with Will."

I still won't call him that, but Mum hates it when I say "the boy" or "Logan," so I don't call him anything.

"Be nice to him," she says. "He needs to like it here."

I used to love my family, but they don't feel real anymore. Will is a dream, Mum's always pretending, and Dad is super sad. I still love my brother, even though he's gone, and every night I talk to him.

You must go somewhere when you die or what's the point? That's why I apologize and tell him how bad it is now, because I know he's listening. I can't apologize to Logan—it's against the rules—so, instead, I ask him about his mum.

"Is she kind?" I say, and he thinks about it, then nods.

"When can I go home?" he asks, and I shrug because we're not allowed to give definite answers. We have to be vague, so he doesn't think this is forever.

"I want to see my mummy," he says.

"My mummy likes to spoil you, doesn't she?" He nods, and I say, "Does *your* mummy spoil you?"

The boy shakes his head, and I'm happy for half a second, because this is important. It's called planting seeds of doubt, and I know I've done a good job.

"Do you have anyone to play with at home?" I ask, and I feel stupid because I shouldn't have said "home," not unless I'm talking about here.

That's a banned word, but there's so much to remember and I'm not as good as I thought.

If Mum was listening, I'd be in trouble, but she's not behind the door, so I relax and watch the boy move some toys around the floor. He looks like he doesn't know how to play, so I show him, and, sometimes, he laughs, and it sounds good because none of us have made that noise for ages. I don't laugh back because I can't anymore, but it still feels nice to hear it.

Afterward, Mum says, "Well done, Amy," and then she locks him in.

~~IIII~~ ~~IIII~~ ~~IIII~~ III

I can't sleep because I can hear Mum's voice through the wall. She reads to him every night, like she used to read to both of us.

I would climb into Will's bed, and Mum would say, "Is there room for three?" and we'd somehow all fit, and my brother would fall asleep to the stories I knew by heart.

I used to love those books, but not now. Mum does the same voices, and I want to bang on the wall and scream, "Stop!" because they're *our* stories. They're Will's stories!

I know when Logan is asleep because the mumbling finishes and the lock slides across.

"Lights out," she whispers, kissing me and waiting for my smile. I try my best because she won't leave until I've done it.

Every night I pray to Will, because he must be listening. It's too scary to think that someone can suddenly be nothing, so I don't.

"I'm sorry," I say. "I made the biggest mistake, and I

hate myself. I wish you'd come back. I wish there were time machines and I could change everything, because Creatures was a stupid game and there was no queen and I should never have left you."

I whisper these things to the dark and see him there. He looks different now. He doesn't run to me or giggle.

He looks sleepy, and I love him, and I'm so sorry.

~~||||~~ ~~||||~~ ~~||||~~ ||||

The sounds don't stop when Mum goes downstairs, they just change. Logan cries, and I bury my head under the pillow and try to think of other things, but it doesn't work.

I thought I only felt guilty because of Will, but I'm not sure now. What if there are some things you can't make better, no matter how hard you try?

Sometimes I'd talk to my brother when he was supposed to be sleeping. We would say funny words that sounded even funnier through the wallpaper, and he would still be giggling when Mum went into his room and sang him back to sleep.

I could talk to Logan the same way and tell him not to cry, but I don't.

I'm scared because Mum said this would make everything better. She said some people needed saving, and the boy in Will's bedroom was one of them.

I didn't want our family to break, so I did what she said, but it's still breaking.

Eventually, the crying stops, but, if I listen carefully, I can hear something else. Logan is mumbling and then shouting and then screaming. He screams the same word over and over again.

"Mummy! Mummy! Mummy!"

But I don't think the one that comes is the one he wants.

𝍸 𝍸 𝍸 𝍸

The days make the nights feel like lies.

In the morning, the boy sits by Will's toys like nothing's wrong, but that's all he does. He doesn't play or bring things to life like my brother did. It's like he's sitting in a waiting room and the toys around him are strangers.

I think of the noises he makes in the dark and move next to him.

"Are you okay?" I ask, and he nods because Mum gets angry when he's not.

I want to ask him things I'm too afraid to say out loud. I could tell him about Will, but that's against the rules. And what would I say?

I think I've made another mistake. I should have listened to the voice that said, "Stop!" but it was a tiny voice, and Mum was louder.

She said it was my fault, and it was, but so is this. I want to make it right because, if I miss Will this much, surely Logan's mum misses him. I know she let him disappear, but we all make mistakes, and I can change this one. I can give Logan back, and Mum will be angry, but he's not hers.

The lock is just a lock that slides in and out. There's no key or secret code, because Mum trusts me, but maybe she shouldn't.

𝍸 𝍸 𝍸 𝍸 𝍷

The bus stop is a bad place. There are no adults to tell the naughty kids off, so they do what they want. And I try to be invisible.

Mum said the best people go to St. Gregory's, but some of the worst do too. They pick on you if you're too loud or too quiet or too big or too small. At school, they ignore you, but the bus stop has different rules.

I needed time off after Logan came, but Mum said it was getting suspicious. She won't keep pretending that I'm ill, and I have to take the 136 bus, because she doesn't drive me anymore. She kisses me goodbye and gives me a look that says, *Don't tell*, and I wonder what they do when I'm not there. Is Logan happier when it's just the two of them? Does Mum try harder and tell more lies, or do they stay in different rooms?

Nia is waiting for me at the school gates, and she beams when she sees me. "Guess what?"

It would only be a sentence. That's how quickly I could say

it. But then what? Mum would be furious, and Dad would tell me I shouldn't have. And Nia can't help, anyway.

"What?" I say.

"I'm getting a little brother."

"What?"

"My mum's pregnant. I'm finally going to be a big sister."

It feels like I've fallen and I can't get up because this must be a joke. The world took Will and then gave Mrs. Nkansa the baby boy she always wanted.

"How's that little brother of yours?" Nia's mum used to ask at the gates, even though they never met.

And I would say "fine" or "great" or "wild" because he was all those things, but not anymore.

Now he's a word I can't speak, and Nia is looking at me like, *Why are you not happy?*

I think back to her mum saying, "You *must* visit us sometime. Nia would love that, wouldn't you, sweetheart?"

I never did, and now I never will. "That's good," I say.

Nia huffs. "It's better than good."

I feel the tears, but can't stop them, and Nia doesn't understand because she thinks they're for her. She thinks I'm crying happy tears so she hugs me and says, "Isn't it amazing?"

"Yes," I lie.

Nia doesn't stop talking about it all morning, but something changes at lunch because she goes quiet, then says, "Are you okay?"

I want to scream, "No!" I want to tell the whole cafeteria what happens when I'm at home and about Will and how I did something horrible and then something worse.

I breathe in and listen to the sounds and imagine how loud I'd have to shout to make them stop.

"Amy?" Nia says. "What's wrong?"

The answer is "Everything," but I don't say that. I don't say anything.

~~IIII~~ ~~IIII~~ ~~IIII~~ ~~IIII~~ II

"We can't," Dad whispers. "I'm sorry."

"Why not?" I ask.

"Please stop talking about this, Amy."

When Mum walks in, he looks scared, and I don't think he loves her anymore.

Logan is holding her hand, and he sits in Will's seat and smiles at me. I smile back because none of this is Logan's fault and, if Dad won't help me, I'm going to do it on my own.

"What do you want for breakfast?" Mum asks, but she's only talking to one of us.

"Crunchy Nut," Logan says.

He never says please, and Mum never corrects him. This isn't really her son, so she doesn't care about manners. She never tells him off because she thinks, if she's always nice to him, he'll eventually forget the truth.

When he's back in his room, I go in because it's only locked at night.

"Hi," I say.

"Hello."

He seems happier today, but I look closely and his eyes are still sad. "Do you like it here?" I ask.

Logan nods. "Your mummy is lovely."

"*My* mummy?"

"Yes."

"What about *your* mummy?"

He stares up at me and says, "She's gone away. I'll see her again when she's back."

I almost don't say it, but I have to because this is a chance I can't waste.

"She's back now. Do you want to see her?"

Logan's face lights up, and I move closer and whisper, "But you can't tell anyone. Not even my mummy. Do you understand?"

"Yes."

We need to go now, because he'll say something if we don't. Will could never keep secrets, and I don't think Logan can, either, even if he *is* the secret.

I hear the front door slam, which means Dad is going to work. Mum stays home, now, but she's not always watching. Sometimes there are tiny chances, so we have to be ready.

I should be at the bus stop in five minutes, but, instead, I hold my finger to my lips and, when Logan sees, he smiles and follows me downstairs. He thinks this is a game, and that's good, because the only times Will was ever quiet were during hide-and-seek.

Mum is in the kitchen with the radio on, but the stairs still creak and the front door seems miles away.

"Hurry up, Amy!" she shouts, and I freeze and wait for her to find us, but she's still loading the dishwasher. The glasses clink, and I can breathe again. Logan giggles until I tell him no with my eyes.

I touch the door handle and turn it, then pull him into the outside world and run.

~~IIII~~ ~~IIII~~ ~~IIII~~ ~~IIII~~ III

"Come on!" I shout, but Logan can't move as fast as I can. Our street is empty, and I'm relieved because we need to get farther away from Mum before we tell the truth. I could take Logan to the bus stop, but the other St. Gregory girls would ask questions—and not nice ones. "What are you doing?"

It's Mum. She's behind us, and I've failed. She looks scared and angry and kind all at once, but I know which one will win when we're home.

I open my mouth, but no words come out. Logan talks, instead, and what he says isn't good. "Amy said my mummy's back."

"Did she?"

Mum stares at, me and I don't want to follow her, but what choice do I have? She doesn't say anything. She just points at the house, and, this time, when the door closes, she locks it and puts the keys in her pocket.

"Go upstairs, honey," she tells Logan and then, to me, "How dare you." She doesn't speak it. She spits it.

"I'm..."

"Don't you dare say you're sorry. Do you know what you did? You almost destroyed this family."

Mum is crying, but not because she's sad. She's shaking, and I'm scared she's going to hit me.

I wish Dad was here because he'd understand and calm her down. He'd make things safe again, even if Mum is a volcano. But Dad won't be home until late, and anything could happen by then.

"Do you still not understand?" Mum says. "I've told you before...if you'd been a better sister...*he* wouldn't be here."

She means Logan, but I'm not sure anymore.

I used to think that, if I'd done my job, Will would be upstairs, Logan would be with his parents, and Mum would be Mum, and Dad would still love her. But *she* left *us*. She didn't do her job either.

Mum has another lock, and I watch as she drills the holes, then swears and tries again.

"Get in," she says, pointing at my bedroom, and, when the door closes, I hear the metal thud against the wood.

I wait half an hour, then pull, but the door doesn't move.

I'm just like Logan, now. I'm trapped.

~~||||~~ ~~||||~~ ~~||||~~ ~~||||~~ ||||

I can't listen at the top of the stairs anymore. But, if I close my eyes and push my ear against the door, I can sometimes hear bits of what they say.

"I had him, Chris. I'd won him over. And she ruined it."

When Dad replies, it's mostly mumbles.

"Now what? I have to start again, and the damage might have already been done. She told him his mother was back. He's not going to forget that."

I thought Logan's mum was bad because she ignored him. But mine's a lot worse.

I try to think about Will, but it's not easy when my head is so full. He usually comes when I'm calm, slipping through the open doors of my dreams. When I need him most, he's somewhere else.

In the end, it's not Will who comes, it's Dad. He unlocks my door and sits on my bed, but he won't look at me.

"I'm sorry," I say, and he holds his head and shakes.

I want to touch him, but I'm scared. I have a fake brother, and it feels like I have fake parents too. This isn't my dad. This is a broken person, and Mum's a dangerous one, and everything feels wrong.

"I know why you did it," Dad says. "You had to try. But that's it, now, Amy. Logan is here to stay."

"He doesn't want to be here."

"He will eventually. And Mum will forgive you if you let her. You just have to play along."

But this isn't a game. This is a nightmare.

"*You* could take him back," I whisper, even though I already know his answer.

I can see it in his eyes. Mum has won the argument, and Dad will do what she says.

That's why he stands up and says, "I can't do that, Amy." And that's why he locks the door behind him.

𝍸 𝍸 𝍸 𝍸 𝍸

"You will go to school," Mum says, "and you will come home. That's it. If you don't, I'll tell the police what you did to your brother. I'll say it was your fault."

It wasn't my fault. It wasn't. It was an accident, but no one saw except me. The truth is inside, but there's no way to get it out.

Every day I think about telling Nia so she can tell her parents and they can do something about it. But I can't get Mum's words out of my head. Everyone will believe her because she's an adult, and she's better at lying than I am at telling the truth.

All Nia wants to talk about is her almost baby brother, and it hurts so much. But I can't cry every time she mentions her mum's tummy and how you can see it move if you time it right. I can't hear that without thinking of Will and how, when I put my hand on Mum's bump, I'd feel something, and she'd say he was high-fiving his big sister.

Those memories used to be magical, but now they sting.

Nia still asks if I'm all right because she's a good friend, and I still tell her I am. But I can see she's getting annoyed.

"Just tell me," she says. "What is it?"

"Nothing. I'm fine."

I walk away because the lie is a force field that doesn't last long. And I keep walking away until, eventually, Nia stops coming.

𝍸 𝍸 𝍸 𝍸 𝍸 𝍷

I try again while Mum's giving Logan a bath because Dad is stronger when she's upstairs.

"Please," I say, but he shakes his head.

"It's too late."

Whenever we talk about this, it opens the door to Dad's tears, but I'll keep saying it until he listens. He could be the hero, but he's chosen not to be so I hate him. He could wait until Mum was asleep and take Logan wherever you take lost boys who've been found. He could do it in secret, but he doesn't do anything.

"Nia's going to have a brother," I say. "A real one."

Dad stares at me until I blink, then he says, "Oh."

I know where to look so I can see all his memories of Will. They're like flickers in his eyes, and they do different things to his face. Some make him smile and some make him cry and some make him make the face that scares me. It's the same face Mum has. Except, she wears it most days while he usually keeps it hidden.

"Don't tell your mother," Dad says and I nod, even though that was never the plan.

I told him because I hoped it might change his mind.

Once upon a time, Logan was somebody's good news, just like Will was for him and now Nia's brother is for her. But nothing can make Dad do anything anymore.

Instead, he turns the news on, and I ignore it because it's boring. And then Logan is on the TV. The newscaster is talking about a missing-person investigation, but I don't hear all the words. I'm too busy looking at the smiling boy in his school uniform. He's never smiled like that here.

His uniform is blue, and his hair is longer, and the reporter says his name is Logan Connolly. Then his mother is sitting behind a table with the police and she says, "Please, I just want my boy back."

Dad makes a weird sound, and, maybe, this is the moment. Because Mrs. Connolly is broken, and she's not a bad mother, and I stole a boy whose smile used to fill a whole TV.

I want to shout, "Give him back to her!," but Dad speaks first.

"Amy..." But that's all he says because his eyes shoot to the door and any fight in him pops like a bubble as Mum marches past us and switches off the TV.

When she turns, her eyes are wet, but her words are hard. "That's enough of that," she whispers.

𝍸 𝍸 𝍸 𝍸 𝍸 𝍷𝍷

"Don't forget the truth," I whisper through the wall. "We're not your family."

Sometimes Logan talks back, but, mostly, it's just me, reminding him he has another mother that doesn't lock him in at night and bribe him with sugar.

When I do hear something, it's not Logan; it's Mum, and she's shouting, "What have you done?"

There's a thud on the wall, then scraping, and Dad's muffled voice. "What's wrong?"

The lock slides back on my door and Mum looks furious. "Come here," she says, pulling me into Will's room and pointing at Logan. "Do you see what he's done? Can you *see* what *you* made him do?"

I can because it's everywhere. He's written all over the wall that we talk through, and it says *HELP ME* a million times.

"Cover it up," Mum says.

"But we don't have any paint."

"I don't care. I want it gone tonight."

Logan is staring at the carpet, and I'm proud of him, because he won't let her win.

If I look for too long, I get scared, because it feels like the wall is shouting at me. It feels like all those tiny words make one huge one.

When I'm back in my room, I can hear Dad papering over the damage. But I know it's there forever, now, just like Logan.

𝍸 𝍸 𝍸 𝍸 𝍸 |||

"Happy birthday!" Mum says, and Logan looks confused because he doesn't think that's right. He can't know for sure because Mum hid the calendars and won't let him watch TV, and the only way to guess the month is by looking out of the window.

Logan might not know what day it is, but *I* do. It's unforgettable because it's my brother's birthday...if you still call it that when they're gone.

Mum has decorated the living room with banners saying 5 TODAY!, and she made a cake and there are presents all over the rug. I feel sick, but we have to smile like this is totally normal because Mum's anger is worse on special days.

This is the *most* special, even if it's a lie.

Logan won't open the presents until Mum sits with him and puts one in his lap.

"They're all for you, Will," she says, and he doesn't say that's not his name because he knows what happens. He rips the paper, then looks at me, and I try to be happy because I have no choice. Dad's smile disappears before it gets to his eyes, and they tell the truth that we're all too scared to say.

I don't know if they bought the presents together, because Dad doesn't really speak to me anymore. He still says things, but they're not conversations. It's just the words that get you through a day like, "You'll be late for school" and "Dinner's ready."

Logan opens the presents and says, "Am I five now?"

"Yes, darling. It's your birthday."

"Where's my..."

Logan's mouth hangs open and his eyes go wide. If he says it, something bad will happen. He wants to say "mummy," and I pray that he does. It's the most dangerous, scariest, stupidest thing, and, if we get caught, everything is over, but I still want him to say it.

He doesn't, though. He just picks up one of his new toys and fiddles with it, and I wonder when his real birthday is and what his real mum will do on that day.

~~////~~ ~~////~~ ~~////~~ ~~////~~ ~~////~~ ////

"It's your favorite...remember?"

We're sitting round the table with Will's birthday meal, except Will's not here, and the boy in his place doesn't like it.

"What is it?" Logan asks.

Mum says, "Half-and-half pie. We have it every year."

She looked delighted when she put it in front of him, but now she's disappointed and her words sound like questions.

I remember when Will was two and Mum asked him what he wanted for his birthday tea.

"Pie," he said, and, when she asked what type, he shrugged.

"Chicken," I said.

"Steak," said Dad.

And Will said, "Yep," so Mum did both in one, with a pastry wall in the middle.

I had some from my half, Dad had some from his, and Mum and Will had a bit of both.

I thought our traditions would stop when my brother died,

and I wish they would. But Mum wants everything the same... or, at least, the same as it can be.

The cream and the gravy are leaking together on Logan's plate, and he makes a face and says, "I don't like it."

That was what Will liked best, so Mum says, "Just try a bit."

Logan shakes his head, and I wait for the explosion. But Mum cuts his dinner into smaller bits and holds one out to him and whispers, "Please."

"No!"

Mum looks at Dad, pleading with her eyes, and he puts his fork in Logan's food and takes a bite.

"Delicious," he says.

When he used to say it to Will, he stretched it out much longer—"*Deeeeeelicious*"—and my brother would laugh and clear his plate. But Logan doesn't know that, so he looks at Dad and says, "No."

It's smaller than the one he said to Mum, but, somehow, it's worse. And Dad doesn't try again.

Mum looks at me, and I want to cuddle her because she's so sad. The tears she hides must have washed away the anger, and all she wants is Will back. But that's impossible. Dad has his head down, and Mum looks lost. This used to be the best day, but now it's the worst. Mum used to sing and dance and look at Will like he was treasure. And Dad used to laugh and joke and hold Will up like he was the World Cup. So I think of something, and then I say it out loud.

"I used to know someone who loved this pie."

I can feel Mum's eyes on me, but she doesn't speak, so I keep going.

"He was a little boy...like you. And this was his favorite dinner."

Logan tilts his head. "Really?"

"Yep. He would have eaten it every day if he could. But it was special, so he only got it once a year."

Logan pokes the dinner with his fork, so I say, "I love it as well. Don't you?"

He looks unsure, and his eyes jump to Mum, then back again.

She's staring at me with a look I've never seen before. I don't know what she's thinking, but that doesn't scare me because there's nothing bad behind her eyes.

Logan takes the tiniest bite, and I say, "See?"

He nods and eats a bit more, but none of us finish ours. Mum cries quietly while Dad's shoulders shake, and I wonder if I've done the right thing.

This is still Will's birthday, even if he's not here to celebrate, and I want what's left of my family to be some kind of happy.

𝍸 𝍸 𝍸 𝍸 𝍸 𝍸

"I'm sorry," I say with my face buried in the pillow. I want to scream it, but my parents would hear, and I don't want to ruin a day I think I've just saved.

I can't remember the last time we talked about Will. His name feels like a forbidden word, so I didn't say it out loud, but I brought him back to life for a few wonderful, horrible seconds. It was nice talking about him, but now it feels like I've picked a scab and the bleeding won't stop.

Logan is asleep, and Mum and Dad are downstairs, their words turned to mumbles by the carpet.

Whatever they're saying, they are talking to each other, and it's been ages since that happened. The sounds are low then high then low again, which means this is an actual conversation.

Part of me wants to be there too. I want to listen and join in, but I'm scared because everything is so fragile here. After what I said at the table, Mum squeezed my hand, and it was the perfect amount and I knew what she meant. She was saying thank you, and I squeezed back and she smiled. It was a broken smile, hanging off its hinge, but it was real, and I almost said, "I love you."

Before I try to sleep, I think of Will's giggle and his eyes and everything else that made him perfect, and I whisper, "Happy birthday."

~~||||~~ ~~||||~~ ~~||||~~ ~~||||~~ ~~||||~~ ~~||||~~ |

One day, we give up. We can't all do it at once, but that's how it feels. It's as if Dad and Logan and I all wake up one morning and think, *Okay, this is life now*, and we stop fighting it.

By now, most of our battles are with ourselves, anyway. At least that's how it feels to me. I can't remember the last time any of us fought with Mum because she always wins, one way or another.

They don't lock Logan in anymore. The first night, no one told him. But, at some point, they did, and he stayed there, anyway. All the other doors and windows were locked, so he couldn't get out if he'd wanted to. But he could have smashed the glass or called for help. Instead, he slept and waited until morning and ate his breakfast, and, a few months later, Mum said, "I think it's time we sent you to school."

"Really?" Logan said.

"Of course. You're a big boy now. There's so much to learn."

There *is* so much to learn, like his name is William Christopher Pearce and that he was born on the twenty-second of June and that we're his real family.

Mum has been teaching him for months, and he's getting good at it. If he answers to Logan, or doesn't answer to Will, there are consequences. But he hasn't had those for ages.

Sometimes I'm scared that he's starting to believe the lie, and, other times, I think he's pretending. What if he's faking it until Mum leaves him alone long enough for him to give us all away?

A part of me hopes that's true, because my life used to be light, but now it's so heavy. Maybe it always will be, because my brother's gone and it's my fault and Mum is so different now. But, sometimes, I still think it would be better if we just told the truth and dealt with it. They'd send us to prison, but we're already there.

I'm thinking all this as Logan stands in the hallway in his new school uniform and Mum looks so proud. Dad seems lost, like he's joined our family by accident. And I stay in the shadows and watch my fake baby brother grin for his first photo since we took him.

"Remember everything I told you," she says.

Logan nods. "It's okay, Mum. I remember," and she looks at him, then at me, and she's crying.

She looks proud and broken at the same time, and I think I know why. She knows this isn't real, but it's all she's got.

It's like when we used to play Creatures, and Will knew what I was telling him wasn't true. But he *wanted* to believe it so he did, just enough to keep playing.

Mum drives us to school, which means I don't have to get the bus. She drops me off first, and Logan says, "Bye." And I hope, hope, hope that he's a good actor.

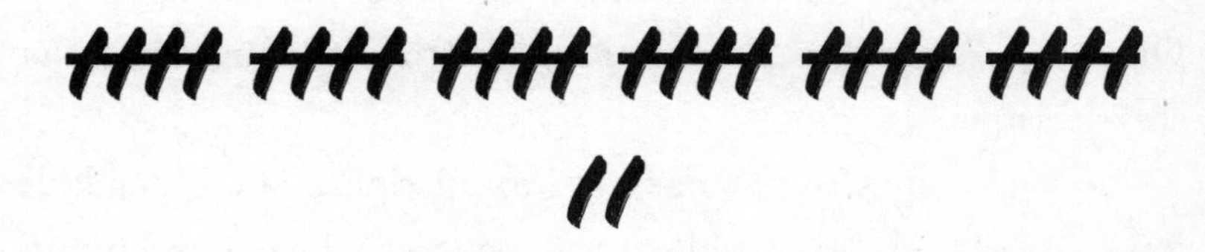

I can't remember the last time I learned anything at school. I don't even know what my teachers said this morning.

At lunchtime, I sit on my own like I always do. Nia has new friends, now, and I wonder what they talk about. Sometimes I'm jealous because she does things that remind me of before, like laughing so hard that she snorts or pulling on her blazer when she's nervous.

If Nia's mum wasn't pregnant, maybe we'd still talk. Or maybe I'm so sad that I can't pretend to be happy around anyone, not even my first best friend.

I wonder what Logan's doing now? Is he answering when his teacher calls him "William"? Is he enjoying school or has he told them everything?

I feel the nerves rise in my stomach and climb up my neck, filling my throat with the lunch I managed to choke down. I try to blink the image away, but I can't, so I squeeze my eyes shut and think of anything else. But everything I imagine breaks apart, so I picture Logan in his uniform. I'm scared that he won't say anything...and I'm scared that he will.

It should be my brother at school. It should be him in the clothes that are a bit too big with the wonky smile and the everywhere-hair. It should be him I come home to tonight, telling me about his new teacher and his friends.

"It should be him!"

I don't realize I've screamed until I see people staring at me. One of Nia's group says something and they all laugh, but Nia stays serious.

No one comes over to ask if I'm all right. The older kids have already forgotten while my classmates whisper and point, because I'm the weird girl, now.

I walk to the bathroom and stare at the mirror, and then I scream again, except it's not words this time. It's just noise, and it echoes off the walls. I don't care who hears. I scream until my throat is sore, and then I do it again, feeling the burn of something I can't put out.

I want to punch my reflection and watch it crack. I want to shout in the face of every teacher who tells me I'm quieter than I used to be. I want to be happy again.

But it's like what Mum used to tell Will: "Want doesn't get."

~~////~~ ~~////~~ ~~////~~ ~~////~~ ~~////~~ ~~////~~ ///

He wasn't pretending. Logan is Will. He's in fifth grade, now, and this isn't a nightmare I'm going to wake up from. It's my life.

We all broke him, but Mum did it the most. She brainwashed him, and what's left is a dress-up game that lasts forever.

Dad hates it. You can see it every time Mum says their dead son's name. He flinches, and part of me wants to hug him better, but I don't because he's weak. He had the chance to stop this, and he didn't.

If I disappeared, would Mum replace me too?

The knots of our family unraveled years ago. Now the only knots are the ones in my stomach and the one wrapped tightly around the truth.

Years are strange things. They can stretch for an eternity or disappear in a blink, and that's what happened to us...both at once.

So many times, I nearly said it; so many times the words

started to come, the silent sound of a confession before it's uttered; and so many times I stopped myself because of Mum... and Dad...and Logan.

I should say me as well. I should say that, for all my desire to tell the truth, I couldn't take a hammer to my life. When I was a kid, I might have. But now, knowing what I know, it's a step too far. I've been feeling guilty for years and, at some point, I stopped wanting to confess and understood that the consequences were far greater than the pain.

What I didn't realize was that Dad was going the other way. I went from guilt-ridden to numb right about the time he finally stood up to my mother.

~~||||~~ ~~||||~~ ~~||||~~ ~~||||~~ ~~||||~~ ~~||||~~ ||||

Pippa doesn't know me as the screaming girl. She and her friends think I'm cool, and they run over to me at break and lunch and talk about their dramas.

I used to tell myself I'm only a seventh-grade mentor to tick the school's volunteering requirement box in my planner, but the truth is different. If Will was alive, he would only be a couple of years younger than them, so this is a glimpse into a future we'll never have.

Logan talks in riddles and walks on eggshells, but Pippa and her friends are carefree and I feel light when I'm with them.

You only need to meet once a week, and you only get one mentee each. But Pippa's friends have adopted me, or I've adopted them, and we talk every day.

I wish I'd had a mentor when I was eleven. Maybe they could have stopped the screams and got me to speak the truth before it became too heavy to lift.

Pippa doesn't talk to me like a big sister. She already has one of those, so she speaks to me as a friend. They all do, although *they* do most of the talking.

On the school field, surrounded by seventh graders who think I'm so much cooler than I am, the world feels a little bit better. But, at parties, surrounded by people my own age, it's as if I've wandered into someone else's story.

It's another form of escape, but I don't enjoy it. I want to lose myself in the night like the strangers who used to be my friends, but I'm always on the outside. I watch Pippa's sister Evie, who is in the year above me, and I watch Nia, whose replacement friends have shrunk to just two. I watch them, but I never join in, because what would I say? They don't ignore me. They just don't realize I'm there.

My homeroom teacher, Mrs. Strauss, is sort of the reason I go. She told my parents she was concerned about my lack of "positive peer relationships" and asked me where the "bubbly freshman" went.

That girl is trapped inside other people's quotation marks. She died along with her brother. But I couldn't tell her that, so I go to the parties, and Mum seems happy that I'm keeping up appearances.

卌 卌 卌 卌 卌 卌 卌

It's on the fifth anniversary of Will's death that Dad says, "I can't do this anymore." If "anniversary" is the right word, because I used to think that was only for things you celebrated, not nightmares you'll never forget.

Mum curls her lip the way she does when she's getting ready for a fight, and I want to leave, but my legs won't move.

"You can't do *what* anymore?" she spits.

"*This*, Jane. I can't do *this*. We have to give him back."

Logan is asleep, but he'll be awake soon. My parents are getting louder every second this argument continues. They start off whispering, then talking, and then, eventually, they don't care who hears. If the woman next door wasn't so deaf, I'd worry, but she's the perfect neighbor. We only have to look like nice people. It doesn't matter what comes out of our mouths.

"It's too late for that," Mum says. "He doesn't even remember what happened."

"Of course he does. You just force the truth out of every conversation. We *all* remember."

Dad looks at me, and I'm praying he doesn't ask me to speak. We *do* all remember. How could we not? But that doesn't mean I want to talk about it. Not with my angry, grief-stricken, fucked-up mother who has built a wall around our past.

Mum sighs and sits down, but she's not calm. She's recharging her anger, and we all know it.

She never used to be angry. She absorbed whatever Will and I threw at her and smiled like it was no big deal. That didn't mean she was a pushover. The quieter she got, the more trouble we knew we were in. But, now, her rage is like fire on her skin. It flickers constantly and roars whenever she's provoked. I don't think one thing changed her. I think it was everything—the lies and the deceit and the grief and the truth she can never bury deep enough.

"I've told you what would happen if you betrayed us," Mum says, and Dad stands over her, looking almost brave.

"*You* betrayed us, Jane," he whispers. "You made our daughter complicit."

She laughs like, "Ha," and says, "Complicit? *She* let him die. *She* walked away from him. She's only here because I saved her."

I look at Dad, hoping he'll defend me, but he just looks broken.

I flash back to my training and all the kids I approached and all the lines I learned in case I was caught. She didn't save me. She used me.

Mum isn't the only angry one in this house. I have anger, too, and I feel it rumbling deep inside. I don't wear it like she does, but what if I let it out? What if I do what Dad never does and stand up for myself?

She always says it's my fault, and some of it is, but not all of it. *They* were the adults. They had choices, and all of them were wrong.

Mum stands so she's eyeballing Dad and says, "You have two options. You can forget today ever happened, or you can do what you want to do and face the consequences."

Dad tries to stay tall, but I can see him shrinking like she's punctured his bravery. He turns away from her, but he won't look me in the eye.

It took him years to be this strong, and it took her seconds to beat him. Mum wins every...single...time.

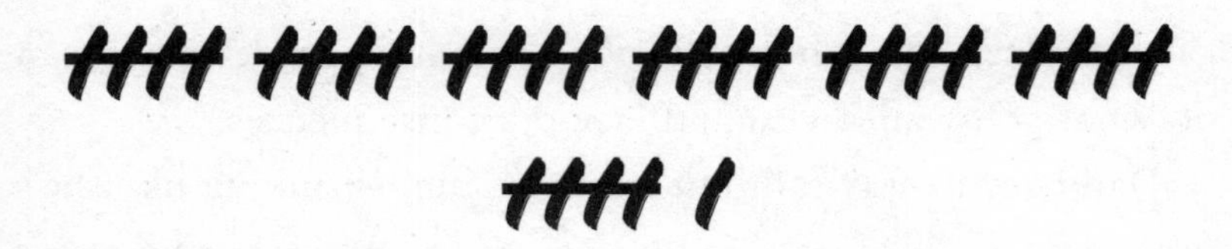

Dad is standing in the hallway with blood all over his face and an eye that looks like an oil spill.

"What happened?" I ask and he shakes his head. "It's okay, Amy. I'm all right."

But he's not. He needs to go to the hospital or call the police, but all the things normal people do in emergencies are dangerous for us. Instead, he goes to the bathroom and holds cotton balls on his cuts and tries not to cry.

"Please, Dad. Who did this?"

"I don't know. They took my phone and my wallet."

"Fuck," I whisper, but Dad doesn't notice because he's a mess. "Can I help?"

He shakes his head and winces, and I touch his shoulder and say, "Do you need a doctor?"

"I'll be fine. It's just a few cuts and bruises."

But it's not, because, when he tries to sit in a chair, he holds his ribs and moans, and he doesn't stand up unless he has to.

He stays silent until Mum comes home, and, when she sees him, she says, "What happened to you?"

He stares at her for ages. "I was mugged."

"Mugged in the middle of the day," she says. "I thought this was a safe neighborhood."

They're playing a game that I don't understand, because I can see it in their eyes. They're saying things with their silences and their stares, and it feels like I've walked in halfway through an argument.

I want to scream at her—"*Why aren't you helping him? Why don't you care?*"—but I keep quiet and watch her and wait.

They're like boxers, sizing each other up, and I squeeze Dad's hand because I've picked my corner. He squeezes back, and I know we could take her if we were strong enough, but Dad isn't strong on a good day. He used to be, but not anymore.

Mum goes down to the kitchen and comes back with antiseptic cream and bandages.

"Here," she says. "This will help."

Dad takes it from her, but he looks suspicious, like it's a trap.

"You should go to your room," Mum says.

She's not looking at me, but I stand and walk out.

Mum whispers at first because she knows I'm still listening. Then her voice gets louder and I think she wants me to hear.

"I'm sorry this had to happen, but I told you there'd be consequences," she says.

I can see Dad's face through the crack in the door, and he looks betrayed even though he should know better by now.

"What did you tell him?" Dad mumbles.

"I think you know."

"You're sick. Do you know that? I'm your husband."

"And *I'm* your *wife*. But you were willing to take him from me. All you had to do was love him."

I don't understand what's happening. Who is Dad talking about? Was he mugged, or did something else happen? And who is "him"?

"So you told Amy it was a mugging," Mum says.

"What else could I tell her? That I knew the man who did this to me…that he accused me of…"

Dad's face looks like it's going to shatter. I can only see a slice of it through the door, but it's enough to know something's horribly wrong. He can't finish the sentence because he's sobbing, and I want to run to him. But I need to watch this play out.

"What did you tell him?" Dad asks.

"*I* didn't tell him anything. It was an anonymous little birdy that told Simon Wells his daughter was getting friendly with a man who should know better."

Simon Wells. I know that name. He's Pippa and Evie's dad. He owns the garage, and Mum flirts with him when the car has its emissions check.

What does Mum mean about one of them getting friendly with a man who should know better? Is Dad that man?

"I would never…" he whispers.

"But *he* doesn't know that. And, seeing what he did to you, I'm assuming you didn't get the chance to deny it."

"Why?" Dad says. "What do you get from making up lies

about me and an eighteen-year-old? Is that the kind of husband you want people to think I am?"

The bathroom is quiet for a while. All I can hear is my father's frantic breathing. Then Mum clears her throat and says, "I don't care what they think you are, Chris. But *you* should. Because, if I want to, I can ruin you. I can spread rumors about half the girls in the village.

"For now, it's just one...and I'm assuming, after today's incident, that Mr. Wells won't want the police involved. But others don't react with their fists. That's why I picked him. I knew he'd punch first and think later. Evie is probably telling him right now that it's made up. But, if enough people hear a lie, it starts sounding like the truth.

"If you *ever* threaten to break up this family again, I will make sure *you* are the only one who suffers."

Logan sits by his window as the sound of the night ripples through his room.

I stand on the landing and think of all the times there was a locked door between us. He knows I'm here, but he doesn't turn around, and I don't speak. Instead, I watch him and hope he's okay. No one in this house is happy—okay is the best we can hope for.

Once I asked Logan why he keeps his window open even when it's cold. He looked at me for a long time, and I saw so many things flash behind his eyes. Then, finally, he said, "It helps."

Later he sits between Mum and Dad on the sofa, and, if you were watching, you'd think they were normal, but they're not.

My mother is the closest to happy. She got what she wanted even if she knows it's a lie. But Dad's and Logan's smiles are fake. My make-believe brother got lost in the game, and my father has been scared into submission.

That leaves me, watching and wondering how it all got so monumentally fucked. I still dream about Will, and, sometimes, he's laughing, but mostly he's dead. His wet, lifeless body weighs me down, and I can't push him off. The more I try, the heavier he feels until, eventually, with all I have, I force him off with a scream that must wake the whole house.

No one comes to me to ask if I'm all right. The locks have gone, but we all stay in our own rooms and silently wait for morning.

I write a note to my brother every single night and tuck it under my pillow and, the next day, I fold it twice and put it in a box under my bed. They all say the same thing with different words, which is that I miss him and I hate this and I'm sorry.

If Mum ever found them, she'd flip because it's evidence. It's saying out loud what we wrap up in layers of silence and tuck in the furthest corners of our minds. But she won't find it because she doesn't come in here. She doesn't tidy my room or sit on my bed or tuck me in like she used to. Sometimes she stands by the door, but that's it.

After what happened to Dad, I'm not brave enough to see what she'd do to me. That's why I speak to Will through pen strokes and doodles. And it's why I hope that, unlike the tooth fairy, he sees what I write in the notes I sleep on.

𝍸 𝍸 𝍸 𝍸 𝍸 𝍸 𝍸 |||

Logan doesn't whisper through the wall anymore. We communicate in a different way, now, but only when it's safe, which means when Mum is out and Dad isn't listening.

It's not Logan's fault that he was brought into this mess, and you can't blame something you broke for not running away.

"Tell me a story," I say, except what Logan says isn't pretend. It's a memory we hide in plain sight.

"There once was a woman whose hair was made of plastic," he says. "Sometimes it was blue, sometimes it was pink, and sometimes it was both."

I've heard this story before, but I don't mind because it's one of our favorites.

"The woman didn't know what she looked like anymore, because she couldn't see," Logan says. "But she was always happy when visitors came."

The first time he told me this story, he cried and wouldn't tell me why. It was ages before I figured out the woman was his great-granny and the plastic in her hair was because she had curlers.

It's a dangerous game. If Mum finds out, even now, I'm scared what might happen. But it's what we do to make things better.

As well as the woman whose hair was made of plastic, there's the man who could bring anything to life and the lady who cried an ocean.

I think the man is Logan's granddad and I think the lady is his mum. Every time, there are more clues, some spoken but most behind his eyes. He doesn't often talk about that woman, but I know the story by heart.

She misses someone so much that she cries and cries until the distance between them is filled with her tears. She's so tired from crying that she falls asleep and is carried on the ocean she made. And, when she wakes up, he's there…the boy I stole.

I think it's supposed to be a happy story, but it always tears me apart because I'm the reason she cries. We all are.

When Logan tells tales about his grandparents, I think about my own and wonder what might have been if they were still alive.

Their absence made our secrets so much easier to keep. Dad's parents died before I was born, and Granny and Grandpa are just faces in photos. I knew them but not enough.

The few friends Mum and Dad still had were easy to leave behind.

I'm not sure how much Logan remembers is real. He's been here so long, and Mum has rewritten so much of his history that his memories are a mixture of truth, make-believe, and lies.

But I'll keep his real memories, and the boy he was before us, alive however I can.

𝍸 𝍸 𝍸 𝍸 𝍸 𝍸 𝍸 ||||

When Mum says we're moving, I don't believe her, because it doesn't make sense.

Moving means shaking the dust off our secrets, but she points to the house on the corner and says, "It's a fresh start," and then, when she sees the look I'm giving her, "He's never going to properly forget until we leave this place."

She means Logan, but I don't think moving is the solution.

"This place has some happy memories, but..." Mum stops and there's a tear in the corner of her eye. She blinks it away, but not before I see what she used to look like.

I loved her so much. I loved all of them. But that version of my mother is like watching an actress play a character you haven't seen in years.

The "but" she can't speak is Will. It's the garden she never goes into and the fence painted a different shade of brown where the hole used to be. It's the flickers of memories we all get at certain moments of every day...of Will bounding up the stairs or lying upside down on the sofa or laughing that beautiful, contagious, everywhere laugh.

That's why Mum wants to move, and I get it. She wants a fresh start where all her memories will be of Logan: the boy who could never live up to my brother.

That's how Dad finds the notes. He's off work, sorting through my room while I'm at school, and, when I come home, he sits on my bed, pulls them out, and says, "You shouldn't have done this, Amy."

"I'm sorry."

"If she finds out…"

Dad can't finish the sentence because he isn't sure *what* she'd do. Would she take it out on me or on him? Would she read the notes and remember, or would she burn them unopened? Mum is a mystery I wish I didn't have to solve every single day.

"What are you going to do with them?" I ask, and Dad sighs.

"I'll keep them safe."

"Please don't throw them away."

It's Dad's turn to cry, now, and he doesn't stop like Mum did. He lets the tears fall on my duvet and then takes two deep breaths. "I would never do that."

He opens one and we read it together, then another, and we forget that, at any moment, Mum could come home. We don't care because we're with Will.

"I'm sorry," I say. "I'll never not be sorry."

Dad squeezes my hand. "It wasn't your fault, Amy."

All the words fall out of my world, leaving me to stare at him until he says, "None of this…Will…Logan…is because of you. Don't ever forget that."

I cry harder than I have in years because he sounds like he used to, when he promised me everything would be okay and he meant it. That's not a promise he can keep anymore, but Dad's hug is like a wall around me, and I hope he never lets go.

Mum said it was my fault over and over again, and Dad never argued. The proof was in his silence, but now I feel a sudden surge of strength.

I look at the box of notes and wonder if Dad has his own hiding place...if there are things he does that Mum will never know about, like the stories Logan tells that aren't really stories at all.

If Mum finds the notes, Dad will suffer again, and I can't risk that. Last time, she threatened to ruin him, and, next time, I'm terrified she will.

When I realize what we have to do, something shatters inside.

"We have to burn them," I say.

"What?"

"If you hide them *for* me...and she finds them..."

I don't have to finish the sentence, because Dad knows what could happen.

"I can make them disappear," he whispers.

"No," I say. "I'll do it."

In the garden, I lay the notes on the barbeque and set them on fire. If anyone found them, they'd know Logan isn't Will, and, from there, the pieces would fall quickly. We need to hide what we are or risk losing what's left.

𝍸 𝍸 𝍸 𝍸 𝍸 𝍸 𝍸 𝍸

The new house is too big, but maybe that's the point. Perhaps our secrets will keep growing and the only way to hide them is to have more rooms to keep them locked up in.

We couldn't move in right away, so we stayed in an Airbnb while the builders finished up. Mum wanted a new bathroom and every wall painted white, except the new wall around the whole house that's made of bricks and spikes. It's supposed to make us feel safe, but it just makes us feel trapped.

I hate it here, because nothing reminds me of Will. He didn't draw on any of these walls or run around these rooms. We didn't cuddle up in this living room, watching cartoons, or play in this garden before that last horrible time. This is a house without my brother, which is exactly what Mum wanted. But our fresh start already feels stale.

Mostly I stay in my room and think about everything until my head hurts.

I'm repeating a year at school, because my grades dropped,

and St. Gregory's doesn't put up with anything lower than a B. They've offered us a tour, and Mum said we should do it—one more attempt to look like a normal family.

It's different from my old school, lighter and friendlier instead of red-bricked and suffocating. And the teacher who meets us is super keen and cringey.

"Mrs. Pearce," he says, "this is Tom. He'll be showing you around this morning."

Mum smiles, squeezes my hand like a warning and says, "Pleased to meet you."

~~||||~~ ~~||||~~ ~~||||~~ ~~||||~~ ~~||||~~ ~~||||~~ ~~||||~~ ~~||||~~ |

Mum speaks for me, and it feels obvious that she's hiding something because who talks like that? She's too eager and too fake, but the boy doesn't know that. He smiles and nods like this is a totally normal conversation.

I guess we all have our secrets, because it looks as if he's carrying a lot more than his backpack.

His name is Tom, and he's not the type you'd normally expect to do a school tour. Nervous energy comes off him in waves and crashes into my own. A few times, he catches my eye, but I'm scared what he'll see if he looks too deep. So I stare at the ground.

Something about him is different. He's weighed down.

He looks like he used to be broken. He looks like me.

I was scared everyone here would be like everyone at St. Gregory's. I thought I'd be the weird one from my very first day because I'm tired of faking it so I don't even try. But maybe I don't have to.

Back in the car, Mum says, "What did you think?"

"It's different."

"It's your only choice," Mum says, but she doesn't look mean. She looks like she's worried about me.

I think back to the day I got into the Academy and how proud my parents were. Will wasn't sure why we were celebrating, but he was the keenest of all. And then we went to the castle, and that was maybe our last perfect day.

𝍸 𝍸 𝍸 𝍸 𝍸 𝍸 𝍸 𝍸 𝍷𝍷

My brother and Logan used to be the only boys I thought about, but not anymore.

Tom's face floats through my mind, over and over, but what I see isn't good. I see sorrow and doubt and insecurity. He has my reflection, and I want to know him, so I do something I haven't done for a long time. I try to make a friend.

It's not easy to cover all your cracks, but I don't want to be alone in this school too. There's something in Tom's eyes that gives me the courage to try, so, when my guidance counselor mentions this buddy thing, I ask for him. She says, "We don't usually get requests. Do you know each other?"

"Not yet," I say.

She smiles. "I'll see what I can do."

Whatever she does, it works, but Tom looks at me like I'm weird.

"I know what you're thinking," I say.

"You do?"

"Yep. You think I'm weird because last time I was moody and, this time, I'm…"

I don't know how to finish the sentence, but I don't have to.

"Hyper?" Tom says, and I laugh because it's been a long time since anyone described me as that.

Will was hyper for both of us. He was off-the-charts exhausting, and I was his audience.

Tom is already backing away, but I'm sure I'm right about him. He looks different from the others.

"Meet me at break," I say, and I think he will.

~~||||~~ ~~||||~~ ~~||||~~ ~~||||~~ ~~||||~~ ~~||||~~ ~~||||~~ ~~||||~~ |||

Everything happens around me, because I'm too late to be important.

All the friendships have been made, all the private jokes and famous stories have been written into our school's history. All I can do is answer my name when roll is called and try not to think how long a year can be.

I go back to the reception area, and he's there, looking a lot like he doesn't want to be.

I try my best smile and say, "I'm here for the tour."

He tells me the truth all the way around, which only makes me like him more. Then he shows me the sports field and says, "That's Simon Marlow's head-start line," and the way he looks at me changes.

Most people don't look at me at all. But something in Tom's eyes feels lovely and awkward at the same time, and I stay quiet because whatever I say will spoil it.

He tells me a story about a dead boy, and I imagine what would happen if I did the same.

This boy has a line drawn in the grass and a story repeated over and over again, but Will doesn't have anything like that. Simon Marlow isn't a secret like my brother.

Tom tells the tale like someone recalling their own experience rather than rushing through someone else's. I give him a hug because he's sad and nice and cute, and, if he has more stories, I might not feel alone in my own.

"Do I scare you?" I ask.

"No."

"I will," I say, because I think we could be friends, and I'm worried how much I already trust him.

𝍸 𝍸 𝍸 𝍸 𝍸 𝍸

𝍸 𝍸 𝍷𝍷𝍷𝍷

Dad hands me a box and says, "I made you this."

At the bottom, on a square of paper, are two words: *I'm sorry.*

"What is it?" I ask and he bows his head.

"It's a way of talking to Will…without raising suspicion. If anyone finds this, it's just an apology."

I don't understand at first, not until we're in the garden and Dad whispers, "I miss you so much, my son. I couldn't say that word for a long time. It may only be three letters, but it's the biggest word in the world."

And then, even quieter and only to himself and to a boy I desperately hope is listening, Dad says, "I'm sorry." Then he writes it and lays it on top of the first note.

When it's my turn, I stay silent for a long time because I don't know what to say. In my room, alone, I can talk to my brother for hours, but, with Dad watching, I feel scared to open my mouth. Eventually, I try something in my head, then out loud.

"I feel guilty every single day. I messed up. I made a mistake. But those are just words, and they're not enough. What happened is bigger than words. I know this doesn't change anything, but I am so…so sorry."

Dad hands me the pen, and I write my apology, put it in the box, and close the lid. Then I watch him hook it on a tree Will never got to climb.

He would have loved it here. He would have worn himself out a million times, then begged for one more.

"No more secrets," Dad says. "This is the place for us to come when we want to speak to your brother."

"Even Mum?" I ask and my father sighs.

"She has somewhere else to go."

"What do you mean?"

Dad doesn't answer for a long time and, when he does, it looks like he's fighting back the words that break through anyway.

When he's finished, I hug him and say, "Thank you for telling me."

"You can't speak about this to anyone," Dad whispers. "It's all I have."

I draw two invisible lines on my chest. "Cross my heart."

𝍸 𝍸 𝍸 𝍸 𝍸 𝍸 𝍸 𝍸 𝍸

Tom is a nice surprise, but he's also dangerous. He looks at me like I'm a puzzle with the middle missing. I could fill in the blanks for him, but then he'd look at me differently.

I could walk away, and, maybe, he'd forget me because that's how school works. If you don't speak to someone for enough days, eventually you're replaced or forgotten or both. But I *want* to talk to him. I *enjoy* talking to him.

That feels strange after so many years of keeping quiet. I lost a part of myself when my brother died...we all did. But Tom is like an open hand, reaching out to who I was and who I might be, and, sometimes, I want to reach out my hand, too, and let him pull me back.

I could fall for him, but that's not allowed. I have to keep my fragile, fucked-up "family" safe...not because I love them, but because I have no choice.

All his words and all his looks are tiny spades digging at

what we've buried. And that's when I realize there's a part of me—the smallest, quietest, deepest part—that wants him to find out the truth.

PART FOUR

73

Even the most normal houses can look terrifying when you know the truth. Amy's new home gave me the shivers when all I had were suspicions. Now it chills my blood.

There are clips of Logan Connolly's mum on YouTube, pleading for the safe return of her son. There are news stories about the disappearance. And there's a photo.

If you stare long enough, and know what you're looking for, you can see him. His hair is longer and two front teeth are missing. He has a chubbier face and a cheekier grin. But there's no doubt.

Logan is Will. Amy took him. But, unlike the boy in the shopping center, she didn't give him back.

Some mysteries are kept alive for years, but not this one. The news reports stopped after a few weeks, and Mrs. Connolly's grief continued off-screen. The police talked about a nearby river and the likelihood of Logan being washed away. The officer in charge said they would leave no stone unturned, but some stones are harder to lift than others.

My head is spinning, and I run to the toilet and throw up, then sit on the floor, trying to steady my breathing.

The rest of the house is asleep, and I don't wake them because I need to figure out what to say. Is it enough to show them a picture of Logan? Would they recognize Will as quickly as I did? I stare at the photo again and start to doubt myself. He was four, and now he's ten. They look so similar, but I have to be certain.

If I call the police and I'm wrong, everyone will be angry. Not just the Pearces but Mum and Jay. I can already imagine them whispering through the walls: *We need to do something about his anxiety. It's unhealthy being this paranoid. It's not normal.*

I think I'm right. But I so desperately want to be wrong. My phone vibrates, and I jump, but it's just Zak talking about a new Netflix show that he's binged in a day. How do I reply to that? How can I pretend everything's normal? Instead, I write a message to Amy, then wait because I can't send it yet. Should I give her the chance to explain, or would they run again, farther this time?

I pull out the list of clues and go through them slowly.

The locks on the outside *were* to keep someone in. They were on Will's door *and* on Amy's. Is she guilty or is she another Logan?

The words under the wallpaper—*HELP ME*—were a plea from a boy who *had* been washed away, just not like people thought.

The stick drawings—one big and one small—a child and an adult. A son and his mother. Logan did them over and over again because he hasn't forgotten. How could he?

He counted hundreds of horrible days with the tally marks surrounding those drawings.

And Amy's journal, when she said I can't possibly know the truth.

I almost wish I didn't.

74

I delete the message to Amy, because there's another way. Instead, I go back to the spot below Will's window. Except that's not the name I plan to say if he wakes up.

The stones clatter against the glass, then fall into the space between me and the wall. If Jane or Chris comes out, I'll tell them what I know and hope it scares them away. But no one comes. Their house is so big and the space between the rooms so vast that I'm left alone to wake their "son" for as long as it takes.

Eventually, the curtain twitches, and he looks down at me. I sign for him to open the window, but he just stares. Is this the boy that needs saving, or am I making a massive mistake?

There's only one way to find out, so I say, "Logan," then again, louder this time, making sure my lips are exaggerating the sounds.

One shout, that's all I get. Any sound can be "just a noise" in the night, so I take a deep breath, dare myself, then yell.

The first syllable is swallowed by the darkness, but the second echoes…before joining the buzz of the street lights and the hum of whatever comes out at night.

He heard it. The whole street heard it. Most of them will fall straight back to sleep, convinced it was in their dreams or someone shouting as they stumbled home from the pub. But Logan doesn't. He looks at me, and I wait for something, anything. I wait for him to tell me I'm right.

Instead, he shakes his head and disappears behind the curtain, leaving me alone on the street, staring up into the darkness.

75

I wake up to the smell of Sundays, and, as I roll over, the list of clues crinkles beneath me.

Aaron's laugh comes first, then Nia's voice, then the dull mumbling of the radio.

Mum loves Sunday, because it's the day we feel most like a family. Aaron has been here all night, and his sister has woken up happy, and Jay "gets things done."

Mum fills the house with the waft of bacon sandwiches, and it's the time when our horrible past feels both the closest and the furthest away.

"Here he is," Jay says, and Mum turns and grins.

Sometimes, for a few blissfully weird seconds, we feel like the families on TV. That's why saying this is going to be so hard.

"Sit yourself down," Mum says, scooping bacon from the pan.

I do what I'm told and watch silently as everyone joins me.

I don't know when it happened, but I've started to enjoy

this life more than I ever thought I would. I assumed I'd always be the outsider because Mum had Jay, and Nia had Aaron, and I was the odd one out. But that's not how it is now.

Maybe it's seeing the Pearces and feeling the horrible tension that fills their walls like invisible portraits. Maybe it's digging so deep into Amy's life that I realized ours is held together by more than hope.

Mum closed her eyes and put one last pin in what she hoped was forever. And she won. That's why I can't tell them. Not yet.

Every time I open my mouth to say Will is really Logan, Mum's smile or Aaron's giggle or Jay's laugh stops me. This is an almost-perfect moment, and I can't take it from them. So I eat, and I speak when I'm spoken to, and I try to laugh as loudly as everyone else. Even if, in the back of my mind, Logan's face is haunting me.

Does he want to be rescued?

I think of all the times Mum could have escaped the bad people in her life but didn't because something holds you in the most horrible places—the fear of what might happen if you leave.

Is he happier now? Does he remember his life before?

Even when you have an answer, the questions don't stop.

"Are you okay?" Mum asks.

"He's probably daydreaming about Amy," Jay says, and the look I swap with Nia says he's right but not in the way he thinks.

"Does Tom fancy Amy?" Aaron asks, and his sister can't help but laugh then.

"I'm not sure it's that simple," Nia says, and then, looking straight at me, "is it?"

I push the fingers of each hand together under the table, then make sure all ten digits are touching the narrow strip of wood around the seat.

"I don't fancy her," I tell Aaron.

He blows a raspberry and says, "Finished."

"So what do you say?" Mum replies.

"Please may I get down?"

Mum nods without looking at Jay, but Nia doesn't give her evils like she used to. She doesn't think my mum is stealing their mother's job anymore.

Looking through my window for so long, I'm starting to realize what others see through their own.

Aaron is outside before his feet have touched the ground and we watch him run round the garden with his arms out, then find his football and kick it against the back fence.

Mum starts clearing the table, and I practice what I'm going to say in my head. It doesn't need to be perfect. It only needs to sound true. I don't want to ruin her Sunday, but, whatever day I say it, things will change. And I don't want to wait too long, just in case.

Nia pats me on the shoulder as she gets up and whispers, "Keep thinking, Sherlock." She has no idea I've already solved it.

Proper detectives wouldn't be scared to shout the truth. It's what they're there for. But that's not my job, and the proof suddenly feels like a lie.

"Mum?" I whisper, but Nia is talking over me.

"Where's Aaron?" She's looking through the patio doors and something's different. There's a hole in the fence where there wasn't one before.

"What *is* that?" Nia asks.

When Jay comes closer, he says, "That's weird."

I follow them outside, echoing them as they call for my stepbrother. But he doesn't come back.

On the ground next to the hole is a round piece of wood with nails poking out. It's the same color as the fence on one side and it fits the gap perfectly.

"Aaron!" Jay yells louder this time and then, when he pokes his head through the hole, "Shit."

"What is it?" Mum asks.

"This isn't another house. It's something else."

Jay runs back down the garden, and Mum stares at him while Nia keeps searching. I kneel down and look through the hole. On the other side is a pool of water surrounded by bricks, and there's a large building with metal pipes looped round the top. But that's not what I'm looking at.

At the opposite end of what we always thought was someone else's garden is a gate and a padlock lying cracked and open on the ground.

There was another hole, one we didn't see until now. It's only big enough for someone small to climb through. But the gate moving back and forth in the wind is large enough for anyone to walk out of.

I'm still staring when I see Jay walk into the area from the other side. He's out of breath and, when he catches my eye, he looks terrified.

That's when I turn to Mum and Nia and say, "I know who has him."

76

"Will is someone else," I say. "His name's Logan Connolly. The Pearces kidnapped him."

"What are you talking about?" Mum asks.

"I'm talking about Aaron. I think they've taken him... because I found out about Logan."

I can see all the tiny bridges I've built with Nia crumble and fall on the grass between us. She's looking at me like I'm insane.

"My brother is missing," she says, "and you're still talking about Amy fucking Pearce."

Mum doesn't respond. She's acting like I'm speaking a foreign language.

"He's not here!" Jay yells from behind the fence.

Nia snorts. "Your stepson thinks his girlfriend kidnapped him."

"It's not..." I say, but the rest of the words won't come.

This doesn't feel like a Sunday anymore. My head is spinning, because Aaron is missing, and there's only one answer, but they won't hear it.

I should have told them sooner, when we were all sitting round the table. Now they won't even look at the photo on my phone that I'm desperately trying to show them.

"I'm coming back," Jay says. "Call the police."

I start to say, "No," but that doesn't come out either. It stops in my throat and won't budge. If the police come now, will it scare Amy away? Or has that already happened?

Did Logan tell her I know and this is my punishment? I think she's already taken one boy from his family, and my eyes burn when I think what this might mean for Aaron.

But where can they run? We know where they live, and I know their secrets.

We *should* call the police. I'll show *them* the picture and they'll understand because it's their job.

That's when my phone pings with an unknown number. "Is that him?" Nia asks, and I shake my head and move the screen before she sees the warning.

> Come alone. If you tell anyone where you are going or what you know, he will disappear.

77

I could wait for the police, but they never helped Mum when she needed it. Even if they come, they would fill the most important minutes with questions I don't have the patience to answer.

"I'll search the streets," I say.

No one asks me to explain myself. No one says, "Who's Logan Connolly?" Their panic has swallowed whatever I tried to explain, and all I'm thinking about is Aaron because, if I'm right, the Pearces are good at making kids vanish.

The electric gate is open before I get there and, as I step through, Amy rushes into me.

"Tom, I…She has Aaron."

"Where is he?" I ask.

"I'm so sorry."

"I know about Logan. Is that why you took my brother? I won't tell anyone, I promise. Just give him back."

Amy stares at me, and those eyes that are normally so beautiful look like pits of despair.

"You think *I* took him? It wasn't me, Tom. I was coming to tell you."

"So tell me! Where is he?"

She shakes her head and sobs into her hands. "I don't know."

I want to believe her, and she looks frantic, but this isn't helping.

"Who took him?" I shout.

Amy crouches on the ground and pushes her fingers against her temples.

"Your mum's nice," she whispers. "Mine isn't."

78

"What's she going to do?" I ask. "She won't get away with it. I know everything."

Amy shakes her head. "No, you don't. You know some things. And I'm glad because it feels so fucking heavy. I wanted this to stop, because can you imagine? Christmas dinner when I'm forty, and we're still pretending my brother isn't dead."

I gasp and step back, and Amy's lips form the slightest sad-smile before she says, "Yep. He's dead, and it's my fault. And Logan took his place because my mother is very persuasive."

"I..."

"You're what? You're sorry? No, you're not. You thought I needed saving. You thought my dad was another abusive twat, but *I'm* the dangerous one. I let my brother die, and I took Logan. And, at some point, I stopped feeling completely, insanely upset because it hurt too much.

"I used to hate myself, and then I didn't even feel that. I was numb because my life is a lie, and then you came along and...I felt something. I think you brought me back to life. So, when you started digging, I let you. I didn't walk away because I *wanted* you to find out. Maybe, that way, this would be over, if we actually took responsibility and Logan went home and we went...wherever you go when you've fucked up this badly.

"I'll help you find your brother. She won't hurt him."

"How do you know that?" I ask.

"This is what she does. It's a warning. She wants you to know what she's capable of if you ever reveal what you've found out."

I check my phone, and too much time has already passed. "Where has your mum taken him? You said come alone, and I did what you asked."

"What?"

"The message. You said he'd disappear if I didn't come alone."

Amy runs back into the house, moving from room to room and mumbling to herself. Then she goes upstairs and the mumbles turn to shouts.

When she comes down, she says, "I didn't send that message. Mum must have got your number from my phone."

"Why would she want me to come here?"

"She didn't," someone says behind us and, when I turn, Amy's dad is there with two phones in his hands.

Handing one back to his daughter, he says, "I know where she's taken him."

79

"Where the fuck are you going?"

Nia is standing in the Pearces' driveway, and I run to her and say, "Jane's got him."

My sister stares past me at Chris revving the engine and Amy looking through the back window. "Are you sure?"

"We did it," I say. "I figured it all out, and this is her fighting back."

Nia looks over her shoulder, and I imagine her running back to wherever Jay is still searching, and then Chris driving off forever. But she doesn't do that. She grabs my hand, pulls me toward the car, and says, "Come on."

Chris's face is a mixture of focus and fear while Amy can't even look at us.

Nia doesn't say anything until we've been driving for fifteen minutes, then she turns to Amy's dad and says, "If your wife has hurt my brother in any way, I'll ruin her."

80

We drive for a bit longer, then pull up at the side of a road covered on all sides by trees.

"Where are we?" Nia asks, but Chris doesn't reply.

Instead, he walks through a clearing and Amy follows. "This is stupid," I whisper. "You have seen every horror film ever, right? You never go into the woods."

Nia sucks in a breath, holds it, then slowly exhales. It's what Mum used to do before she was brave, and I remember the day she vowed to leave Martin forever.

I used to think only men were scary, but that was before we met Jane.

What choice do we have? If Aaron is in there, we need to follow Chris and hope this isn't some horrible trick.

Nia grips my hand. "Come on."

The sun fills the gaps between the trees, but I hardly notice. The anxiety that is normally a stone in the pit of my stomach has grown into a boulder, pushing the sickness I'm feeling up my throat.

Chris and Amy are a few steps away from us, their feet crunching the leaves that cover the trail.

They are whispering to each other, but I can't make out the words. Chris looks like he's been here before, and Amy copies his steps, their eyes fixed firmly ahead and their bodies dodging the branches while Nia and I parry their spiky jabs.

This doesn't feel like a well-trodden path. There are no dog-walkers and no signs of life except the birds singing above us. Sometimes the trees rustle then settle as something unseen escapes, like they know what's coming.

I look for footprints or any other sign that Aaron came this way. But the ground is hard and completely covered, and there are no carvings on the trees or clues that he's been here.

If you didn't know where to look, this place would be a dead end. That's why I follow Chris and Amy, silently hoping we can trust them. But Nia is done being quiet.

"Where are you taking us?" she asks.

"To your brother," Chris says without looking back.

"How do you know where he is?" Nia asks, and, this time, he doesn't answer.

"Amy?" Nia says, and she shivers at the sound of her name but doesn't reply.

I wonder if this is the first time they've spoken since they were friends. I can't imagine them being close, but, then, we've all had lives before this one.

Eventually, we reach a clearing and Chris clears his throat and says, "He's here."

For a moment, I think he means Aaron, then, as Jane appears alone and smiling, I realize he means me.

81

"Hello, Tom," Jane says. "I see you brought company."

"Where's Aaron?" I ask.

But she just smirks and says, "All in good time."

"Where is he?" Nia asks. "What is all this?"

"This," Jane says, "is what happens when your nosy brother won't stop digging. This is what happens when he doesn't get the message."

I look at Amy, but she's watching her father with an expression I can't interpret. At first glance she looks angry, but there's something else underneath. I thought they were bringing us here to rescue my brother. But Chris is now standing next to his wife like they were both in on it.

"So you figured it out," Jane says. "Well done for that. But it ends now. You will never take my son."

"He's not your son," I say, and Jane grins with all her teeth.

"Of course he is."

"I know what you did."

I'm not sure who I'm talking to, because it's not just Jane; it's Amy and her dad as well. They're all guilty, because how could they not be? They took Logan and turned him into Will, and something that horrible takes a lot of effort.

Jane steps forward. "I will do anything to protect my family."

"*Your* family?!" Nia shouts. "What about *our* family? Where the fuck is my brother?!"

Jane's mask slips, and I see something else in the corners.

She looks sad, and I wonder if Nia is breaking through. "You really love him, don't you?" Jane asks.

"Of course I do. I'd do anything for him, including going clean through you. So stop pissing about and tell me where he is."

"I love my family too," Jane says. "And I would go clean through anyone if I had to. Tom has started terrorizing my children."

"Terrorizing—" I say, but Amy's mum cuts me off with a stare I've seen before. It's the look of someone you don't push. It's the warning I saw too many times in Martin and Gary—the one that says, *Be careful*.

"Throwing things at William's window? Breaking into our garden?"

I try to act calm because Jane knows. She must have seen what we moved that night, or maybe there are cameras we didn't notice. Whatever the reason, she knew what I did at the dinner party, but sat on it until now.

"Where. Is. My. Brother?" Nia asks again.

"He's safe," Jane says. "And he'll stay that way if you

promise to leave us alone. I've shown you what I can do. There are a lot more holes for a boy to fall through if you're not careful."

"Are you threatening me?"

Jane turns her stare from me to Nia and whispers, "Yes."

82

"Stop it," Amy mumbles. She's crying, and I want to go to her, but I can't move.

Jane turns to her daughter, who shrinks even deeper into herself. Amy is terrified, and, whatever Chris has to do with this, I know she didn't want to bring us here.

She glances at her father again, and I expect to see a look of betrayal, but it's not there. Instead, there's almost a warmth to her face—one that freezes the moment her mother speaks.

"I'm not the one who needs to stop," Jane says. "Have you been helping him? Or did he really work it out on his own?"

I think of all the lies Amy told, all the times she said she didn't need my help and tried to convince me that I had the wrong idea. She wasn't lying to be mean. She was hiding like Mum used to because she thought it was too late to be saved.

"She didn't tell me anything," I say.

I don't think Jane believes me, but she stays silent, pacing the clearing, then crouching at a spot in the corner. "It seems we're at an impasse," she says, not looking up from the ground. "I brought you here to show you something, and I hope you start seeing things from my point of view."

I can feel Nia's rage burning beside me. Her arms tighten, and her eyes are focused on the woman who took our brother, but she doesn't move.

"This is where I come to remember," Jane says.

She has her hand on the ground, and, when I look closer, I see the edge of a stone poking out from between her fingers. Only when she steps back do I see the letters carved into the gray—W. P.

At first, I don't believe it. Then, as Jane's features soften, I realize where we are.

"He's here," I whisper. "Will."

"Will is looking after Aaron," Jane replies. But the tremble in her lips gives her away.

I think they buried him here. They've brought us to his grave to warn us, and, if I don't stop, Aaron's could be the next initials in the middle of nowhere.

"I will do whatever it takes to protect my family," Jane says. "I'm not scared of what you think you know. Knowledge doesn't always give you the upper hand, Tom. Sometimes it makes you an easy target."

Nia jumps forward too quickly for me to stop, but I grab her hand and pull when she's half a step from Amy's mum.

"Don't fucking threaten him," Nia says. "Tell us where Aaron is or I swear to God..." She looks fierce, but I can feel her shaking.

Jane smiles. "Of course. But that's the end of it. Tom is not to see Amy again. He will not try to speak to Will. And, if you call the police, I'll show them the evidence I've compiled."

Before I can ask what she means, she steps forward and holds out her phone.

"This is security footage of the night you and your friend broke into my garden. And these are photographs of the two occasions you stood below my son's window and damaged my property."

When Jane sees my face, she leans in too close and says, "You weren't the only one watching."

83

Nia reaches for her phone and says, "I'm calling my dad."

"And telling him what?" Jane replies. "You don't know where you are. And I have your brother. This would go a lot more smoothly if you accepted my terms and we took you home ourselves."

"I'm not getting in a car with you. You're a psycho. We'll walk."

"That would be a mistake," Jane says. "We didn't choose this place by accident. There's nothing for quite some time."

Nia's fingers curl into fists, and, for a moment, I think she's going to attack. Instead, her knuckles tighten then soften, over and over again, until eventually she says, "Whatever you want. We'll do it."

Jane smiles like she did at the dinner party, when I mistook her menace for delight.

"Excellent," she says. She reaches down to what I think is a gravestone and whispers something, then leads us through the clearing and back to the cars.

I do my best to remember what's around us, but there's nothing out of the ordinary. Everywhere is just trees and bushes and silence—the perfect hiding place for an unspeakable secret.

If they really wanted to keep this place secret, they could have blindfolded us. But they didn't, and that's when I realize what Jane is.

Martin never tried to lock us in because he knew he didn't have to. We stayed because we were terrified what would happen if we tried to leave. And now Amy's mum thinks we're too scared of her to fight back.

I try to see the thoughts behind Nia's eyes, but she won't look at me. She's staring at the road, her lips moving just enough for me to understand. So I do the same through the other window, remembering every tiny detail of where we are and where we might have been.

Jane isn't with us. She left in her own car while Chris and Amy sit silently in the front seats of this one.

I reach out and hold Nia's hand and she gives me the briefest sad-smile and a squeeze.

"I'm sorry," I whisper, and my sister squeezes harder. She doesn't look scared. She looks furious.

84

Jane's car is in her driveway as we pull in, and I can see Aaron's face through the back window.

Nia yanks on the handle, but it won't budge.

"Open the fucking door!" she yells, and, when Chris turns off the ignition, she bursts out and runs to her brother.

She's saying something I can't hear through his closed window, and that's when I notice Logan sitting next to him.

He could run. He could bring Jane's lies crashing down. But time and fear can change people, and I'm not sure he knows who he is anymore.

Aaron clambers out and giggles like this is all a game.

"Where have you been?" Nia says.

She hugs him so hard that he says, "Ouch," then looks at her funny as she sniffs away her tears.

"Are you okay?" he asks.

She breathes out and says, "I am now."

"We were naughty," Aaron says. "But Will's mummy found us."

Jane is staring at us with that terrible fixed grin, and I hate her because she's thought of everything.

"I found them wandering the streets," she says. "Lucky I was there to bring them home."

Nia turns to me, and I can see the fight flicker and fade behind her eyes. I hear a shout, then turn to see Mum and Jay running toward us.

Jay pulls Aaron into a hug his son tries to wriggle out of. But he holds on, his eyes pushed tightly closed as if he's terrified that, when he opens them, his boy will have disappeared again.

"Where was he?" Mum asks.

Before we can answer, Aaron says, "I was with Will. He showed me the hole in the fence, but then we got lost, and I was a bit scared but not really. Then Jane found us."

Nia looks frantic, and I want to scream the truth, but this is a warning.

"We should leave you to it," Jane says.

"Thank you so much," says Mum.

Jay stops looking at Aaron just long enough to hug Jane and shake Chris's hand, and I feel sick.

Nia clears her throat, and I think she's about to explode, but I remember Jane's face in the woods and how easily she took our brother.

"Not yet," I whisper, and Nia stares at me but doesn't move.

Amy looks helpless, and I want to take her with us. She doesn't follow the others back into their house. She stands in silence, and I know what she wants to say because we all do.

"Amy," her mum says, "come on."

If you didn't know better, it would sound caring. Before she closes the door, Jane turns and waves. Whatever she's done to Logan and Amy and Chris to make sure they keep playing her horrible game, she thinks she's done it to us too.

Mum crouches next to Aaron and says, "You really scared us. Don't ever run off again, okay?"

Aaron nods, then looks serious because his dad is crying, and Nia and I know exactly what Jane has done.

We won't tell anyone, because, next time, we won't get him back.

85

I don't want to live here anymore.

There are stick figures carved inside my wardrobe and pleas behind the paint and holes in a door we might never replace.

This place is a warning. It's a scary story you tell to make kids behave. And it's our life.

My curtains are closed, because I can't look at Amy's house either. Everything is a reminder of a truth I can't tell. If I do, there's no guarantee the police will do their job before Jane keeps her promise.

"I'm sorry," I whisper into the darkness, and then I go downstairs and check everything over and over again until I want to scream at myself to stop.

But I can't, because my doubt swallows my certainty the moment I step away from a door or a window. The voice that tells me the house will flood if I don't check every tap or that there'll be an electrical fire if I don't turn off every socket is louder than it's been for years. And it's all because of Jane.

"Are you okay?"

The voice makes me jump, and, when I turn, Nia is there. I feel both embarrassed and relieved. I don't want her to see my rituals, but I'm scared I'll be doing them all night without a distraction.

"Not really," I say, and Nia points to the chair next to hers. The moon is low and full tonight, and its glow fills the kitchen.

"I'm sorry I didn't believe you about the holes," Nia says. "If I'm honest, I didn't *want* to believe you…even when we saw the words on the wall."

"What are we going to do?" I ask.

Nia draws invisible patterns on the table with one hand and rubs her eyes with the other. "We need to stop that woman."

"She's smart," I say. "She didn't take Aaron. She got Logan to do that so it would look like a game."

"And our parents fucking thanked her," Nia whispers. "We can't let her get away with it. She thinks she's so strong, but there must be a way of taking her down."

Mum used to talk about strength. She would whisper to me as we fell asleep in the same bed, just a door between us and the devil roaming the rest of the house.

"We need to be strong," she would say. "Can you do that for me?"

I was only a kid, so it wasn't easy. But I tried. And, eventually, Mum's bravery held just long enough for us to break free.

Nia looks like Mum did the day she'd had enough. "Jane will get what's coming to her. All we need is proof that Logan isn't who she says he is."

"We'll need his DNA for that," I say. "You heard her. She

won't let them anywhere near us now. I missed my chance." I wanted to save Amy, and I failed. I was in Logan's room, and it would only have taken a second to pick up a hair from his pillow.

"I messed up," I say. "And now Aaron...I'm so sorry, Nia."

"It's not your fault. If we'd listened to you, we could have caught her sooner. But we still will."

Aaron is back with his real mum, now, but there are so many weekends to come.

If Mum and Jay find out the truth too soon, she'll call the police, and he will charge around to the Pearces. I don't think either scenario would end well.

Jane hid the death of one child and the theft of another for years. She manipulates people, she lies with the perfect smile, and the police won't be able to search her house or test Logan without evidence.

If we report her now, with a crumpled list of clues and a few absurd sounding stories, we'll lose.

"Unless..."

Nia waits for me to finish, and, when I don't, she nudges me and says, "Unless what?"

But I can't speak because, despite what I thought in the woods, Jane wouldn't be that stupid, would she?

86

"We need your car," I say down the phone.

"*Just* my car?" asks Zak. "Or will you also be requiring a driver?"

Nia laughs, and he says, "Am I on speaker? Because you should always warn people if they are. I could have told you what I really think about your stepsister."

"We all know you love me," she says.

Zak snorts. "Are you doing group chats now? I thought..." He stops because he is this close to insulting at least one of us. I know what he means because me and Nia huddled around the same phone isn't a sight he's used to. But a lot has happened since yesterday.

"We need your driving skills...and your secrecy," I say. Zak is quiet for a while, then he says, "This is another Amy thing, isn't it?"

"Sort of," Nia replies. "Are you coming?"

"This is very odd," he says. "Listen for the honk."

Fifteen minutes later, Zak is out front, and Nia shouts goodbye before Mum can ask where we're going.

We quickly stuff what we need in the trunk, and, when Zak sees, he says, "What is that for?"

"We'll explain everything," I say. "Please just drive."

Mum comes to the front window with a strange look on her face, because this isn't how she expected us to spend the first day of the school break.

"She's going to ask questions," Nia says.

"*I'm* going to ask questions," says Zak. "What's happened to you two? Are you…friends now?"

"We have a common enemy," Nia says and then, when she sees my face, "but yes, you could say that."

I check my phone, then tap a zip code into Zak's GPS. We have it all planned. Last night we searched Google Maps for hours, looking for anything that stood out from our road trip with the Pearces. I fell asleep before Nia did, but, this morning, she woke me with a smile that said it worked.

"Where are we going?" Zak asks.

"I'm not sure. But we'll know when we get there."

He looks at Nia through the rearview mirror and says, "How the hell did he convince you to get involved?"

"Amy's mum is a psychopath," my sister tells him. "She kidnapped Aaron just to show us what she'd do if Tom didn't stop digging."

"What the fuck?"

"We should probably tell you about Logan," I say.

87

"So you were right," Zak says.

I was, but, just like when Nia said it, I'm not pleased. I didn't *want* to be right. I want Amy to be happy and Logan to be with his real family and Will to be alive.

The thought of losing Aaron terrifies me, so I can only imagine how Will's death could twist a family inside out.

"I recognize this," Nia says. "It's not far. Look out for where we parked."

"There," I say, and Zak pulls in so fast we all jolt.

We don't get out right away. We sit in silence, because we're scared and excited and uncertain.

I run through what happened yesterday and wonder if this is another trap. Except there was a rock with Will's initials on it and Jane looked different. When she bent down and whispered to the ground, she seemed almost at peace.

Would they really be that stupid, showing us where Will was buried just to prove a point? Maybe they underestimated our sense of direction, or perhaps they don't care because they thought Aaron's abduction was enough to keep us quiet.

"Okay," Nia says at last. "Are you ready?"

I'm not, but maybe I never will be. I don't want to see what's buried beneath that stone, yet it's the only way to protect us. Jane's threat will be like a scar on everyday Aaron visits until we stop her.

I nod and open the car door, then watch Nia go to the trunk and pull out a spade.

"When do I get an explanation for that?" Zak asks.

He's still trying to make jokes, but I can see how scared he is. He knows what the spade is for, but is desperately hoping for a different answer. The truth is: so am I.

I can't say it. I can't even think it. I just follow Nia through the woods and try to stay calm.

It takes longer than I remember. But we don't have someone guiding us this time. Instead, we follow the flattened grass and the dried dirt until we finally reach the clearing.

I'm half-expecting Jane to be there, waiting for us, but it's empty. There's nothing except the song of a single bird hidden in the trees and the distant hum of cars.

Nia picks up the stone and hands it to me. Up close, the carving looks similar to the patterns on the box we found in Amy's garden.

W. P. William Pearce. This is the closest he'll get to a gravestone.

I hold out my hand. "I'll do it."

The sound of the spade hitting the dirt makes me shiver.

"Are you sure you want to do this?" Nia asks.

Still digging, I say, "What choice do we have?"

"We could tell the police. They could find...whatever's in there."

"And, if there's nothing, we're the ones that look wrong. We need evidence. Jane has footage of me and Zak breaking into her garden and of me throwing stones at her windows. What do *we* have?"

Zak makes a face. "They recorded that? Is there anything else I should know?"

"Sorry...but you're safe, provided we..."

"Don't do anything else stupid?"

He's right: this *is* stupid. It's reckless and insane, but we need to do something.

After a while, Nia takes the spade, and we swap places. The earth is softer, now, but, no matter how deep we go, there's nothing but dirt.

Finally, Zak gives a sigh. "My turn," he says, and Nia hands him the spade and flexes her fingers.

He keeps digging long after I've realized we're wrong. There's nothing here except a stone with Will's initials on. Jane brought us because it wasn't a risk. She didn't take us to the scene of the crime. This is just where she comes to remember.

"I'm sorry," Nia says, and so am I, a little bit. But I'm also relieved.

I didn't want to dig up a dead body. I want this to be over without seeing the truth.

I start filling in the hole because, the next time Jane comes, she'll know what we did. Even with the ground level again and the stone back in place, it looks different.

She will know what we came looking for, and she'll know that we failed. We just have to hope it rains hard or she doesn't come here often. Only time and nature will cover our tracks.

"It was always a long shot," Nia says.

"So that's it?" Zak asks.

"No," I say. "We just have to think of something else."

We don't leave right away. We sit on the forest floor with our sweat and our fear and our failure and try to figure out another plan.

When we get home, Mum will ask where we've been and she'll know if I lie. She always knows. It just depends how important the truth is to her. Perhaps it will be enough that I'm with Nia. Maybe she'll think this is our blended family finally slotting into place.

Mum waited years for this life. She told me it would come, but I didn't believe her. She said it would get better, but I thought "better" was a week without threats or bruises or broken things. I thought it was an undisturbed bath or a laugh my mother could actually finish.

When "better" finally happened, it was a release. It was freedom. And only then did I realize how trapped we'd been.

People like Jane think they're unbeatable. They think no one is ever going to fight back. This time, we tried, but it wasn't enough.

Zak jumps, looks behind him and whispers, "What was that?"

"What?" Nia asks.

He tilts his head. "I think I heard something." We all listen but it's just the same sounds. "There." He points toward the hidden path.

There's a crack, then another, the slow crunch of dried leaves until it's unmistakable. Someone is coming.

88

"Shit," Zak whispers, and I freeze because I can't believe my eyes.

"Amy," Nia says, and then, her body bristling, "is this some sick game?"

I look between the trees, searching for Jane or Chris and trying to figure out what the hell is going on. But Amy steps forward with her hands held out and says, "It's not a game."

She looks behind us, at the fake grave we dug up and refilled, and says, "You figured it out."

"There's nothing there," I say.

"No. But it's still important."

Amy walks past us and stares at the ground, then picks up the stone with her brother's initials.

We were here less than twenty-four hours ago, but it feels so different this time. Yesterday Amy looked terrified; today it feels like she's the one in control.

"How did you know we were here?" I ask.

Amy passes the stone between her hands, then finally says, "I heard the car beep."

Zak looks uncomfortable, and she says, "Don't worry. She's not here. I knew you'd come back, Tom. I saw the moment you figured it out, and, when I saw Nia with the spade this morning…"

The girls swap looks, then Amy says, "I'm so sorry for what she did to Aaron. We never wanted that to happen."

"Really?" Nia says. "Because your dad knew exactly where he was going, and you didn't put up much of a fight." I want to defend Amy, because my sister doesn't know what she's been through. She doesn't realize that some people's fight mode broke years ago. But I flash back to Chris and his daughter whispering as they led us here. If they weren't talking about betraying us, what were they discussing?

Amy crouches next to the dirt we've just packed tight, rests the stone to one side, then reaches for our spade.

"What's happening?" Zak mumbles, and Nia and I shake our heads.

We thought we'd come here and find the proof that could finally save Logan and Amy. But now she's the one digging.

I step forward and ask what she's doing, but Amy doesn't answer.

"Can I help?"

"Yes. But not yet." We watch as Amy digs and then kicks at the dirt.

When she finally sits back and slows her breathing, her hands are muddy, and her face looks washed out.

"What are you doing?" Nia says. "Your mum will go mental when she sees this. She'll come for Aaron again."

"No," Amy says. "She'll come for Tom. And we'll be ready."

89

Back on the main road, Chris is in his car, and Amy walks over and sits in the passenger seat. They don't turn to each other. They both look at the three of us.

Zak whispers, "This is proper creepy."

And Nia says, "What if it's a trap?"

They're trying their best not to move their lips because Chris and Amy are watching us as they pull away.

"It's not a trap," I say. "Jane is really, really good at this. She came to our house for dinner. She tricked Mum and Jay. And she brought us here because she thinks we can be broken like Amy and Logan were. But they're not as broken as she thinks."

"Or she's completely brainwashed them."

"No. Amy's right. If we want to win, we need the right people on our side."

Something surges inside me—a mixture of excitement and panic—as I say, "We need to tell our parents."

"Dad will go ballistic," Nia says. "He'll knock their bloody door down."

"Not if we do it right. We tell them everything, and we make sure they listen. Jane thinks her family is untouchable because of what *she's* done to them. But she's never met ours."

"Yeah!" Zak says. "Sorry. But that was a pretty good speech."

Nia laughs. Then we drive home to the people who have no idea what we're about to tell them.

I think of Amy the whole way, kicking myself for not seeing it sooner. I pushed and pushed, asking her questions she was too afraid to answer. I forced her to remember a brother she could never get back and another who wasn't real.

The best times were when I stopped asking.

Nia catches my eye in the mirror and says, "I'll back you up."

It feels good to hear, because, for so long, I didn't know what was real and what wasn't. I didn't know what was worth worrying about and what was just creepy coincidence.

Now we're all in this together.

90

"Tom has something to tell you," Nia says, "and you need to listen to all of it before you freak out."

Everyone's in the living room, even Zak, who walked in without a word and is making his most serious face.

When I'm done, Mum grips my hand and Jay stares in silence. He looks at each of us in turn then, finally, he says, "They took Aaron?"

"Logan took him. But Jane made him do it. It was a warning."

"And there's a grave?"

"No," I say. "I think it's a shrine or something. It's where Jane goes to remember, but..."

Mum glances at the dirt in my fingernails and I don't have to finish the sentence.

What would we have done if there was a body? If I close my eyes, I can imagine what we might have seen, and I have to open them again before my insides shatter.

"And Amy..." Mum says.

"She was coming to warn us. And now she has a plan."

"I don't like it," Jay says. "It puts you all at risk. Why won't she just tell the police?"

"Because Jane is good at hiding the truth. She'll twist it so Amy's the one who suffers, or she'll show the police the videos of me on their property and convince them I'm lying."

"Amy is all the evidence they need," Jay says. "She can bring them Logan. He can speak out."

"He won't. It's too late for that," I say. "Jane needs to be caught red-handed."

When Amy explained everything, it made perfect sense.

But, now, with time to think, I'm scared it won't work. "It's this or nothing," I say. "She probably won't come back to school, anyway."

Was that the real reason she left St. Gregory's? Did someone get too close to the truth, and Jane threatened them before enrolling Amy at our school?

"I could speak to her," Mum says.

"And say what?"

"I'll tell her I know exactly what it's like to feel trapped in your own house. I'll tell her I remember how it feels to be terrified every second of every day. And I'll tell her I don't feel like that anymore. There's a way out. She just needs to be brave and tell the police herself. Jane controls that family. I know what that feels like. But I also know things can change."

Mum hasn't been this honest with me for a long time, but it's more than that. She's talking about our horrible history differently, now. She isn't scared of it. She's in control.

Mum left her old life behind when she married Jay, but she didn't forget what happened to us. She kept it close, the memories of all the tears and bruises and terror making her stronger somehow. She promised that, if she ever met another monster, she'd win. That's why we had to tell her, because, if anyone can help us stop Jane, it's my mother.

"We could figure out a way to get Amy alone again and convince her to speak out," Nia says. "I'd rather that than risk Aaron getting hurt."

"It's not that easy. The house is a fortress. You only get in if they let you."

"Or you jump over the wall," Zak mumbles, and I shoot him a look, but he shrugs. "What? We've done it before."

Mum's look is a mixture of confusion and concern, but she doesn't criticize me. Instead, she says, "No one does anything else foolish. Tom's right. If we go to the police without the evidence for them to get a warrant, Jane and Chris could run and take Amy and Logan with them. We need to bide our time and have faith in Amy's idea. She knows her mother better than anyone."

I can feel the anger coming off Jay in waves. His arms are pulled tightly against his body as though he's suppressing the urge to fight. Nia sees and rests her head on his shoulder and, slowly, his shaking stops.

He's a good man. Even now, knowing what he does about Aaron's disappearance, the part of him that won Mum over is winning again.

I think of Amy frantically digging up the dirt where we thought her brother was buried and say, "Jane will come here. We've made sure of it."

"How can you be certain?" Jay says.

"What's the one thing even the cleverest monsters can't control?" I ask.

Mum looks concerned, then her face changes, and I see a thought sparkle and settle behind her eyes. "Anger," she says.

91

I can't sleep or eat or think about anything except the pretend grave that Amy spoiled just enough to make it obvious. What happened there wasn't a mistake. It wasn't caused by an animal or a stormy night. It was done by someone wanting to send a message.

Whenever the doorbell rings, I picture Jane on the other side. Every night, when I do finally dream, I see Aaron locked in a room like this one. He screams, but no one hears him. And then Jane whispers, "I warned you," and I wake up, sweating and breathless.

I always wanted to be brave. But the Pearces aren't something to escape. They are something to catch, and that's a lot harder.

I don't know how often Jane visits the shrine, but, the next time she does, I'm expecting a knock on the door. I'm desperate for it, because this won't work if she doesn't explode.

Jay wants revenge for what happened to Aaron. "What are we waiting for?" he asks.

And Mum says, "Trust me. We need to be patient."

It's what she said to me, over and over again, while she planned her escape from Martin and then Gary. I didn't believe her, then, but I do now because I've seen it.

I wonder if Amy is scared or if she knows her mum well enough to sit back and wait for it to happen. I'm worried about her, but it's too risky for us to message each other. She hasn't come back to school, and I miss her. My feelings are still there, wrapped in so many others, but bright enough to shine through the gloom.

I miss the way she smiled when she meant it and how she looked when I wasn't searching for her secret. I didn't see it then, and I hate myself because Amy was happiest when we were talking about other things—like how my mum met my dad or the squirrel park—and when she danced at Sensorium.

Everything was tinged with sorrow, and her happiness was temporary. But it was there, and I wish I'd made more of it.

I think I loved her, and maybe I still do. And that makes what we're trying so much harder. If we catch Jane, we catch all of them.

We could have walked away. We could ignore the big home on the corner like we ignore all the other houses on our street. We could forget in order to feel safe. Except we'll never feel safe and we'll never feel happy. How can we when we know the truth about a mystery the police called a tragic accident?

Logan Connolly's mum thinks her son was washed away. But the tide comes in eventually.

When I go downstairs, Mum is at the table.

I don't do this in secret now. She watches me in silence, even when I check the back door twenty times because there's a hole in the fence, and Jane could fit through if she tried.

I haven't told Mum my biggest fear: that, on the day the Pearces handed over the keys to our new home, they kept one for themselves. As if she could read my mind, she asked Jay to fit bolts, but the thought still fills me with dread.

When I'm done, I kiss Mum's cheek, and she smiles but doesn't move.

I close my bedroom door and slide the lock across. The one I bought to prove my theory—now I use it, just in case.

92

I can't message Amy in case Jane has her phone, so I do something else and hope it works.

The sign on my window says: WE ALL NEED A HEAD START SOMETIMES.

Even if Jane sees it, she won't know what it means; not unless Amy told her.

I keep thinking about what she said the day Aaron went missing.

"I didn't walk away because I *wanted* you to find out. Maybe that way this would be over, if we actually took responsibility and Logan went home..."

Amy wants this to end, and I want to help her. But I'm still terrified about how it could play out. If things go wrong, I might never see her again. And, if they go right, we might not get the chance to say goodbye.

That's why I leave the note by the head-start line. If anyone else finds it, it will be nonsense.

> I wish we didn't have secrets and could have just been whatever you wanted us to be. I wish I hadn't pushed you so much to answer questions you must have hated. I'm sorry. I'm thinking of you. Please write back x

I don't know if Amy will find it, but I have to try. I need to know that she's all right and hasn't been hurt or locked in.

And I want her to know I'm still here, even if her curtains never open and school feels empty without her.

93

When Jane finally comes, it's not how we expected. She doesn't look angry. She looks calm. Until her words give her away.

"What did you do?" she whispers.

"What do you mean?" I ask, stepping back and hoping she follows.

Jane thinks she knows this house better than anyone.

She feels safe here. But she shouldn't. "You know full well."

My heart's racing, and I can feel the sweat under my arms as I try desperately to stay cool. Jane needs to be the one who breaks, not me.

"Where is he?" she asks.

Her eyes dart all over the place, her fingers pull at her clothes, and I know it's worked. All she needs is to say it.

"I said, where *is* he?"

She's still whispering, but something is rumbling below the surface, and I take another step back.

"Do you mean Jay?" I ask.

Jane says, "Where's my *son*?" The last word is the quietest and the sharpest.

I glance at the painting above the fireplace where Jay fitted one of the hidden cameras the day after we met Amy in the woods. There are three in total: one filming the front door, the second that I just checked and a third with Jane front and center. This is how to be certain that, when the time's right, you can trap a monster.

Upstairs, Jay can switch between the cameras on his laptop or have all three on a multiscreen like security guards looking for thieves.

"I won't ask again," Jane says, trying to push past.

"I don't know who you mean."

"You know damn well what I'm talking about. You went to the woods and you dug up…"

She stops and looks over my shoulder. Then she shakes her head and mumbles something I can't make out. She's furious, but her tears are coming hard now, and she looks scared as well.

"Give him to me!" Jane screams.

She moves so fast that I don't realize she's scratched me until I feel the sting. I touch my cheek and my finger comes away red. She lunges again, and I step away this time.

"Why would you dig up my son?" she snarls.

I try to keep my voice strong, but it cracks at the end. "What do you mean?"

Jane clenches her fists, and I brace myself, but she doesn't move.

Instead, she takes a long breath out. "You think you're so

clever, but you're not. My son died six years ago, and no one has any fucking idea."

"*I* do," I reply.

Jane laughs. "'*I do.*'"

She's mocking me because I'm scared, and she thinks she's the reason. But I'm terrified she'll leave without saying everything.

I think of Amy when she told me what happened to Will. She lost something she can never get back. They all did. But she doesn't want to live that lie anymore.

"What about Logan?" I ask.

Jane stares at me like I'm prey. "What about him?"

"He has a mother. A *real* mother."

"*I'm* his real mother. And his name is William."

She's calmer now, and, if you didn't know better, you would think this was a normal conversation.

"It wasn't always, though, was it? You took him."

Jane shakes her head and says, "We both know that's not true."

I could stop now, but Amy wants this. She said it's okay to say her name. She said it's vital.

So I open my mouth and force out the words because this tape is a confession, and Jane's isn't the only one.

"Okay. Amy took him. But *you* made her do it."

"She had to," Jane says. "It was the only way. You must understand, Tom. Remember how your family reacted when I took Aaron for an hour? Imagine that with no end. I had to do something. I'm sorry you found out, because Amy really liked you. But you know you can never tell. Give my son back and stop digging."

She's crying again, now, and I risk the quickest glance at the camera. But she catches me, follows my gaze and says, "What have you done?"

Jane's eyes are tiny specks of fury, and there's movement behind her. I see them before she does.

"Mum," Amy says. "Stop."

94

Amy and Logan are standing in the doorway, and Jane looks from them to me and back again. “They took him…” she whispers.

Amy touches her mother’s shoulder. “They didn’t.”

The anger falls from Jane’s face, replaced by confusion. “But…”

“It’s over,” Amy says. “I’m tired, Mum. We all are.”

I hear the floorboards creak, and I imagine Mum, Jay, and Nia upstairs, discussing what to do. But I hold my hand to my ear—our secret sign that I’m okay—and the creaking stops.

Amy looks at me, and she isn’t scared. She looks strong, and I want to hug her and tell her I’m sorry for not figuring it out sooner. I want to hold her because it worked. We have Jane’s confession on tape; at least enough of it for Amy to fill in the gaps.

The sound of sirens breaks the silence. Usually, it surges and fades, but, today, it gets louder until I know exactly where it is.

"We should go," Amy says. She pushes her lips together and nods, then leads her mother down the path.

Logan doesn't move for a moment. He looks at me, and I want to say the right thing. But what is that? Then he turns and follows Amy and Jane, and I walk to the end of the street, where the police car is parked in the Pearces' driveway.

The gate isn't locked anymore, and the front door is open. Chris stands with his arms crossed, and I think of him that day in the woods, when Amy set this plan in motion and he didn't stop her.

"Tom..." Mum says from behind me. She hugs me and Nia joins in and Jay stands a few steps back.

"That was intense," says Nia.

People are starting to gather in the street, talking in hushed voices. Then another police car arrives, no siren this time, no flashing lights, just two officers who stride quickly inside.

Amy was the one who had to release the truth, and, today, she had the strength to turn the key in the lock and finally open the door.

95

Not everything ends with an explosion.

For a while, with Jane threatening to charge through our house, I thought it might. But the truth is a lot calmer.

That night, the police knock on our door and Mum hands over the recording.

I write a statement that sounds ridiculous when I read it back. I can see the disbelief on the officer's face. Then his partner shows him the picture of Logan Connolly before he went missing, and another of him now.

Whatever the policeman was about to say evaporates.

In its place, a single sound: "Oh."

And now we're all watching from my bedroom window as police tape is stretched around a house that suddenly looks smaller.

Amy has already left, her and Logan driven off in different cars for different destinations. I don't know where she's gone, but I desperately hope she comes back.

I always wondered why she chose me—if I really was a random first friend or if it was more than that. It definitely was for me.

When the final car pulls away, Mum and I are still watching. We're used to looking through windows more than Jay and Nia.

"We did it," Mum says, but we don't feel happy. How can we when we've just destroyed a family?

It's not until I think of Logan's real mother that I smile. I'm not naive. I know whatever happens next is not going to be easy. But I hope the damage Jane caused isn't irreparable. I hope Logan remembers his mother as more than just a stick figure carved into a wardrobe.

It was just the two of them—like Mum and me—and then they didn't even have that. They were two broken souls, each grieving for the other. Two lives made dark and lonely because of a tragedy that shattered three more.

96

"If you thought this was going to have a happy ending, you weren't paying attention."

I laugh down the phone because Amy's right. Sometimes, for the briefest moments, I still imagine her as my girlfriend. I picture a life that's impossible, like most of the lives we dream. Whatever Amy dreamed of, I doubt it was this.

Her parents are awaiting trial, she's going to be a witness, and Logan is probably back with his real family now.

There was no emotional reunion on the news. Whatever happened was in secret, although, remembering how Jay swept up Aaron when he disappeared, I imagined an eruption of relief and a hug that lasted hours.

Maybe one day Pauline Connolly will reveal how it feels to have her son home. But some wounds are too deep to fully heal, and I think she and Logan will always be unknown to the rest of the world.

"How's your dad?" I ask, and Amy is quiet for a long time.

"I don't know."

"I still can't believe he let you do it."

"I used to hate him for not standing up to Mum. But I guess he got the better of her in the end."

"It's not a win, though, is it?"

Amy sighs. "We don't deserve to win."

I think back to that day in the clearing, when Amy told me her plan. Her dad had told Jane that he buried Will in one place when he'd actually hidden him in another. I thought it was to protect his family and to give her a safe place to grieve without ever risking the truth coming out.

It looked like a smart move when Jane got so confident that she brought us there. But Amy destroying the shrine lit a fuse under her mother she knew wouldn't be stopped. She would explode, she'd blame me, and all we had to do was film it.

"Dad wasn't protecting Mum," Amy says. "It was the one thing he had over her. I didn't know if he would ever use it. But, the day Mum took Aaron, we knew we had to escape. I hated her for making your family suffer. The police found Will's real grave. Dad told them everything."

"Was it really you that took Logan?"

Now that Amy is miles away, just a voice in my ear rather than a mystery to solve, I can ask the sort of questions that always stalled before. I don't think I can upset her any more than she already is.

"Yes," she says. "I took him."

I don't reply, because there's nothing I can say that's right. Instead, I wait until she says, "I feel different now it's over. Not better, just different."

"I'm sorry," I say, because I am.

Sometimes saving someone doesn't end well for everyone. Sometimes it doesn't end well for anyone.

When she doesn't speak, I ask, "What's it like there?"

"It's okay. It still feels like everyone's pretending, but...not like before."

She's staying with a new family now—a temporary one that looks after people like Amy. They have two kids of their own, but she doesn't talk about them.

"It's not forever," I reply, and then, "Nia says hi."

They talk on the phone, too, but always behind closed doors. I don't know what they say to each other, and I won't ask.

Sometimes Nia tells me stories about Amy before the accident. She feels guilty for not realizing the change was more serious than kids' stuff, but it's not her fault. My sister is making up for lost time, now, and I can feel Amy's smile down the phone when I mention her name.

"I miss you," I whisper.

"Me too."

I still see her in the gaps she used to fill. I picture her behind the curtains in a house that's now a crime scene. I remember her smiling at me from across the courtyard at school. And I feel her when I sit by the head-start line and repeat the conversations we had before I dug too deep.

What Mum says about memories—that a few, some good and some bad, become tattoos on your soul—well, Amy is one of those tattoos.

97

We spoke a lot about moving because, even when you buy new doors and wardrobes and replaster the walls, there are some things you can't change. Houses have echoes, and this one has more than most.

But Mum wanted to stay. "We can't change what happened here," she said. "But we can write a new story."

Nia raised her eyebrows at me because it *was* pretty cheesy, but, out loud, she said, "Cool."

And that was that. We stayed.

"Whose choice is it?" Jay asks.

Aaron yells, "Tom's!"

I used to hate the pressure of being in charge of family film night. Whatever I picked would piss off someone—usually Nia—and Aaron would be huffy that he couldn't sing along. But, tonight, I'm happy to choose.

I used to wait to be invited into a circle of four. And, even then, I'd feel awkward. Now I don't wait because this is my home.

When the film's over, Nia tucks her brother in while Mum and Jay tidy up.

So much is the same as it used to be. But not everything.

I stand outside the bedroom and watch my sister play some tunes and whisper made-up stories. Then I come in without asking and sit next to her on the bed. She smiles, then carries on whispering because Aaron won't sleep until he's happy with the ending.

When he's not, he suggests alternatives, and Nia laughs and says, "Whose story is this?"

There's not enough room for all of us on the bed, but we manage anyway.

Aaron listens, wide-eyed, to every single word while I close mine and think about Mum.

She used to tell me stories in bed, then fall asleep next to me, not by mistake but because it was our safe place. I knew she was protecting me, but I didn't always know why.

Sometimes I have to remember that Jane was a mother, too, turned desperate by tragedy. I don't think I can ever say that out loud because of what she did to Logan and to Aaron. But that's what I think as Nia finishes her story and kisses her brother good night.

"Are you coming?" she asks, and I look at Aaron and imagine what might have been.

"Not yet."

98

"Are we nearly there?" Aaron moans because we've already walked past the lake and the cafe and the playground, and his excitement slipped a notch with every, "Not yet."

"Soon," I tell him.

As we turn right, Jay looks at Mum and says, "I didn't even know this was here."

The trees are in full bloom, now, and there are people sunbathing and having picnics and playing with their kids. When we find a space, Mum lays out a blanket while Jay and Nia unpack the food.

"This is nice, mate," Zak says. "Thanks again for the invite."

"No worries."

"Look!" Aaron yells, pointing at the squirrel running over at full speed. It stops right in front of us and waits.

I crouch next to my brother and say, "He's not the only one."

Aaron looks to where I'm pointing and we see more of them dashing between other groups and racing up and down trees like they own the place. I realize, now, that they do.

"This is brilliant," he says.

"Do you want to feed them?" asks Nia.

"Yes!"

I think of the day Amy brought me here. She said she used to visit with her brother, but I was imagining the wrong one. I wish I'd known the truth, then. And I wish she was here now.

Aaron laughs as more squirrels bound over, and Nia looks happier than I've ever seen her. Zak is feeding them, too, watching as they grab things, then scarper.

"They're like furry ninjas," he says, but I don't join in.

I feel grateful and sad and heartbroken because we're happy, but not everyone can say that.

Amy's family shattered, and what was left was a lie and then a horror story.

I'm still thinking of her when Jay touches my shoulder and says, "How are you feeling?"

"This was her favorite place."

Mum is watching us, smiling, and Jay says, "Maybe it can be ours now."

He looks uncertain because this is new to both of us and we still don't know the rules.

"I think so," I say.

I watch Nia chase Aaron, his giggles filling the park. Then I close my eyes and imagine Amy playing here with the brother she lost far too soon.

Will's silhouette dances away from me, a shape I can't fill

in. But Amy's is crystal clear, and she looks beautifully, blissfully happy.

I know she's not that person anymore, but I hope that, one day, if she wants to, she'll come here with us.

ACKNOWLEDGMENTS

Thank you to my wife, Rachel, for your unwavering support. From the moment I told you I dreamed of being an author, you have encouraged and believed in me, and that means the world.

To Charlie—you are the smartest and funniest person I know. Thank you for filling every day with laughter...and for sleeping so I could write this in the gaps between our adventures. And to Lucas—you may have only just arrived but I am so pleased you got to see this book's publication. Thank you for completing our family.

Thank you to Claire Wilson, who is undeniably the best agent in the business. I am so grateful for everything you do, and I now have two books that only exist because of your faith and support.

Thank you to everyone at Sourcebooks who has played a role in bringing this book to an American audience, including Steve Geck, Cassie Gutman, Beth Oleniczak, and Meaghan Summers.

I am so grateful to Nicole Hower and Kelly Lawler for designing such a wonderful cover. It might just be my favorite one yet.

I owe huge thanks to my UK editor Carmen McCullough at Penguin Random House. I will never forget your reaction when you first read this story. Writing a second book is scary and incredibly uncertain, but your feedback immediately calmed my fears. I have loved working with you on this one from the very beginning.

Thank you also to Millie Lean for working so closely with Carmen. Your enthusiasm for these characters was clear from the outset, and your notes were invaluable.

Wendy Shakespeare—your brilliance is no secret, but I will add to the praise regardless. Thank you and everyone on your team for the intricate work you do to ensure this and every book is as good as it can be. That includes my copy editor Jane Tait, whose eye for detail is amazing, and my proofreaders Marcus Fletcher and Leena Lane.

Thank you to everyone else who has worked with me at PRH, most notably Maeve Banham, Anne Bowman, Toni Budden, and Harriet Venn.

Thank you so much to Emily Hayward-Whitlock and Fern McCauley at the Artists Partnership, and to Miriam Tobin and Safae El-Ouahabi for all your work at RCW.

Tig Wallace—I will thank you at the end of every story I am lucky enough to write because you took a chance on my first novel.

Thank you to my mum, although those two words really don't do justice to all the things you have done for me. I am beyond grateful for all the sacrifices you made and the encouragement you gave. I appreciate everything I noticed at the time and everything I have realized since.

As always, I am incredibly grateful to everyone who reads this story. Thank you!

ABOUT THE AUTHOR

Vincent Ralph has been writing in one form or another since his teens and always dreamed of being a novelist. He owes his love of books to his mother, who encouraged his imagination from an early age and made sure there were new stories to read. Vincent lives in the UK with his wife, two sons, and two cats. He is also the author of *14 Ways to Die*.